The
Black
Squirrel Ball

A Samantha Cummings Mystery

AMY LIPTAK CARUSO

iUniverse, Inc.
New York   Bloomington

The Black Squirrel Ball

Copyright © Amy Liptak Caruso

iUniverse books may be ordered through booksellers or by contacting:

iUniverse
1663 Liberty Drive
Bloomington, IN 47403
www.iuniverse.com
1-800-Authors (1-800-288-4677)

ISBN: 978-1-4401-8010-1 (pbk)
ISBN: 978-1-4401-8011-8 (ebk)

Printed in the United States of America

iUniverse rev. date: 10/26/2009

To my paternal grandparents, Louis and Margaret Liptak.
They worked hard and always had fun along the way.

ACKNOWLEDGMENTS

My husband Vinny, who consistently supported me throughout the past year and bought me a new desk and computer—just the push I needed to start pulling my ideas together into a story.

My father Louis, Aunt Nancy, and Aunt Jane, who helped me craft the initial plot and provided historical references to round out the details.

My mom Marylin, sister Sharon, brother Dan, and nieces Elizabeth and Olivia, who supported my creativity and provided encouragement when I was stalled with writer's block.

In addition, my friends Delphine Soucie, Tracy Lynch, and Jack Anderson provided editorial review and great suggestions. They helped me move the manuscript from a rough draft to an actual publication.

And special thanks to Homer Perkins, a contemporary of my grandfather's. Many of his stories and suggestions have been woven into *The Black Squirrel Ball*.

PROLOGUE
AUGUST 1968

THE EVENING STARTED OFF JUST flawlessly.

Raul and I hosted a large fund-raising event for the park—The Black Squirrel Ball. Mr. Cummings, Peaceland Park's superintendent, requested that we help raise money for the first ever end-of-summer celebration.

What a spectacular evening I expected! We planned on wonderful music by a fifteen-piece orchestra and dancing under the stars. I was so looking forward to dancing the tango with my husband. He has incredible rhythm, and when I'm in his arms and the music begins, I feel like I am floating on a cloud.

There was a violent rainstorm last night with thunder, lightning, and high winds, and I was worried that the worst of the weather was going to continue tonight, but the sun was shining this morning, and the park staff was able to have everything just right for tonight's event—not a pine needle or a rose petal was out of place. It was about seventy-five degrees with a slight breeze, just like I remember from my family's mountain house when I was a *niña* in Mexico. It was perfect for dancing and strolling through the park.

In order to raise the most money possible, Raul and I developed a large invitation list of colleagues from Formula 333—the household cleaning chemical company we both work for—local dignitaries and vendors from both Peaceland Park and the company. Approximately 250 people attended, and we hoped to raise about $10,000. That would be quite a sum for the park and Mr. Cummings would be *muy feliz*—very pleased.

I am one of the top salespeople in the northeastern division of the company, and I also provide training at the summer weekly sessions which are held at this beautiful park. From June through August, my sales colleagues come to Westfield to learn about the new products my husband and his research and development team of chemists create.

I love when they come to town, and I take on the unofficial role of hostess along with the other executives. Because of my success at Formula 333, I like to think of myself as a role model to all the young women starting their careers with the company. I have invited many of them, and I am happy that some made the journey to western Massachusetts for this wonderful event just before Labor Day.

As I was dressing tonight, I was thinking about what a fulfilled life my Raul and I have. We have not been blessed with *niños*, but our lives are very full with good friends and lovely colleagues here in our home away from home. We have been very successful with our work, and Raul showers me with gifts. Only last week, my darling gave me the most exquisite ruby and diamond necklace to wear tonight, and, thankfully, I was able to find a red silk dress to match it on such short notice.

Lately, Raul has been preoccupied and tense. And although many wives would be happy to have their husbands come home early from work, I was wondering what was causing him to him be so on edge. He is constantly doting over me, almost to the point that he is checking on my whereabouts all the time. And whenever we get the chance, he takes me to our beach house on the Connecticut shore that he purchased as a surprise for me earlier this summer.

He was home especially early today, and we arrived at the ball to properly greet all the guests. My dear *madre* taught me that to be a gracious hostess, you have to be prompt and make sure everyone feels welcomed. I wanted to say hello to each guest as they entered Peaceland Park's path from the parking area through the rose garden and continued toward the lawn and pavilion area where the ball was held.

This event was not only a fund-raiser, but also an evening of appreciation for all the good people who work so hard at Peaceland Park. The groundskeepers, kitchen staff, and security officers deserve the accolades they receive. They do help prepare for the evening, but they also bring their guests to enjoy the *fiesta*. I was a little worried that the young laborers and their dates from the park might not mix well with the executives and their families, but Mr. Cummings told me that I shouldn't worry. I'm not sure he is aware that at the events for the sales staff, the sales team members can be rude and condescending to the hard-working park crew. I think it takes a good deal of self-control for the laborers to hold back from responding. One day, this tension is going to come to a head.

I enjoyed seeing the park crew and the handsome young men who drive our summer guests back and forth to the local hotels. Tonight they dressed up in their best suits and well-shined shoes and danced the night away with their sweethearts. At the end of the night, they will have to help clean up and also provide transportation to our out-of-town guests, but I don't think they will mind. My favorite driver is Bobby Dorion because he is so polite. Jake Cerazzo and Paul and Frank O'Connor are fine drivers, too, along with the other young men who jockey the executives around town and to appointments in Springfield and Hartford, Connecticut.

After the ball, the gentlemen from out of town, including two New York City investors, and the Formula 333 executives, and Raul, would join Mr. Cummings for a post-*fiesta* poker game, and therefore I was planning on having Bobby drive me home. I left him a note to meet me at the top of the waterfall at the end of the night—which I expected to be a little after 11:30 when the band ended.

My favorite part of the evening was after the presentations by the dignitaries and Mr. Cummings acknowledging Raul and me for our hard work and dedication to the first Black Squirrel Ball—an event that was so successful he wants it to become an annual festivity. Mr. Cummings then asked the guests to clear the floor and the band to start our favorite song, a tango. Raul put on his top hat, took me by the hand, and twirled me out on the dance floor. The dance floor cleared, and the guests gathered around to watch. Once the music started and my husband held me close to him, it was like we were all alone. I looked into his lovely green eyes, and we shared one of the most sensual dances ever.

We have been married for almost five years, and although our marriage is excellent in many ways, I don't recall ever feeling so physically exhilarated as we did at the end of that tango.

The end of the evening came much too soon, and I wished Raul was not joining the gentlemen for the poker game, but I knew it was important for Raul to socialize with the other men—especially since he has been so anxious lately. He usually enjoyed his microscopes and chemical formulas far more than smoking cigars, drinking scotch, and playing cards.

As I was waiting for my driver by the waterfall, leaning against the wooden railing, I felt a stillness from the silence of the park that vastly contrasted to how lively it was just a half an hour ago when the band was playing and people were enjoying the evening. The only thing I could hear was the soft sounds of water trickling over the many rocks from the top of the garden path down to the large pond almost two stories below.

I was trying to relax, leaning against the wooden railing waiting for Bobby, but my body was still tense from that dance, and I couldn't wait to go home, take a bath with lovely scented rose petals, and stay up for Raul to end the evening very late, but very passionately.

I closed my eyes and took a deep breath to try to slow my heart rate. I noticed the beautifully smelling flowers from the breeze coming through the trees by the pathway.

It was quite later than 11:30, and I was wondering where Bobby was when the carillon bells rang midnight. The loud noise and vibrations from the tower startled me so much that I grabbed my hands to my chest, grasping my lovely pendant around my neck.

Then I felt a tightness around my neck and everything went black.

CHAPTER 1
MAY 2008

I was just about at my wits end. Another day in the corporate world, wondering what I was going to do in this misery—a gray cube about 3½ square feet in size, thirty feet away from the nearest dark-tinted window, at the end of the aisle where the water cooler conversations were only surpassed in interest by the many people's butts I had a view of as they bent over to hit the cold water button.

And most of all, there was no opportunity for creativity in that land of mediocrity.

As I started to wallow in self-pity and sing "Take this Job and Shove It" silently in my head, Aunt Reggie called.

"How would you like to do something more rewarding than that high-paying soul-killing job that you have now?" she asked.

I had dinner with my aunt the previous week, and she said I "was showing." Not that I was pregnant, but that I looked miserable and that it showed.

"The Black Squirrel Ball is going to flop if we don't get organized and raise more money. And we need someone like you to get it done. The committee agrees that this year we need a professional. I know this is a shot in the dark, but I think you should quit your job and go back to fund-raising."

I was a fund-raiser right out of college. The job had a tiny budget; it was a small organization, but there were some great opportunities. I got a little burned out after a few years and thought a corporate job might be the way to go. That job had better benefits, a big title, and the opportunity to travel—all the glamour. It turned out to be all a drag.

I was more than burned out. I was like the cinders that are stuck to the back of the bottom of the woodstove. I was done.

"Sure. I told my boss a few months ago that I would stick out this God-

1

forsaken project, and it will be done next week. I doubt if she would care if I only gave her one week's notice," I responded. I doubted if she cared if I got up from my desk and never came back. But that wasn't right. You should always treat people the way you would want to be treated, not the way they may deserve to be treated, as my mom says.

"Don't you want to know the pay and lack of benefits?" she asked. I knew the pay would be lousy, but she had been talking about the Black Squirrel Ball and how this event is going to be the talk of the town for the year. I could take this on, raise a bunch of money, get reacquainted with people outside of the corporate ivory tower I had been sequestered to, and then get another full-time job when it was finished. Just like that. I had a plan to escape this sentence.

I thought, "Plus, if I'm working on the Black Squirrel Ball with Aunt Reggie maybe she'll feed me a few meals a week and my grocery bill won't be too big. I'll survive."

"I know you'll take care of me," I said.

My family members are all great cheerleaders and sources of encouragement for me. I know many people say that about their family, but this is for real. My mom is always willing to do errands or shopping for me. My dad listens to the police scanner to tell me if there are traffic jams and gathers the local business scoop from the guys who stop by his work garage to hang out for hours on end, or as my brother calls them, the garage flies. And my aunt Reggie is always there for good career advice.

After Aunt Reggie retired from Formula 333, she was just as busy with volunteer work. In addition to The Black Squirrel Ball committee, she was active with the Rosary Sodality and as a greeter at the elementary school near her house on the north side of town. She doesn't have time to exercise, but based on her metabolism she doesn't need to because she's still the one hundred pounds she was forty years ago when she got married.

She said, "Great. Our first meeting is at seven o'clock tonight."

"How about I stop by for dinner?"

"Golumki are already in the oven," she said.

"My favorite!" I said.

When I exclaimed my excitement for golumki—the Polish people's version of meatloaf-like comfort food—my co-workers looked up from their water cooler conversation like they never knew I was there before. In addition to not being interested in the water cooler butt contest, I tended to show a lack of interest in most things at work lately.

She continued, "I know they are your favorite. And like you always say, always have a backup plan. I didn't know it was going to be that easy to get you to say yes so I had the golumki made as soon as I got approval for your salary this morning—which by the way is not much, but this will be a great opportunity."

The Black Squirrel Ball is an annual event that celebrates the mascot of Peaceland Park in my hometown of Westfield, Massachusetts, about ninety miles west of Boston and a few miles north of the Connecticut line. The park is the jewel in this small city.

And the squirrels are well known throughout the western Mass area. Some say that the squirrels were purposely introduced to the park, but my family knows the real story because my family pretty much grew up in the park. Not just my siblings and me, but my cousins, and my Dad, Aunt Reggie—or Regina as she was baptized—and Uncle Joe.

Grandpa worked in Peaceland Park since the 1940s, and that meant everyone in the family worked in the park, too. Whether it was helping build the original flagstone walkways in the early days, taking care of the horses, or cooking in the pavilion kitchen for the summer picnics, everyone had a role. The park was part of the family, and the family was part of the park.

I loved going to Peaceland Park when I was little. I remember my grandmother picking me up from the school bus stop and bringing me to her house every day when I was in half day kindergarten. She would bake me a treat and tell me to go play "out back." To some kids, playing "out back" may have been a quarter-acre square of grass, but for me it was a huge park with a pavilion, duck pond, rose garden, carillon tower, and a lily pond, soccer fields, wild flower gardens and wooded paths to the Enchanted Oak. "Out back" was a labyrinth of stories that could be played out from my imagination.

I was planning on letting Peaceland Park go to my imagination again. That was just what I needed — a good dose of creativity to get my juices flowing again. Nothing like a little fund-raising medicine to cure the corporate culture woes.

Aunt Reggie told me about the committee members at dinner the week before —after I verbally puked all over her about my work wretchedness and gave her the ammunition to go to the committee and convince them to pay me 20 percent of the $50,000 budget.

There was Frank O'Connor, the nearing retirement finance coordinator at Formula 333. Aunt Reggie said he wears the same clothes that were in fashion in the 1970s because she remembers him wearing the clothes when they worked together back then, and he has a buzz cut that he must do himself since it is always uneven. She said that he doesn't want to spend any money on himself or the ball, and he thinks that everyone who has attended in the past will come this year just because it's the fortieth anniversary. With his snow-white hair and very fair skin, she said he is quite the typical Irishman.

Doree Bowers, the newcomer to town, was in her mid-thirties and very energetic. Her husband Richard was recently recruited to Formula 333 as the VP of finance. Aunt Reggie said that Frank doesn't care for her because she's young, has new ideas, and, most importantly, her husband took the job he felt Frank deserved for the final few years before he retired. Doree is thin and fit with a great tan, has shoulder-length blond hair with sunglasses always on the top of her head to hold her thick locks back from her face, and wears clothing straight off the racks of Nordstrom's.

It sounded to me like she was the anti-Frank.

Aunt Reggie said, "He is jealous of successful people. He thinks since his father, George, was the CFO for years that he is entitled to live on the O'Connor legacy at the company and the park. Unfortunately for Frank, he doesn't have nearly the amount of charm, character, or smarts as his father. He's nothing like George."

And then there was the saving grace of the committee, Esther LaFluer, who was the chairperson. Esther helped in the office of her family's dairy business for all her working life, retiring when her older brothers sold out to a locally based dairy conglomerate. She's been a longtime friend of my mom and Aunt Reggie and attends all our family events with her husband Dax. When I think of Esther, her jet black hair with a slight wave that parts to the left comes to mind. Her hairstyle has been the same for decades, and yet she always looks eternally classic.

Aunt Reggie told me that Esther hoped to raise the most money for Peaceland Park this year by having the loveliest, most attended, most publicized ball ever. And since Aunt Reggie told them if they paid me $10,000 to run the event it would be more organized than last year's traffic snafu, have better food service than the year the champagne fountain tipped over on the mayor's wife in her handmade white silk dress, and that I would help raise more than ever … $100,000, I guess I better help make it happen.

$100,000.

Compared to the last three years, which raised $35,000, $40,000, and then $38,000, the goal was going to be difficult to achieve

But I thought I could do it. "Sure I can," I thought to myself with a 'can do attitude,' imagining my face on the Rosie the Riveter poster.

Even in my best year of fund-raising, I don't think we netted $100,000 with multiple events and an annual appeal.

But then again, if I couldn't make the ball a huge success, it's not like they were going to fire me.

But I thought I could do it.

And although they couldn't fire me since it was a consulting job for only a few months, I wouldn't get another job in the area if I screwed it up. I took a big chance. I like to be a risk taker on tasks and initiatives but not on job security.

So into fund-raising/special event planning mode I went. I had to go through the Rolodex, make sure I was at all the community networking events pronto, and get ready for some serious schmoozing. I had to make it happen, I thought, or else I would need more than a few meals from Aunt Reggie in a couple of months—I may have to move in with her and Uncle Paul!

And I definitely had to get to the gym. Whatever I wore to the event, I had to look fantastic. With the schedule I'd been keeping and the fast-food diet I'd been consuming, my body fat content was a bit more squooshy. Not that I'm overweight, but I could tone up a bit, I thought.

I made a list to get a florist and a rental company for tents, chairs, tables, and linens. Maybe a band—but I had hoped the committee had one already—traffic coordination from the police, publicity sponsors, get the invitations printed, and enlist volunteers for the event and table fund-raising chair people. And that was just the 'to-dos' for the first week.

I really needed a big break. A huge gift. Something that no one would expect. I needed a $50,000 donation to really make it happen and get to $100,000. That would get the committee to realize they didn't make a mistake in hiring me, and also position me for the next big thing. I might even be able to get rid of my clunk of junk car if I could upgrade to a better job.

I quickly jotted down an agenda on some scrap paper for tonight's meeting. I didn't have time to type it up, but considering it was 3:00 p.m. and I was still supposed to be working at my current job, I figured the committee would let that detail slide for the first meeting.

At the next meeting—which should be early next week—we would cover the next deliverables, including the budget, ten new names from each committee member for prospecting, and a project plan.

Feeling a little bit more confident as I stared into the muslin fabric of my dead-end cubicle, I said to myself, "I'm Samantha Jane Cummings. I'm organized, and I'm the Black Squirrel Ball coordinator. I'm ready to make it happen."

CHAPTER 2

I LEFT WORK A LITTLE early and drove home to change and get my laptop. After months of practicing my "I quit" speech on the way home every day, I was happy to crank up the radio, open the sunroof, and let my shoulder-length auburn hair flow in the wind. Hootie and the Blowfish were on the radio with their live version of "Mustang Sally," and I was joining the backup singers.

What a feeling of exhilaration to be free of that place! Well, almost. I'd be free in about a week.

It's funny how you wouldn't think twice about leaving a job where your physical safety was at risk. If you were a window washer on skyscrapers and didn't have proper harnessing, you would call OSHA. But we think it's tolerable to work with people who are evilly motivated and just downright mean because "that's the way people are." They can demoralize us and get to our souls, and yet, because we need a paycheck, we stick it out.

Straight out of college, I joined a small nonprofit as a fund-raiser and PR coordinator. I didn't know any better than to be intimidated, but I used my naïveté and gung-ho tenacity to raise about $100,000 a year and a ton of in-kind donations. The in-kind stuff, like roller skates, sporting goods, movie tickets, new household items, furniture, and school supplies helped the agency, which served families in distress, make their limited funds go a little further and the children to have a better sense of normalcy. It may not seem like much, but having a bike to ride or sneakers that fit are very important for young kids and their self-esteem.

And with regular PR in the local press, we were able to increase the number of people who donated on a regular basis. That was a big deal, because right before I left, we kicked off a capital campaign that was pretty successful. They raised about two million dollars. That's huge for a small organization.

But then I was called one day and asked if I'd like to go to the corporate world. One of our funders had a job opening, and I thought it would be a great place to transition to. The benefits were good and the opportunity for advancement was pretty much endless. I could also go to graduate school—maybe even law school—and get either option paid for. So why not leave the nonprofit world and follow the money?

Looking back now, even though the last six months were horrible, the previous two years were pretty good. I did earn my MBA and worked on a number of high-profile projects—which made my manager look great and resulted in her getting promoted. After awhile, doing all the grunt work and not getting any of the kudos for good results sucked the positive energy out of me, and I was turning bitter.

But it was time to switch gears and to get in control of my destiny. I wasn't going to let energy-draining thoughts have a place in my life. I really needed a change of pace, and working on the Black Squirrel Ball was just what the doctor ordered. Or in this case, just what Aunt Reggie ordered.

It was going to be interesting working with volunteers again compared to my first job out of college. I was a little more mature than I was a few years ago, but in some ways I felt like that tenacity I had was a distant memory, along with my confidence.

Having to play office politics really sucks the positive energy out of you and makes you question yourself and your skills.

I was so ready to use my energy in a positive way. And maybe I'd even be the belle of the ball. The Black Squirrel Ball!

When I got home to my apartment, I had about fifteen minutes to run in and change clothes. I thought I should start off with my lucky suit. A simple navy-gray pin-striped pantsuit. Mom always says, 'dress for the job you want, not the one you have.' I might be working for the black squirrel's favorite snack—peanuts—but I needed to look like a million bucks. Or at least a hundred thousand bucks.

On my way into the apartment, I saw my landlord, Mr. Zilenski. He is a lovely little old man—about five feet tall, mostly bald, and he walks with a shuffle. I especially like that we share our Polish heritage, even though my last name showcases my smidge of Irish bloodline, and I'm also Slovak.

"Hey, good lookin'," came from a booming Mr. Zilenski. For such a petite man, he has such a boisterous voice. He moved here a few years ago from Kentucky to be closer to his daughter and grandkids. He bought a large two-family house on Western Avenue in hopes that they would all live there together, but his daughter wanted to stay in her subdivision cookie cutter house in the latest and greatest development in town. She visits at least once a week and brings him cookies and artwork made by the kids.

"Hey, Mr. Z," I said.

"Hot date tonight?" he asked with a little hint of optimism in his voice.

"Nope. Not tonight." Not in many nights. My boyfriend of three years, Jonathan, was on another long-term assignment in New York City, so we hadn't seen too much of each other lately.

"I'm taking on a new job. I'm going to organize the Black Squirrel Ball."

"The what? You folks come up with the wackiest things to celebrate. In Kentucky, we don't celebrate rodents. We eat them. I can make the best stew from squirrel and 'possum. If you'd like, I can type up my recipe for you," he said.

"I think I'll pass this time. But maybe you can save me some the next time you make it," I said with my fingers crossed behind my back. I like to encourage his adventurousness without actually having to participate in it.

I stopped at the back door to my apartment and explained, "The Black Squirrel Ball is the biggest fund-raiser for Peaceland Park. Don't worry, you'll get an invitation."

"I'll only go if you save a dance for me," he said. He was so loud, I thought the neighbors two streets over heard him.

"You bet, Mr. Z. How about a nice two-step?"

"That or a polka," he said. "I may be a redneck from Kentucky, but I love to polka."

"Sounds good. I have to run. I only have a few minutes to change, and then I have to go to Aunt Reggie's for golumki," I said.

"A new job, a dance card with my name on it, and golumki. Are you sure you didn't win the lottery?" he said.

I may not have won the lottery, but I am pretty lucky in many ways, including my living situation. I live in the apartment on the back of the house and Mr. Z lives in the main part of the house. I think he was planning on living in the apartment and having his daughter live in the main part of the house, but considering his trouble walking, I think it's better he is in the main house where the stairs aren't as steep as mine.

My kitchen and living room are on the first floor, and then the bathroom and bedroom are on the second floor. When you walk in from the driveway, you enter into a small mudroom that has a stacked washer and dryer. I knew I was really a grown-up when the delivery man came that special day. Nothing is better than starting a batch of wash and going to bed on a Friday night instead of having to spend your Saturday morning at the Laundromat.

I'm really a simple girl.

After walking through the small mudroom, you enter a plain white kitchen with splashes of my favorite color—red. I like red for just about everything except cars. I like black cars.

The living room is pretty small. Just enough space for a loveseat and two chairs. Not just any chairs—I have a lovely seashell-backed chair that I reupholstered in a community class at the high school. It was my great Aunt Caroline's from my mother's side of the family. She was a nurse for more than forty years, and I always feel calm in that chair. I call it my thinking chair because I feel like I can settle into it and let the chair suck me in. It's a comfortable spot where I come up with some of my best ideas. I knew I'd have to start sitting there more often if I wanted this project to be a hit.

After I ran up the stairs, I quickly pressed my suit pants, fluffed up my hair a bit, re-touched my makeup, got changed, brushed my teeth, and darted out the door again.

Mr. Z was sitting in the backyard looking out toward his azaleas. It was mid-May and they were all shades of pink, coral, and purple.

"See you later, Mr. Z. I'll shape up the evergreen shrubs this weekend if I can use your electric trimmer," I said.

I like to help Mr. Z around the house, especially when it comes to making the yard look nice. Maybe I have a little of my grandfather's horticultural skills in me.

"You got a deal!" he yelled.

I jumped in my car and took off for Aunt Reggie's.

CHAPTER 3

"YOU'RE GOING TO BE THE Black Squirrel Ball head cheese?" Uncle Paul asked me when I got to the door.

I could smell the golumki as soon as I drove into the driveway. The browned ground beef mixed with rice, rolled up in a blanket of cabbage, covered with tomato sauce, and then topped with bacon. Yum! The bacon really makes it. Everything is better with bacon.

"Yup, I told my boss today that I would be leaving in a week."

My boss was a bit surprised. I don't think she actually thought I had something in the works. She didn't need to know that I didn't have anything in mind until about fifteen minutes prior.

"Everything works out for a reason. I was finishing up a project at work; I was miserable, and Aunt Reggie came to the rescue."

Plus, I'm pretty good at this stuff.

That's an understatement.

I'm actually *very* good at this stuff. I organize like no one else. Well, that's not quite true. My mom is the best organizer of them all, but she says she can't ask for money. So I'm the most organized paid fund-raiser I know.

A former co-worker once teased me that I had a list for everything. The next day, my mom sent me an Excel spreadsheet for that year's upcoming Easter Saturday meal. It included who was bringing what item and what temperature and time it needed to go in the oven. I sent the list to him and told him my organizational skills were genetic.

Anyway, I enjoy fund-raising for things I believe in, so raising money for Peaceland Park would be fun. And working on this might just help me build my confidence to land the next "real" job.

Uncle Paul said, "So, what are you gonna to do first?"

Just like Uncle Paul. All business—not much chitchat. He was a shipping and supply manager for about forty years at a local sporting goods company. And he was a Marine for two years. I think he was a cook, but every Marine was trained to fight, and he took it pretty seriously—especially now that he is retired. He gets all spiffy in his dress blues and goes to the schools for the Memorial Day and Veteran's Day services. Uncle Paul doesn't have time for too much dillydallying.

"I want to get a list of all the old-timers from Peaceland Park and Formula 333 to collect old pictures and stories so we can have a slide show on the big screen—oh yeah, that would be cool." I kept going with thinking out loud and soon realized that I had a great idea percolating. I continued, "Plus, it would be cheaper than printing the advertising books they used to have." I was quite impressed with my first great idea of the day.

We immediately sat down to the dinner table. In addition to golumki, Aunt Reggie made a salad and had warm rolls just out of the oven. And I smelled something chocolaty coming from the oven.

Their house was modest in a nice neighborhood right near two schools on the north side of town. It was a ranch with three bedrooms and one full bathroom until Uncle Paul retired. Then he added a bathroom in the basement. It always seemed odd to me to have it built at that time. They raised three kids in the house with one bathroom and yet with just the two of them, he wanted his own. Some men like hot rods for their retirement present or fancy gold watches. He wanted his own bathroom.

"But would the committee go for the slide show idea?" I wondered to myself. "They may want to just stick with the same old ideas and not break into anything new. Or they may want to do everything new and not appreciate any tradition."

Ah—the beauty of working with volunteers, I thought as I squirted Heinz ketchup all over the golumki and took my first bite. It had just the right proportion of cabbage, ketchup, meat, and bacon.

I hoped there would be a similar balance of chemistry with the volunteers as there was with my dinner. Volunteers can be awesome if they are positive and hardworking, but if they are negative, then there's no chance to do anything new and the project can be ruined. It's just like good golumki; if you have too much bacon it's too greasy, and the meal is a disaster.

"Aunt Reggie, do you think we're going to have any luck getting this committee to take on new ideas?" I asked.

"You bet. But Frank won't get on board with anything new, so we'll just override him. Esther has the archives of Peaceland Park in Dax's study. After he retired, he decided to take all the pictures, programs, and newspaper clippings and put them in some order. Then, he wants to have them saved in the archive department of the library."

11

"What a great idea. That way we can get Dax involved, too."

Dax is Esther's husband. My grandfather hired him as a groundskeeper when he was just a teenager, and he just retired a few months ago as the superintendent. After Grandpa died, Dax stepped in. Dax said that Grandpa's shoes were too big to fill, but he would gladly take his shovel and dig in to the job.

Aunt Reggie said, "I think we should also honor Dax for his retirement. He said he didn't want a party, but we could have him work on the archiving and slide show, and then honor him at the end. It would be like he would be putting together his own gift."

"Don't you think that's a bit cheesy?" I said with a schwinchy face—my eyes got squinty and my lips puckered toward my nose a bit.

Then I bit into the hot buttered rolls. Not homemade, but almost as good. It had been awhile since I had a meal like this. With work being so crazy, I'd been living off pizza slices and frozen dinners at nine o'clock at night.

Aunt Reggie said, "I don't think it's cheesy at all. Dax wouldn't trust those archives to anyone else. He takes great pride in the history of Peaceland Park, and he wants to make sure he has those archives in tip-top shape."

"I wouldn't expect anything less from Dax. Grandpa was lucky to have someone like Dax take over after he died," I said.

"And Dax was lucky to have Grandpa," Uncle Paul said with a little smirk and roll of his eyes.

"What do you mean by that?"

"Dax was not the best kid. Actually, I take that back; Dax didn't have the best parents. His mother died when he was young, and his father was a truck driver. He was always on the road, and that left Dax to fend for himself," Uncle Paul said.

"He spent a lot of time at our house, but there was only so much Grandma and Grandpa could do," Aunt Reggie said. "It wasn't like we had too much extra money for shoes and clothes. There was always plenty of food at our house and plenty of chores to do at the park and the farm. And there was plenty of love, too."

She continued, "Dax and your father and Uncle Joe used to run around that park and raise hell, and then catch hell when they got home. Grandma would shout out a bunch of chores to the boys, and he would just join in. Dax and your father were in charge of feeding the pets of the park."

"Wait a minute," I said. "I didn't know the park was a zoo."

"No, not zoo animals. Pets of Mr. Smith's," said Aunt Reggie with a slow and punctuated tone to her voice. "Mr. Smith would collect animals from his travels and colleagues who lived in the Midwest, Mexico, Canada, Europe, and South America. There were birds, dogs, cats, and four black squirrels. He kept them as pets."

"How could you keep a wildcat or a squirrel as a pet?" I said with a voice of disbelief. Here comes one of those stories that's going to be contradictory to common known history, I thought.

"They were all in cages," Aunt Reggie said. "And then the squirrels started to be found in and around the park."

"So how did they get out of the cages?" I asked. It seemed to me that Aunt Reggie and Uncle Paul were leaving out some important facts—like there was some secret mystery coming to light.

"One night your father and Dax fed the squirrels, and then the critters just happened to not be in their cage the day after," Uncle Paul said.

Aunt Reggie gave him a roll of the eyes and said, "OK, you say it the way my brother trained you to tell it," she said. "Anywho, your father and Dax said the squirrels were mean. Your dad said that they would bite and hiss at them. They told me the cage had a "complicated latch," but I think they left the cage open one night and the squirrels got out so Dax and your father didn't have to feed them anymore. Within a few years, the squirrels mated and migrated throughout the park."

"And it took almost twenty years for them to get across the river," said Uncle Paul. Westfield has a clear delineation between the north side and the south side of town. The north side has always been considered the more industrial area. It's where the turnpike exits and where the National Air Guard base and a few large distribution centers for retailers are located. The south side is where downtown is—with the town green ornamented with large elm trees, the library, post office, shopping centers, the college, and, of course, the jewel of the city, Peaceland Park.

Westfield is known for a number of things. Columbia bicycles, buggy whips, H. B. Smith boilers, Peaceland Park, and black squirrels. And now, you'll see a gray squirrel with a black tail or a red-tailed black squirrel.

"So my dad and Dax are behind the black squirrel phenomenon in Westfield? They're responsible for the whole black squirrel population?" I said with great surprise.

"That's right. Your father—and Dax, of course—were like social integrators for the black squirrel population," my uncle said with a highbrow look to his face, like he was stating an academic truth.

"OK, so now that we, I mean, now that I know about how the black squirrels got all over Westfield, how can we get that into the ball planning?" I asked.

Aunt Reggie sighed and started speaking a little slowly to me, like I needed a bit of extra help understanding. "Why do you think Grandpa started the Black Squirrel Ball?"

I shrugged.

"He started the ball to raise money, but he called it the Black Squirrel Ball not to honor the little rodents, but to honor your father, Dax, and all the people who worked at Peaceland Park. Sure, the park was first started by Mr. Smith, and it couldn't have happened without him and the funds he raised from his sales teams, but it was the workers at Peaceland Park and those who lived right around the park who really made it what it is today. And, more importantly, what it was sixty years ago. The black squirrel represents the "little guy" and the "everyday people" with a lot of energy who made the park so great."

"Tell me about it back then." I said. And after I said that, I realized I sounded like a little kid asking for my parent to tell me a bedtime story, but I love these stories. I love to hear "how it was back in the day." I get inspired by it all. And if I was going to raise $100,000, I needed inspiration to motivate me.

"The first Black Squirrel Ball was quite the celebration. It was a celebration of many, many years of planning, hard work, and fund-raising to build Peaceland Park to Mr. Smith's vision," my aunt explained. "The park started with just a few acres, and slowly Mr. Smith acquired more and more land. Then he started to hire a few guys. One of the first tasks was to create the One Acre Lawn."

"What was the significance of the One Acre Lawn?" I asked.

"I don't know, but I bet Dax and your father would. Or if not, I bet it will be in the archives that Dax has."

She continued, "Anywho, first it was the One Acre Lawn, then the two nearby pavilions and the walking paths. Then, in the 1960s, the ponds were re-done. Dax can definitely tell you more about the ponds. And in the 1970s, the covered bridge was built, the blacksmith shop was added, and the waterwheel. You can get all these facts from Dax, but to get back to my main point, Grandpa knew he had to keep the fund-raising going and make sure his crew's morale was in good spirits, so he figured that he could throw a party for his workers and let other people pay for it."

"You mean, Grandpa started the Black Squirrel Ball really for the workers?" I asked with a little sarcastic tone. My grandfather was always scheming up something. One of his favorite quotes was "make it what it ain't." He would take an old truck that couldn't get out of second gear, shine it up nice, and drive through town waving like he was in a parade. No one thought he couldn't go any faster—they just thought he was friendly. They thought he was just being Grandpa.

"That's right. Grandpa put on this elaborate ball. Or the lady volunteers did, and he would make sure all the workers and their dates had a great time," she said.

Uncle Paul interjected again, "A great time on the donors' dime."

"Well, no," she said. "It wasn't like he embezzled funds. The volunteers knew the workers didn't have to pay for their tickets. They set up the tents, got the park in perfect shape, and cleaned up the mess the next day before the park reopened again."

"How did they get up that early? Knowing how Grandpa liked to have a good time, I would imagine the park staff liked to drink and carry on, too," I said.

"I think they just moved the party down by the river, built a big bonfire, and stayed there all night," said Uncle Paul with a bit of an unexpected belly laugh.

Again my aunt said, "No. Now you're just talking foolishness. I don't know how they used to do it, but I do know that the caterers take care of cleanup nowadays so we can sleep in the next day."

"You mean Frank hasn't cut that part of the budget?" I asked sarcastically.

"No, but he may cut your salary's budget if we get to the meeting late. We better get going," she said.

"But we haven't had dessert yet," I whimpered. I had passed on a third golumki in lieu of the chocolate dessert that was baking through dinner.

"Well, you're not getting any," Uncle Paul said matter-of-factly. "That's for the church bingo bake sale tomorrow night."

I was horribly disappointed, and my face must have shown it.

"Don't look at me like I just killed your goldfish. We'll go for ice cream after the meeting," Aunt Reggie said.

"That was not quite the same as some homemade chocolate baked goods, but a treat is a treat, and I knew I shouldn't be picky. Beggars can't be choosers," I thought to myself.

Chapter 4

I walked into the meeting room with Aunt Reggie, and I was a bit intimidated. I knew Esther, but I had only heard about Frank and Doree from Aunt Reggie. However, from the descriptions she provided, she hit the nails on their heads.

Doree was wearing a pair of skintight ankle-length taupe slacks with a matching sweater set and an oversized set of red sunglasses serving as a headband to her thick golden hair, and Frank was wearing a threadbare short sleeve plaid shirt with every color in it except red and blue, which were the colors of his wide striped tie. The two of them couldn't have been more opposite in fashion sense. I had hoped that they would be able to come together on planning this event.

Yet they were all waiting with solemn faces, and the tension was as thick as my mom's pea soup.

"Good evening," I said in the perkiest tenor I could come up with.

Aunt Reggie introduced me to the group. "This is my niece, our new coordinator, Samantha Cummings."

"You can call me Sam," I said as I was hoping to ease a bit of the friction in the air. But the meeting's tone continued to feel tense.

"Why do we have to go with that band?" Frank immediately asked Esther and Doree. "It's not like we're bringing Elvis back from the dead. Why are they charging so much?"

"Frank, we need to have good music so that people will dance all night," Esther said. "Nothing's worse than a party where everyone is just sitting around looking at each other. We want to see you get your groove on."

We all chuckled a bit. Everyone except Frank.

Esther is quite lovely and seemed to have an optimistic way to deal with the uncooperative Frank.

"Frank, you know how important it is to use the resources of local companies who have supported Peaceland Park in the past. That band has been providing services to the park for years and knows the ins and outs of setting up here," Aunt Reggie said. "It pays to contract with people who know how to work at the park. Remember the year we went with that other caterer?" she asked Frank with her eyebrows raised and looking over her half reading glasses like an old schoolmarm, emphasizing the word "other." That must have been the year of the see-through dress on the mayor's wife due to the crashed champagne fountain that wasn't set up properly.

With a raised voice, Frank said, "Using that caterer saved 20 percent of the food budget, and we raised the most money ever."

"Yes, but then the mayor and his wife and all their guests didn't come back the next year," Esther said. "How much did that cost us in lost revenue? That wasn't a good plan for the long term, Frank."

"Who cares about that mayor and his prissy wife anyway? He didn't get re-elected last year and I don't care if he ever comes back to the ball," Frank said.

This guy is more cantankerous than an old mule, I thought.

"I have a few names to add to the invitation list. Shall I give them to you, Sam?" Doree kindly interrupted.

"That will be great, Doree. I'll be getting the list from past years and developing a new database, so I can add these as well," I said.

I knew I needed to get across pretty quickly that I wasn't the guest in this group but the person in charge. However, it's not my style to be a bull in a china shop, so I thought it would be best to sit back a little and observe before really jumping in and taking hold of things. That would be for the next meeting.

Esther, Doree, and Aunt Reggie went on to discuss the band, including some songs they wanted added to the set list, and some suggestions for the caterer.

"Here are some color copies of a few pictures I thought we could use as ideas for the decorations," Doree said as she passed out a ten-page packet of copies from various party planning guru magazines. "I especially love the pictures on pages 5 through 8 from the wedding in the Hamptons. Wouldn't it be great to have lighting like that?"

The pictures were from the wedding of a top Wall Street executive—his second marriage—to a very young Long Island socialite. The decorations alone probably cost a quarter of a million dollars.

"I hate to sound like a killjoy, but our budget is nowhere near that," Aunt Reggie said. I thought she was going to say, "I hate to sound like Frank" at the beginning of the sentence, but she caught herself.

Doree looked a little red with embarrassment, and quickly said, "Oh, I realize that our budget is much less, but I thought we could use these as inspiration and for themes."

That was a nice save for the newcomer. She seemed to be trying a bit too hard, but I supposed she was just trying to make a good impression on the rest of us. Maybe she was just nervous.

The rest of the meeting consisted of the group reviewing a few other details that had already been committed so I could get up to speed—which didn't take too long.

I also presented my slide show idea, with some help from Aunt Reggie, and everyone loved it. Even Frank thought it was a pretty good idea because it wasn't going to cost anything.

Esther said, "I love playing tricks on Dax, and this is going to be fun!"

Our next meeting was early the next week, after I had left my current job and could be a bit more focused on all the tasks at hand. We ended the meeting before 8:30; Aunt Reggie took me for ice cream, and I was in bed before ten.

I got chocolate-covered almond chip on a sugar cone. It wasn't as good as whatever chocolately dessert was in her oven earlier that evening, but it was a close second for an early summer night.

When I climbed into bed, I tried to close my eyes, but I could hear the crickets holding an orchestral performance outside my window. With all the ideas I had going through my head for the ball, and reviewing the final things I had to complete before I left my miserable job, I was going to have a few long days ahead of me.

But then I could be totally devoted to the Black Squirrel Ball.

I rolled over, pulled my blanket up to my chin, and let the crickets sing me to sleep.

CHAPTER 5

"THE BLACK SQUIRREL BALL? WHAT? Are you crazy?" asked my soon-to-be-former co-worker Mike with a big laugh while he was shaking his head at me. In addition to Aunt Reggie, Mike had also noticed my miserable attitude lately and had suggested that I clear out of the job sooner rather than later.

"Yes, I'm leaving to organize the Black Squirrel Ball for Peaceland Park. Like you told me last week, I need to get back to my senses, and it isn't going to happen here," I said.

"Well, I saw this in the lobby gift shop this morning—before I heard you were leaving—and thought of you. Now it's even more appropriate," he said.

He handed me a key fob. It was a metal round disk about one inch in diameter attached to a key ring. It was imprinted crudely with two messages: *Live the Life You Love* on one side and *Love the Life You Live* on the other.

"This is quite appropriate," I said as I read it and rubbed my fingers against the smooth metal. "And I might as well start now. I know it's against company policy to solicit donations from co-workers, but may I ask if I can add you to the invitation list? You can decide later if you would like to come to the ball."

"Put me down for six tickets. Kerry and I will take the kids and their dates," he said.

"Don't you want to know the date at least?" I asked.

"It's the second to last weekend in August. When you left me the voice mail this morning, I Googled Black Squirrel Ball to see if you were making it up."

"And? The Black Squirrel Ball showed up on a Google search?" I inquired.

"No, but I bet it will by the end of the week," he said. "I went to the park's calendar of events and it was listed there."

I was already writing this down on my to-do list before he finished the sentence.

Mike works in the sales area, but he is more of a finance guy. I think he happens to have the charisma of a sales guy with more smarts. You make more money in sales than finance, so that goes to show you how smart he is.

His wife Kerry is a local politician in a nearby town and keeps pretty busy with the library commission and the quilting club. Their two children are in college and truly appreciate their parents' doting.

"I already called Kerry, and she put it on our calendar and told the kids to keep the weekend open. I think it sounds like fun."

"That's great. I'll call you in a few weeks to update you on the details," I said.

"Is this a black-tie thing?" he asked with an inkling that he was hoping it wasn't.

"It is, but you can wear a summer suit—anything goes."

I could quickly tell by the look on his face that he would have rather I said black tie, suit, or summer suit—not that he had an option of what to wear. He really does have a wonderful wife because I don't think he can match two black socks, and yet he always looks quite dapper. She probably lays his clothes out for him every day.

"Don't you worry. Kerry will make sure all eyes will be on the two of you while you're dancing the night away," I said.

I switched gears a bit on him to focus back on the ball planning.

"I'm pretty excited about the event, but I'm most excited about the slide show we're going to put together. The former superintendent is going to coordinate pictures and items from the archives and, then we'll show it on a big movie screen while the band plays music from the era of the pictures. I can't wait to hear all the stories about how Peaceland Park was started and the funny anecdotes from the old-timers. This is just what I need to get my head back to what is important. Like your gift says—Love the Life you Live and Live the Life you Love. I need to get there, and I think this is the first step."

"I think you are right, Sam. You're on your way," Mike said with a big smile.

CHAPTER 6

I ENTERED THE MEETING ROOM and no one was there yet. My commute was so much faster with a walk through the park rather than a thirty-minute drive to Springfield.

I had my agendas printed, and my flip paper for brainstorming; the caterer had already sent me sample menus. I also had a map of Peaceland Park blown up to three by five feet so we could plan out what will be going on where.

As I sat at the table in the conference room, I felt at ease. This room used to be Grandpa's office. It was attached to the pavilion and had a huge stone fireplace along one side of the wall. It had a window at the other end and was paneled with the original pine from the 1940s. The smell in the air was quite unique—a mix of woodsy aromas, the fresh peonies and early roses in the arrangement on the table, and just a hint of old cigar stink.

I can only imagine the stories my grandfather could tell about this room—the salespeople from Formula 333 whom he entertained with poker games and scotch, the ice fishing trips he planned, and the young men he hired for their first jobs working at the park. This is where Peaceland Park started. This is where the board of directors met sixty years ago—where the vision of the park was developed.

Uncle Joe once told me how Grandpa came home as the river was rising during the flood—well actually before they knew how bad the flood of 1955 was going to be—and took the family up to the park for the night. They slept in sleeping bags on cots in front of the big fireplace while it was pouring outside. Uncle Joe said they all felt safe and warm and didn't worry about the rain or the flood, even though they were less than a third of a mile from the river. They were all together, they were warm, and that's all that mattered.

I had that same feeling in the room as I sat waiting for the committee members to arrive for the meeting. I didn't have a fire going, but I did feel a little like I was waiting out a potential flood—a flood of uncertainty about my ability to raise the $100,000 we needed to make the event a success. And yet thinking about the past made my soul warm and calm. I might have been apprehensive and lacked confidence on the inside; but I needed to look cool as a cucumber, and I needed to do it quickly.

Frank came in first. No 'hello' or 'how do you do?' He just barked, "I hope the print job for that oversized map which you don't need is out of your pay, because we don't need to waste money on unnecessary expenditures."

I could ignore his crotchetiness and hope he would just let it go, or I could take him head on and demonstrate that I knew what I was doing.

"Mr. Barker made it for me for free," I said. Mr. Barker is the local printer I used all the time when I actually had a budget in my old job.

"Don't you be using up all your chits on useless stuff. We need to raise money not collect extra large pretty pictures," he continued.

"It isn't useless at all. We'll be using this map to plan traffic, parking, security, and staging. Then, we will go over the money raised so far during the meeting," I said, making it clear that I had more than pictures to show for my time and effort.

Doree and Aunt Reggie walked in together. "Good morning," they said in unison.

"It's a great morning, isn't it?" I said and turned toward Frank, raising my eyebrows and hoping for a response but not expecting much.

"I'm on the green side of the grass, so it can't be too bad," he said. I took that as a win for a pleasant conversation starter.

"The grass does look exceptionally green on this lovely May morning," Esther said as she walked in.

Everyone took their seats, and I called the meeting to order. Our first agenda item was for each committee member to add ten new names to the invitation list and for each person to come with a sponsor name.

"Let's start with the invitation list. We need to have this list nailed down by June 10th to have the invitations addressed by June 18th and in the mail by June 20th. I'd like to have them arrive prior to July 4th," I said.

"That makes sense—so we get people's attention prior to the holiday and the peak of vacations," Doree said.

"Right, plus we have a story running in the local paper and TV station this week announcing the event," I said, "and we want to capitalize on the attention that will bring."

Everyone, even Frank, looked impressed with the publicity plan that I had locked in and already started.

Some of the big details of the event had already been planned, like the date, the printer, and the band. I wouldn't have done anything differently. The event is always at the end of the summer; Mr. Barker donates the printing in exchange for two tickets—which is a super deal for us—and the band plays every year. It's an eight-piece band that can play 1940s big band favorites to "I Want to Rock and Roll All Night," by Kiss and everything in between.

"So how did everyone do getting ten new names for the list? Our goal is to add two hundred more names of likely attendees or supporters. I have ten, what about you Frank? Who do you have?" I asked politely.

"Everyone I know is already on the list. I can't add anyone else. My friends have been coming since it started. I'm not going to go try getting anyone new. You should be happy that I can keep people coming back," he scoured. Actually, he doesn't help keep people coming back as demonstrated from his catering/mayor fiasco a few years ago.

"Frank, I hope you realize that I can only do so much. If we want to hit $100,000, there's a formula to reaching that goal. It doesn't just happen." I felt like I was starting to talk to a first-grader who didn't want to follow coloring instructions, but I did need to stick to my guns. I can help the committee raise the money, but they need to help, too. And we need names. Many, many names.

"Doree and Esther, do you have your names?" I asked.

"Even though I'm new to the area," she said like she deserved a gold star, "I was able to get twelve names to add to the list. I'm not sure if they can all go, but I'll keep bringing names until early June. I have been going to more church activities, and I joined the book club at the library so I could meet more people to add to our list."

Doree certainly had a great deal of confidence and was flawless in her demeanor. She wore a beautiful black cotton pantsuit with a white eyelet blouse showing off her backyard pool tan and Tiffany "d" necklace.

"That's pretty ambitious. Not only are you finding time to volunteer with us, but you also are finding time to do other community activities so you can get more names for us. That's quite clever," said Esther. Esther wanted to give Frank a bit of a dig. It must have worked because he just rolled his eyes at her.

Esther continued, "I also have twelve names. Dax and I started going through the archives for the slide show, and we remembered a number of salespeople from Formula 333 who have moved away, but have family in the area. I hope we can get some big spenders to come back," she said. "And there's one person in particular who I really want to get here: Raul Suarez."

"You *really* think you'll get Raul to come back here after what happened to his wife the last time he was here?" Aunt Reggie asked.

"I think it might be good for him to come back—for closure," she said.

"Plus, he loves Dax, and I am going to tell Raul that we're honoring Dax. The two of them have kept in touch over the years, and I think I can persuade him to come."

Nothing like feeling like the oddball out of conversation. "Who is Raul Suarez and what happened to his wife?" I asked.

Aunt Reggie said, "Raul Suarez was the head of research and development years ago for Formula 333. He was a chemist and was known for coming up with many of the early big-selling products. He was very quiet, but he was also a very suave man around town."

"And what happened to his wife?" Doree asked while Aunt Reggie took a quick breath.

"She died." Frank stated quite bluntly.

I felt a little like I did the other night—when Uncle Paul and Aunt Reggie were talking about how the black squirrels "really" expanded around Peaceland Park. I thought we were a pretty close-knit family, but maybe some stories were lost over the years. I'm certainly learning more and more about this place that played such an important part of our families' lives over the years. I was gaining more curiosity on what I would learn about the park and the Cummings as a result of coordinating the ball.

Aunt Reggie's voice snapped me out of the mind tangent I was traveling on. She said, "Pauli Suarez didn't just die. She died of mysterious causes, and no one ever knew what happened. The police deemed her death an accident, but not everyone believed that, and certainly not Raul. He was heartbroken that the investigation ended like it did and he just couldn't take it anymore."

She continued, "He was severely depressed, and back when this happened—in the late 1960s—men weren't really 'allowed' to show their emotions like that. Some say he was institutionalized."

Esther said, "I don't know if he was institutionalized when he first left town, but he isn't now and hasn't been ever since I can remember Dax corresponding with him. He mentioned to me on one of our annual visits to his lavish home on the Connecticut shore that he still goes for counseling. Plus, he never remarried. He loved his wife so much."

"And although he has told us over the years that he enjoyed living here very much and he loves Peaceland Park, when he visited us a few years ago he said he still wasn't ready to go back to the park. He stood at the end of our driveway and looked through our neighbors' yards and just stared at the Kensington Street entrance. But he wouldn't go into the park," she continued.

Now that they were talking about Mr. Suarez, I thought I remembered seeing his name on a plaque near the One Acre Lawn. Many of the employees of Formula 333 were honored with their name on a brick along the walkway in the lawn.

"What happened?" I asked. Now that we were off agenda, I thought, "Why not keep going and find out more about the past?"

"Can we get back to the agenda? Some people work for a living, you know?" Frank spouted off, scolding me like I was a schoolgirl. This guy can really get under my skin.

"Mr. O'Connor, this is part of the agenda. Any opportunity the committee has to share the history of Peaceland Park and what happened here helps me understand where we can and can't raise money. We're all here to make the ball the best it can be, and if I can't ask questions about the past, you must be expecting me to work with my hands tied behind my back," I said very assertively.

Even I was surprised by how coolly and calmly yet directly I responded to his abrupt behavior. After a few years of corporate politics and keeping my mouth shut, I felt liberated.

"If this is a subject you would rather not discuss, I'll take it up with Dax and Esther at another time," I said to Frank.

"Why don't you come over for dinner tonight? I can make my famous chicken potpie, and you can ask Dax all the questions you'd like," Esther said.

"Sounds great. Let's get back to the expenses since that's one of Mr. O'Connor's favorite subjects."

I passed out a budget proposal, which included the previously agreed upon services, like the band and catering. It also included an exceptional quote from the florist.

"How did you ever get such a deal on the flower arrangements? Are we going to have twigs and flowers left over from the funerals of that week?" asked Aunt Reggie.

"I finagled a bit. There are a few plants that the park is looking to get rid of that the florist, a nationally recognized perennial gardener, would like to get hold of, so I made a trade with her. She doesn't happen to know that the park is already planning on thinning the perennial beds she has her eye on. And this is the perfect time of year to split some perennials, so she's going to come over one day with Dax and thin some of the daylilies, herbs, and phlox."

I thought, "Not only is she going to do some of the work, but she's going to save the landscapers' time because it needs to be done anyway. She thinks she's getting the better end of the deal and in exchange is donating much of the floral arrangements for the ball. Now that's resourcefulness!"

The florist is a lovely lady, aptly named Violet Dorion. Sometimes people are named for their callings in life. The photos I shared with the group included tall arrangements of carefree roses in Lucite vases that were about three feet tall. Intermingled in the arrangement were grapevines and wild flowers.

"This is a bit different than previous years," said Doree. "I noticed pictures from the last few years had very low, tailored arrangements."

It was also much different than the lavish pictures she provided the other night.

"I thought the same thing, but here is where it pays to have a tie-in with history," I said. "Violet found pictures from the early days of the Black Squirrel Balls, and there were some that were very similar to these arrangements. We thought it would be a little of 'what is old is new again'. Also, she's going to jazz it up a bit by putting little white lights in the vases so that when the dancing starts, the lights will go on. And she'll also provide the little lights within the tent and lanterns throughout the park—we'll have a beautiful woodsy fairy tale feel."

"How much will the lanterns cost?" Frank asked, as if he thought I would forget to figure those in. I just had to keep reminding myself to kill him with kindness. He was, after all, the person signing my paycheck.

"I'm glad you asked that, Frank. The lanterns will be rented from the florist for a dollar each. The lanterns range in size from six inches in diameter to twelve inches, and they will all be white. If we wanted to buy them, they would range from $10 to $20 each."

"But we only need them once, so why would we buy them?" he quipped. This guy can really push my buttons with his negative attitude.

"You are exactly right, and that's why renting for a buck each is the best way to go. It will also reduce setup and electric costs because they are battery operated. We won't have to bring in extra bark mulch the day before to hide the extension cords," I concluded.

After that budget discussion, I was feeling a bit more confident compared to the first meeting the other night, and so I decided the other items could simply be covered with Esther and Dax at dinner. Talking about the catering menu, more names to add to our list of potential donors, and the slide show were all topics that Frank would just punch holes in.

"How about we adjourn for today? I'll send notes, and we can meet on Friday morning," I said with a hope that Frank had a tee time already arranged.

"I can't meet on Friday because I have an important appointment," Frank said. That was code for "I'm going golfing."

Doree, Esther, and Aunt Reggie all said they could meet, and we agreed that we would start working on the logistics of the parking and traffic plans.

"OK, we'll continue to work on our prospecting list; you can send me what you have and we'll all get back together one week from today. I'll visit Chief Cerazzo to discuss the support we'll need from the police department."

I looked forward to six days of freedom from a man who doesn't have one optimistic bone in his body. Frank could suck the positive vibe out of a cheery four-year-old. So much for escaping all the political negativity in the corporate world.

Meanwhile, I couldn't wait for Esther's chicken potpie and to hear more about Mr. Suarez and his dead wife.

What a great night to look forward to—good food and intrigue!

Chapter 7

Esther and Dax lived around the corner from my apartment, so I walked over. It was a clear night in the sixties and, with a sweater, I wouldn't be too cold on the way home.

As I left the yard, Mr. Z caught me. "Do you have a hot date tonight?" he asked.

Jonathan is still working in the city. I often wonder if Mr. Z believes me when I talk about Jonathan, but he was the one who introduced me to my boyfriend about a year and a half ago. When I moved in, Mr. Z quickly found out from my mom that I wasn't dating anyone. He had a great accountant that he thought would be just perfect for me. Little did Mr. Z know that this accountant was a nice guy who had wanderlust for getting out of town at any opportunity.

Soon after we started dating, Jonathan accepted a consulting position with a big firm that sent him on out of town assignments for three to six months. Sometimes he would be in Hartford, sometimes Boston, or sometimes farther away in Chicago or Miami.

The latest assignment was in New York City, and he loved it. He didn't come home too often on the weekends, and our relationship had become a series of voice mails informing each other when we might be able to talk again.

I was thinking of breaking up with him, but I hadn't had a chance to talk to him about it, and it's not like I was looking for anyone else right away. I did need a date for the ball, but I was figuring I could always call a friend or go with my brother if Jonathan couldn't make it.

Wowza.

Something must definitely be wrong with me. I wasn't the least bit fazed about the possibility that my boyfriend of almost three years might not come to support the project I'd be working on for the whole summer.

"Can I cut some peonies? I'm going to Esther and Dax's for dinner and to work on ball ideas."

"Of course. *Mi casa* is *su casa*," he said. Mr. Z trying to talk Spanish with a Southern accent at a decibel level that can be heard for a mile radius cracks me up. It was like a redneck's version of Spanglish.

I picked about a half dozen beautiful Sarah Bernhardts, a beautiful, full pink flower with ruffly edges to the petals. I mixed in a few late-blooming tulips from the slightly shady side of the yard and started on my jaunt to the LaFluer's house.

As I walked a block east on Western Avenue, I was wondering more about Mr. Suarez. How did his wife die, and why did he desert the place he loved so much after her death? Was it an accident? Maybe foul play? Was he distraught with guilt or lost without the love of his life? And why after so many years is this the first I am hearing of this? So many questions.

But I needed to be careful. Sometimes my curiosity can get the better of me and I come across as nosey or insensitive. I would love to be able to bring this wealthy former Westfield resident back for the ball, but I wouldn't want to seem like I was just gold digging.

As I was getting lost in my thoughts, I almost got run over on the sidewalk by a Strollercise class of eight women in hot pursuit of something that didn't look to be in my sight.

For women with very young stroller riders, they certainly had tight butts in their spandex and lycra shorts. Chatting away loudly, they were synchronized in step with a little skip that looked like they were practicing for a fast waltz. When they got to the corner of Broadway and Western Avenue, they continued briskly down the sidewalk striding in long lunges. That's how they got those buns of steel.

Once I got to Fairway, I took a right and crossed the street. Esther and Dax had a lovely yellow Cape on the corner of Fairway and Vine Street. The houses in the neighborhood are less grand than the large Victorians on Western Avenue, but just as charming, especially the yards.

I remember my father telling me a story about how Grandpa would help Formula 333 executives seed and fertilize their yards, but one man who lived on the other side of Western Avenue, down toward the college, told Grandpa not to help anyone else on his street; he wanted to have the best grass, perennials, shrubs, and flower boxes.

I bet that Dax provided pruning assistance, perennial advice, and fertilizing counsel for the whole block. As I got closer to their house, I felt like I was walking into a peony garden show. There were about ten different varieties in their front yard. As I looked down at my bouquet I felt unimpressed with myself, but I thought the LaFluers would appreciate my gesture just the same

When I turned the corner to enter the side door, Bogey, a beautiful golden retriever, bounded toward me with a happy greeting and a soggy tennis ball in his mouth.

I bent over to give Bogey a one handed hearty rub. "Hello there, buddy. How is the most handsome dog in the neighborhood?"

He danced around me a few times as if to answer me in dog body language, "I'm happier now that you are here." No wonder Esther and Dax are so easygoing—with a dog like Bogey, any stressful day would be instantly cured.

"Ey there young lady. Are you going to give Bogey all the attention, or can I get a hug hello, too?" Dax was about five feet six inches tall with thick wavy white hair and sunken eyes. He always looked like he had a suntan right around his eyes—like he didn't put sunscreen near his eyes but perfectly covered the rest of his face. He was French Canadian and had lived in Westfield all his life with very few relatives, and yet he still had a bit of an accent—just enough to make you question exactly what he was trying to say once in a while but not so overwhelming to hear it every time he spoke.

I almost skipped over to hug Dax as Bogey tripped me with his excitement. "There you go—now everyone has a little Sammy love."

We walked up a brick-paved walkway to a breezeway that was decorated as a breakfast room. Even though it was dinner time, the small white iron dinette set had two place settings with cereal bowls and coffee cups. It was just like Esther to be planning for breakfast before dinner was finished—especially since she's such a good scone baker. She's even won prizes at the local fair for her scones—they're that good.

I handed Esther the peonies as she gave me a welcoming squeeze. Her stout Irish frame was always full of love and laughter, and she surely loved to hug. I wondered what would happen if she tried to hug Frank at the next committee meeting. Maybe that would scare the cheapskate out of him.

"Dinner will be ready in a few minutes. The potpie is just starting to get a little golden brown on the top," Esther said. "We're so excited to have you for dinner. I even picked up your favorite beverage."

Ah, Coca-Cola. Nectar of the Gods. Some girls like champagne or martinis. I love Coke.

Dax poured me a tall glass of the dark bubbly and led me into the dining room. It was set for an intimate holiday dinner. Esther had crystal candlesticks with white tapers lit in the middle of the table and her real silver and Wedgewood china before each chair. I felt a bit out of place wearing my favorite jeans, T-shirt, and apple green fleece. I even had my hair back in a barrette. I wasn't planning on a fancy white linen tablecloth experience. And there were four place settings, not three.

"Oh my. I should go home and change. What's the special occasion?" I was rubbing my lips together as I remembered I didn't touch up my makeup. Then I heard my mom's voice in my head, "You should always look your best—even if you are going to the grocery store at seven in the morning. You just never know who you might bump into."

"We want to celebrate your joining the endeavor for the best Black Squirrel Ball ever," Esther said as she came into the dining room with the salad dishes beautifully plated with microgreens and precisely five grape tomatoes on each of the four plates.

"And I hope you don't mind, but I asked Gareth to join us." Did she think I was going to walk out of this house after I smelled the chicken potpie blub-blubbing away in the oven? She could have invited my arch enemy or even Frank, and I would have stayed to experience that dish with more senses than just smell.

Gareth is their neighbor who happens to be single and about my age. I don't think Esther appreciates that I have a boyfriend. But then again, since Jonathan is out of town more than he is in town, I'm not sure I appreciate him as my boyfriend either.

She continued, in a tone that seemed like she had rehearsed the apologetic explanation, "He is so busy with his business and civic responsibilities that I just don't think he has time to eat well."

"I see him with McDonald's bags too often," Dax said, shaking his head.

I don't know Gareth that well because we didn't go to the same school until I was in ninth grade and he was a couple of years ahead of me, but I do know that Esther and Dax think the world of him. And he takes pretty good care of them—snow blowing their driveway and sidewalk in the winter and helping Dax load up the leaves in the fall.

"We need to keep him healthy and strong if he is going to keep helping me with the snow this winter," Dax said. "That Epstein kid who used to live next door was useless as a neighbor. I'm glad his girlfriend convinced him to move in with her and sell his house."

Esther stopped Dax before he said anything else that she might be embarrassed for. "Dax, the Epstein kid was a fine neighbor. But you are right that Gareth is ten times better. And the eyes on him!" she said with excitement. "Those eyes are like little pools of the Caribbean ocean twinkling with sunlight at high noon."

"Ey—I may be old, but I'm not dead yet. You could at least wait until I'm out of the room to gush over our neighbor who is less than half your age." It was good to see Dax get a little riled up. His French Canadian accent really showed when he got heated.

"Oh, you're the only man for me. But it doesn't hurt to look, does it Sam?" She leaned over to him and kissed his cheek.

I decided to change the subject quickly. "How about Frank today at the meeting? I thought he was going to pop a blood vessel when I asked him for his invitation list additions. I hope he realizes that I'm here to facilitate and do the dirty work, but I need some fuel from the committee."

"Getting down to business so soon?" Gareth asked as he entered the front door after a quick tap on the screen door frame. "I heard voices in the front of the house, so I came in this way." He looked at the dining room table with a similar surprised look as I probably had a few minutes earlier.

"What's all the fanciness for? The last time you asked me over, I got a fluffernutter sandwich, and I ended up pulling your old hot water tank out of the basement. Should I go back home and get some tools for tonight's project?"

Esther almost floated across the Oriental rug in the dining room, which was right off the front hall where Gareth was standing.

"I just thought we should celebrate Sam's new assignment with the Black Squirrel Ball. I have this beautiful room with lovely serving pieces, and I only use it four times a year: Easter, Thanksgiving, Christmas, and our anniversary."

"Yeah—congratulations, Sam," Gareth said. "I hear that you're going to help the committee raise a fortune!"

After Esther greeted him with a little hug, he stepped toward me, reached out his hand to shake mine, and gave me a peck on the cheek. I'm not sure, because the smell of the potpie intensified as Dax brought it into the room and placed it as the centerpiece of the table at the same time, but I think my heart may have skipped just one beat. Those eyes of his really are something else, and the touch of his hand in mine was firm, slightly calloused, and yet a bit gentle as he gave my hand a quick extra squeeze before releasing it.

We all sat down, and Dax said grace to bless our food and all our efforts for a successful ball. Then we immediately dug into our salads. As soon as we were done with the salads, the potpie was sufficiently cooled down to cut, and Esther did the honors of serving. It had big bite-size chunks of chicken, celery, carrots, and red potatoes, with peas scattered throughout the rich and creamy sauce. I could taste a hint of white wine mixed with the medley of rosemary and thyme.

The table was quiet for a few minutes as everyone concentrated on the smells and tastes of dinner.

Then Dax started the conversation I had been waiting for all day.

"So I hear you'd like to contact Mr. Suarez to get him to be your big donor this year?" he asked.

"I wouldn't jump to that conclusion just yet, but I would like to learn more about him and see if you think he would join us this year," I responded.

I did want to get to the same conclusion as Dax suggested, but I wanted to wander down the curiosity path and find out more information first.

"Esther and Aunt Reggie said that he hasn't been back to Peaceland Park since his wife died forty years ago. Do you really think he would come back now?" I asked.

Oh, how I hoped we could get him to come and bring a big check. Fifty-thousand dollars would be nice, but $25,000 might do if I could get a few more other gifts.

Dax said, "I think we need to talk about why he would go back to the park. His last experience at the park was pretty painful, and although he has a great affinity for the park, it's the place where his wife died."

"Whooaa, Nelly! You can't just cut to the chase like that. I could choke on a carrot," Gareth piped up. "Who is this Mr. Suarez, and how did his wife die?"

Perfect. I didn't have to be the curious cat. I had one sitting right next to me.

"It's not the best dinner conversation, but you asked, and I bet Sam is just as inquisitive, so Esther, if you'll forgive me, I'll go ahead," Dax said.

"That's what we're here for, to converse and share stories. Good and bad," Esther said as she took a big sip of her white wine.

"It was the morning after the first Black Squirrel Ball. I was in charge of getting all the big heads to clean up Peaceland Park as early as possible," Dax said.

"Big head, what's a big head?" Gareth asked.

"We used to call the kids who would come to work with a hangover big heads. They stayed late after the ball ended, pulled out their guitars and sang and danced until about three or four o'clock in the morning down by the river. I stayed, too, but I stopped drinking about eleven so I could think straight the next morning."

He continued, "So as I was saying, the next morning, I was walking down the flagstone pathway on the east side of the pond when I noticed a red shoe. I stopped to pick it up, and then after I bent down to get it I noticed something sparkling in the morning sun up in one of the waterfall pools. It was more than just a reflection off the water, so I squinted a little and got a better view of it. It was a piece of jewelry."

We were all fixed on Dax and his story. I was thinking about taking another serving of potpie and thought it might be distracting to him, so I waited.

"I then noticed that the water wasn't trickling down like it usually was. Sometimes a raccoon would go into one of the pools to wash its hands, tip over, and get stuck in the rocks. Then, the flow of water would be different. I climbed through the wooden fence at the bottom of the path and pulled myself up the bank. When I got toward the top I saw the most horrifying thing. It was Mrs. Suarez."

"What did you do?" I asked. I was out of the potpie trance now and back into the "tell me a bedtime story" from the other night.

"I called on the radio to get the security guys there pronto. I didn't know CPR, and I didn't know what to do. I was only about eighteen years old and had never seen anyone like that before."

"Was she dead?" Gareth asked with a probing tone.

"I didn't know," he said with a shrug of the shoulders. "I couldn't tell, and I was so scared I just grabbed my radio and told security to come right away and to call an ambulance. I was so scared of what I was looking at that I was stuttering so much they could hardly understand me."

"Did you know it was Mrs. Suarez?" I asked.

"I didn't know when I first saw her," he said with a stutter. I had never noticed Dax stutter before. Maybe it was because he was having a flashback-type recollection. "But by the time the security guards came, I figured it out by her dress and the piece of jewelry in the little pool of water. She was one of very few women who wore red the night before, and she certainly stood out. She had a large ruby and diamond necklace around her neck that Mr. Suarez bought for her. I remembered that he got it for her because I heard her say that she bought the red dress to go with the necklace."

"Most women get their accessories after their ball gowns," Esther said. "But I guess if you have a husband who can afford a gift like that, you can plan backwards."

Esther thoughtfully added another helping of the potpie to all of our plates.

Dax continued, "By the time the ambulance came, security determined she was dead. I called your grandfather, and we met the police at the Suarez house to tell Mr. Suarez."

"How did she die?" Gareth asked. I loved that he seemed like the nosey one, and I was getting all the information I hoped for.

"It was a deemed an accident," Dax said with an emphasis on "deemed." "The police said the fall didn't kill her, but she fell into the shallow water head first and drowned."

"You don't sound convinced," I said before I realized that it came out of my mouth instead of Gareth's.

"Mr. Suarez was never convinced. I was young and didn't know any better. But over the years, I've always wondered how it really happened. To this day, whenever I walk by that waterfall I remember Mrs. Suarez and that horrible day."

By the time Dax was toward the end of the story, I noticed that we had all continued eating, and my plate was the cleanest. Gareth's was full so I guess he must have served himself thirds while Dax was describing how he and Grandpa broke the news to Mr. Suarez, or he was so transfixed with the story that he didn't eat his second helping. I was immersed in the story, but that didn't prevent me from cleaning my plate.

Dax continued, "I remember how devastated Mr. Suarez was when he heard the news. The Suarezes didn't have any children and no family around here. They were totally devoted to each other and their work."

"She was absolutely beautiful. Long, wavy hair. Big brown eyes like chestnuts and flawless skin," Dax said as he closed his eyes, as if he could describe Mrs. Suarez better if he saw her in his imagination.

"I'm not dead," Esther said under her breath and abruptly.

"And she wasn't just a pretty face," Dax said as he gave an eye to Esther to emphasize that he wasn't just describing Mrs. Suarez as a pretty doll. "Mrs. Suarez was very successful in her own right—she was a top salesperson at Formula 333. She could light up a room and bring in the most revenue of any of the more experienced salespeople every month."

"And Mr. Suarez was a big-time chemist and inventor—right?" Gareth was there again. It was like I could think something, and it came out of this mouth. "I remember my mother swearing by 'Mr. Suarez's spot remover' when it came to cleaning my little league uniform when I was a kid."

"I still use that stuff today," Esther said. "Although not as often now that Dax isn't working at the park and getting grass stains all over his clothes."

"They were both very successful at Formula 333." Dax said. "She was so vivacious and full of life. And then she was gone." His voice got slower, and the words were more pronounced.

Then he got a puzzled look on his face and told us how he never really believed that it was an accident. He didn't necessarily think that she had any enemies, but he wondered why a woman would walk down a slippery waterfall with high heels and a fancy dress to get a piece of jewelry. As he described the scenario, we discussed that all she had to do was get someone from security, and they would have gotten the necklace.

Gareth said. "She was probably worried her husband would kill her if she came home without those jewels around her neck."

"Mr. Suarez would have never hurt Pauli or gotten upset at her for anything. He doted on her every move," Dax said.

"I still can't figure out how the necklace got there," I said.

"She could have tripped on a piece of flagstone and bumped up against the railing, and it could have fallen off of her and then into the water," Esther said.

"Or maybe she was upset at Mr. Suarez for some reason, and she took off the necklace and threw it in the water. Then she realized she made a mistake and climbed over the railing to get it back," I said.

"I think you are all wrong. I think she was pushed over the railing, and the necklace fell off when she hit the rocks," Dax said.

He continued to tell us how the police ruled out foul play and the investigation was open and shut pretty quickly.

"Mr. Suarez told me that he had a cold feeling go up his spine about midnight, and he shivered. He told me that at the time he thought it was just the scotch getting to him. But later, when he got home and Pauli wasn't there, he immediately called the police. He knew she was in trouble," Dax said.

"So why didn't they find her earlier?" Gareth asked.

"I have no idea. It never made any sense to me why the police didn't do anything until the park security called 911 the next morning," Dax said as he shook his head. "And I don't understand why the park security fellows didn't see her when they roamed the grounds after the ball."

He went on to tell us that the park had extra security the night of the ball to ensure that everyone got to their cars and that no one had any romantic interludes in the arboretum.

"I remember this one time when I was a young teenager working the night shift and I came across an elderly couple doing it by the Enchanted Oak," he began to add.

Trying to change the subject back to Mrs. Suarez and away from geriatric locomotion, I asked. "Do you think it was a cover-up? After all, I have never heard anything about this mysterious death until today. My family practically lived in Peaceland Park, and I don't remember anyone ever talking about it."

"No, I just don't think anyone wanted to believe that someone could kill Pauli—especially in the park—and it was easy to believe that it was an accident at the time." Dax looked wistful and disappointed. "Plus, in your family, it was an unwritten rule that we didn't talk about it. It just made your grandfather too upset."

He continued, "I know it was something he took to his grave as a low point in his life and the park's history. Every year, he would always lay flowers on the top of the waterfall on the anniversary of her death, and it is something I continued for him and Mrs. Saurez's memory since he died."

"But I never could figure out how the security guards with the dogs missed her," Dax said as his dark eyes squinted and became even more sunken.

"Maybe it was one of the security guards who killed her," Gareth said as if to pose the question, which he was now taking over, but it was like he threw a grenade that suddenly exploded a heavy silence into the air.

Dax looked at Gareth seriously and said, "I worked with all the men on duty that night at one point or another, and I don't think any of them were actually capable of hurting a fly—never mind a healthy and agile woman like Pauli," Dax said. He described the security guards in their sixties and seventies.

Dax told us that there was Walter, whose wife died decades before and who lived near my parents; Uncle Paul's father, who was a retired truck driver—I forgot what his real name was but everyone always called him Goose—and Mugsy, who was also a part-time gardener.

Dax said, "Mugsy was an interesting character. He was a talented bricklayer and mason in his day, but he was in a snowmobile accident by the river and almost died. He was never the same after that," Dax said. "Your grandfather grew up with him and gave him a job when no one else would."

"Why? Why wouldn't anyone else give him a job?" Gareth asked.

"Let's just say his spark plugs weren't always firing," Esther said. "He was a little odd, and it didn't help that he was crossed-eyed."

"Do you think there was foul play by any of them?" I asked.

"I can't imagine it. Walter was a little man of about five feet tall and maybe one hundred pounds if he had a heavy coat and his work boots on, and Goose had a bad arm. Neither one was physically capable of hurting anyone, especially a spirited woman like Pauli," Dax said.

"Doesn't sound like they could really provide 'security' to Peaceland Park," Gareth said.

Dax started to laugh. "You're right. But they didn't need to demonstrate any force with their bodies because they had Vic and Bach back then," Dax said.

"Who?" Gareth asked.

"Victoria and Bach were the German shepherds that were trained to be the real security guards." Dax said "real" louder and longer than all the other words. "The old-timers just walked the dogs around at night, and if anything seemed out of sorts, the gentlemen would let the dogs loose to bark very loudly, and people would run away."

"But I did always find it odd that neither Walter nor Goose found Mrs. Suarez before I did." I noticed later that he didn't say anything about Mugsy, and Dax continued, "The whole thing was handled poorly, especially the investigation. Mr. Suarez was so frustrated by the police work that he hired a private investigator, but most of the potential evidence was compromised because the medical examiner was fairly new to the job. And no one was about to question the police directly. The police chief was quite the tyrant back then."

Dax said that he remembered the investigation was kept quiet within Westfield so that people didn't get scared off from visiting Peaceland Park. The railing was fixed the same day that Mrs. Suarez was found so that no one else would fall through. "How that railing broke may have helped determine what happened," he said.

I didn't want to ask, but I guessed that Dax was assigned to fix the railing that day. And from the despondent look on his face, it started to sink in for me as to why I hadn't heard this story, even from my own family. They were in a helpless situation, since the police were in charge of the investigation.

With a deep sigh he said, "So, that's why Mr. Suarez hasn't been to Peaceland Park since the first ball, and I don't think we can get him to come to the ball this year. But I am planning on seeing him next week, and I'll ask. We'd love to have him visit, and he does still love the park," Dax said. "I'm convinced that our committee chairperson will get him to support the fortieth anniversary Black Squirrel Ball somehow." And he turned to his lovely wife and gave her a wink.

"I'll try my best. But meanwhile, you need to get on the task of pulling together pictures and articles so that Sam can get a slide show together. She's going to make a display of historic proportion!" she exclaimed with a "can do" hand gesture.

Dax and I went into the den while Gareth helped Esther clear the table. I was amazed by the number of piles of photos and boxes of albums.

Dax said, "I've started sorting pictures by decades, but some of the early years are a little fuzzy. I really wish your grandfather was still here. He could look at any one of these pictures and tell me within a week of when it was taken. He had a memory like a steel trap."

"I bet my Aunt Reggie, Uncle Joe, and my dad would remember some of these. Between the four of you, we should be able to get pretty close. And we can't use all the photos for the slide show, but I can understand that you only want to put these in some order once," I said.

There were black and white photos of the Carillon Tower the winter before it was dedicated, the rose garden when it was a tomato patch, and the swan in the ponds. All these pictures had great stories. Some Dax knew and told with great detail. But some pictures he was clueless about.

After a while of looking through pictures, Esther called us out to the patio for dessert. She apologized for not making a homemade dessert, but she was volunteering at the hospital earlier in the day so she had sent Dax to Russell for a pie made by the new bakery.

"I can't bake better than this, so we might as well support the local economy," she said proudly.

It was a pecan pie with vanilla ice cream, and then she put a little drizzle of chocolate sauce on each one. Yum!

"So what's next on your big plan for the ball?" Gareth asked me.

"I need to get cooking on the big asks for sponsorships. Tomorrow I have an appointment with the former switchboard operator at Formula 333, and a meeting with a fellow I used to work with who was a driver during the late '70s and early '80s."

Lucinda Marino was the switchboard operator, and she's an old mean lady living in a nursing home in Westfield who pretty much has scared away everyone except her immediate family members, and even they are terrified of her.

Tom Marfucci owns a financial advising and estate planning services firm, and he has all the big shots in the area as clients. He even has his own weekly personal finance segment on the local TV station.

The two people I have to meet with tomorrow couldn't be more opposite from one another.

"You are going to meet Lucinda?" Dax asked. "That's courageous. She never gave a dime to Peaceland Park, and I heard that she's as mean as ever."

"I don't want it to seem like I'm taking advantage of her, but her granddaughter Isabella is my hairdresser, and Lucinda has a bunch of pictures of the park in her nursing home room. Isabella is going to meet me there and ask Lucinda to lend me the pictures to make copies. Hopefully she'll also make a donation, but I'm not holding my breath," I said.

"And then I am going to meet Tom Marfucci to get a big sponsorship out of him. I'm not going to take no for an answer with him. My goal for tomorrow is to raise $10,000."

I was thinking that I needed to get home soon and practice my pitch. My meeting with him was at 12:30 p.m. tomorrow, and I only had fifteen minutes with him, so I needed to be on top of my game. I was also hoping that I could get at least another five names out of him for the invitation list.

I scraped my fork along the plate to get the last crumb covered with chocolate sauce, took the final bite, and smacked my lips together with satisfaction.

"Well folks, it was a lovely and informative evening, but I have to get home and get ready for my big day tomorrow," I said.

"Why don't I walk you home?" Gareth said like he had rehearsed it—or maybe he was coached by someone, like Esther.

"That's OK. I can make it back just fine. I wouldn't want you to have to do that."

"But Bogey needs a walk before he settles down for the night," Esther said, and Bogey came darting into the room like he was on cue as well.

"OK, but let's get going," I said. "I need to get my beauty rest."

Gareth put Bogey's retractable leash on, and Bogey took off before we had a chance to exchange hugs and good-byes with Esther and Dax.

When we got to the end of the street and turned the corner onto Western Avenue, we both started to talk at the same time.

"You go first," he said.

"No, you go," I said.

"OK. Don't you think it's weird that the investigation of Mrs. Suarez's death was so rushed?" he asked.

"You bet, and that the fence was fixed so quickly," I said. We continued to exchange our curiosities, including about how Dax didn't mention much about Mugsy and how no one found Pauli until the following morning.

"It just doesn't seem right," he said as he shook his head.

I kept going over what Dax had said to me, and I was so mentally exhausted that I didn't have the energy to say what I was thinking. I thought that maybe there was a good reason this topic wasn't discussed, at least to my knowledge, for so many years, and maybe we should keep it that way.

We continued to walk in silence at a pretty brisk pace due to Bogey's excitement, and soon Gareth was saying good-bye and wishing me good luck on my $10,000 day.

"Let's stay focused on the positive part of the evening, and you planning the best Black Squirrel Ball. If there's anything I can do to help with the ball, you can count me in," he said.

I thought that he might need a date to the ball and if Jonathan blew me off for an 'important assignment' I could have a chance. He would look awfully nice in a white pressed shirt and jacket. Or maybe a Tommy Bahama shirt—I bet he would go for the tropical look.

I had to snap myself out of this wardrobe planning, since I had a boyfriend, and Gareth probably already had a date.

"Thanks. We may need some more help with the invitation list. Do you have any out-of-town relatives who you could invite in for the weekend?"

"All my relatives live within the Westfield city limits, and they're probably already on your invitation list from years past. We treat this event like our family reunion."

Great, I thought. No chance of getting more money from him if everyone he knows has been going for years. First Frank and then Gareth. How am I going to raise this much money if no one new will come to the ball?

But then I got a nice surprise. "I may be able to squeeze a sponsorship out of my partner. You can put us down for a $2,500 table. We'll invite a few clients and write it off as a business expense."

"Great! Thank you for your support. I'll drop off the sponsorship package tomorrow on my way to Springfield so you can review the details." I realized that I was sounding a bit precise in my response—very corporate—and then switched back to being my laid-back, conversational self.

"I had a nice time tonight. I love hearing Dax tell his stories. I just wish it was one of the more pleasant stories to hear," I said.

"Me, too," he said.

"It all just doesn't add up," I said half under my breath but loud enough that Gareth still heard me.

"You're right. Something went down forty years ago at the park, and I bet we'll never know what really happened," he said.

Bogey was getting a little rambunctious in the azalea bushes and Gareth said good night. I felt like there was chemistry in the air—like he wanted to give me a hug or kiss on the cheek—but he just stepped back and said, "OK then, see you soon," and we both looked down at our shoes.

"Yup—see you tomorrow," I said quickly as I entered my kitchen door.

Up until I went to bed that night, I was feeling a bit melancholy about the dinner engagement at Esther and Dax's house. On one hand, I couldn't help but keep thinking that Gareth's eyes were more like the color of the Hawaiian ocean and how it fades into a blue sky rather than the Caribbean ocean.

And I couldn't get the thought of Pauli's mysterious death out of my mind either.

At least I'd get to see those eyes again tomorrow when I dropped off the sponsorship packet.

CHAPTER 8

IT WAS A RESTLESS NIGHT'S sleep. I was dreaming that I was free-falling, but I would wake up before I hit whatever my body was aiming for.

When I woke up for the last time, I trudged into the bathroom and looked into the mirror. By the look of my face staring back at me, it looked like I did fall, and I hit the pavement, because my face was red, and I had puffy circles under my eyes.

It didn't help that I needed an "enhancement" to fade away some of my premature grey. And according to my counting on the calendar I needed to wait another week so then I would get my hair done again right before the ball. At times like that, I really felt like I had a little too much of my mother in me. She can plan her next four series of perms and haircuts around a trip or event eight months away.

It was a high-maintenance morning to be presentable for my meetings. I was especially trying to not let my hair look too terrible since I was going to see my hairdresser. She could have insisted that I come in earlier than I had scheduled. She has a thing about her clients looking their best. Good thing she didn't see me last night without much makeup or this morning when it looked like a Mack truck hit me.

I was able to put my hair up in the front, and I added a little extra mascara to emphasize my eyes compared to the gray roots. I thought I looked pretty good for a semiunemployed professional.

I wore a navy pantsuit with gray pinstripes on the jacket. The pants were plain navy, and I had a great pair of wing-tip-style navy patent leather heels. I wished my hair looked as good as my feet, but we can't have everything every day.

I drove down Western Avenue and then right onto West Silver Street, near my Aunt Ruth's house—my mother's sister—and then past the hospital. Once

I got to the post office, I turned left onto Broad Street. That route was better because there were fewer potholes and manhole covers to avoid on West Silver Street compared to Court Street. Plus, making a right into the nursing home parking lot is much easier than a left across traffic.

I met Isabella in the parking lot at the nursing home on Broad Street. I hadn't been in this place since my mom and I delivered poinsettias to shut-ins at Christmas. A high school friend of mine, Jerry, asked us to visit some of the residents who didn't have any nearby family members. Jerry is quite a character and can persuade the pants off of anyone. That talent is put to good work on a regular basis because as a certified nurse assistant in the nursing home, he has to help the nurses bathe and shower the male residents—who think their body odor is nostalgic.

When we visited in December, the medicinal smell turned my stomach, and I went home immediately after our visits were complete instead of joining my mom for the prime rib dinner special at the new restaurant down the street. It's quite unusual for me to turn down a good meal, but I was nauseated.

"Let's hope I can keep my nose and stomach in check," I thought. I had some mints in my shoulder bag just in case.

Isabella looked as beautiful as ever. Tall, long red hair, and all northern Italian. She was a great hair stylist and she has been very loyal to her clients over the years. She always made sure I had a backup stylist in case of a hair emergency when she was traveling. That's dedication.

Isabella's maternal grandmother, Lucinda Marino, was the switchboard operator at Formula 333 for forty years. I can't seem to stay in one job for more than two years, never mind four decades. How incredibly boring that must have been.

On the other hand, Aunt Reggie said that Lucinda knew everything about everyone because she sometimes forgot to disconnect her line when she transferred calls. That must have kept the job interesting!

"Hello," she said in a sweet, quiet voice when we reached each other in the parking lot.

We exchanged hello hugs and cheek kisses and entered the lobby.

"My grandmother is expecting us. She was quite specific what time to come so she wouldn't miss breakfast or the Wii bowling competition," she said with a chuckle. "She and her partner are in the running for finals. They have matching shirts and everything."

We met Lucinda in the lobby, where Isabella introduced us.

"It's about time," she said with a bit of a scorn. "I can't miss warm-up in forty-five minutes in the rec room."

She was in a wheelchair that had huge rugged wheels—like a dune buggy version—and it was bright blue with a big smiley face painted on the back.

As we walked with her down the hall, she was complaining all the way. I was thinking that she either didn't know the smiley face was on the back of her chair, considering her bad temperament, or that she purposely put it there to be a balance to her face, which looked like it was permanently frowning.

Even though she was cranky and ill-tempered, all her comments were relevant to her surroundings and current events. I was thinking that this woman was quite "with it" and that Dax must have had her mixed up with someone else. She seemed to know which end was up as she led us to her room and said hello to all her fellow residents and the staff by name along our route. However, everyone seemed to ignore her.

"I understand that you are collecting pictures and stories for Peaceland Park, are you?" she asked in a tone that reminded me of the Wicked Witch of the West from the *Wizard of Oz*. I was getting ready for her to call me her "pretty."

I explained to her that I was working on the Black Squirrel Ball, and that we were trying to raise $100,000 for the park this year—the most ever raised—and that we also wanted to put together a slide show, showcasing the history. I continued that all the pictures borrowed would be electronically scanned and promptly returned, and that photos used in the slide show would be acknowledged by the provider on the bottom of the respective slide.

"I hope you don't think you are going to get any money out of me. Every penny I have goes to that administrator upstairs to keep me in this godforsaken dormitory for old people that my children have sentenced me to for life," she said like she had rehearsed many, many times before.

"And how can I trust that you will give me back my pictures?" she scowled. At this point, Isabella rolled her eyes and looked like she wanted to crawl under the bed.

"I'll borrow the pictures from you today, electronically scan—make copies of them tonight—and return them tomorrow. Barring any natural disaster or major emergency that I cannot foresee, your pictures will be back safely with you tomorrow at this same time.

"OK. I find your answers satisfactory. You may borrow my pictures. Isabella, please open my closet and remove those four boxes."

I couldn't believe that she had so many pictures. When I said I would have them back in twenty-four hours, I thought there might be a photo album or two. It was going to take me all night—and that was if I got started as soon as I was done with my appointments.

"Some of the boxes have stuff from Formula 333 and some from Peaceland Park — it was all one big family to me, and I didn't separate it. I expect that you will return the boxes and the contents exactly as I have them now," she said as if she was M in a James Bond movie giving me mission instructions.

My eyes were wide with amazement—both fear that I might screw something up and excitement that I might have access to information that no one else has ever had the privilege of having. That may be a bit of an exaggeration, but after the James Bond moment, I was getting carried away.

"Grandmother, I can't come back tomorrow with Samantha since I have to work, but she'll deliver the boxes back to you and place them in the closet—OK?" Isabella asked with a hint of "oh, I hope you don't want me to come back because you scare the shit out of me."

"Of course—I figured you could only come today since you only come to visit once a week. I know, you are too busy to visit your dying grandmother," she said. This lady definitely could pour the guilt on. She wasn't dying, just getting crankier.

"Fine then. You two have got to get out of here with these boxes. Call Jerry, and he'll put them on a gurney and bring them to your car. I have to get to the rec room for warm-up. I can't Wii if I'm not loose." I thought it sounded funny—the combination of "wee" and being "loose." I'm glad she wasn't snacking on prunes, or I would have really cracked myself up.

I was glad she suggested Jerry because I hadn't seen him since Christmas.

"Hey there, girlfriend," he said in a prepubescent boy's voice as he entered Lucinda's room.

Jerry was every bit a flamboyantly gay man that one could be, and I don't recall him ever being anything but. All the girls in high school asked him for help picking out their prom dresses. No other guy would be caught dead looking at *Seventeen* magazines, never mind having a subscription to it, but Jerry didn't care. He loved fashion, decorating, and baking. I was his home economics partner for a semester, and he made the best blueberry muffins, insisting that we dip them in a little melted butter and then coarse baking sugar to make them sparkle.

Jerry's hair was very spiky blond with streaks of orange upon this visit, but it was drastically different every time I saw him. Isabella took a double-take and her eyes almost popped out of her head when he walked in and opened his mouth. Jerry skipped over to me and gave me a big bear hug, picking me off my feet and twirling me around twice with his Conan the Barbarian arms and stature.

His oxymoronically ripped masculine body and drag queen-like demeanor were enough to make people's heads turn. The funny thing is, the old women in the nursing home love him because he can easily maneuver them out of their wheelchairs and give them hairstyle and fashion tips. I'm not quite sure what attracts the old men to Jerry, but he is always being sought out by residents of both sexes.

Jerry picked up the heavy cartons of pictures so easily—like they were tissue boxes—and placed them on the gurney. He maneuvered it out of the nursing home and toward my car, gave me another big hug that squeezed the air out of my lungs, and told me to make sure he and his new boyfriend were on the ball's invitation list. I wondered which one would wear a dress—maybe both of them.

Isabella gave Jerry her business card and offered to provide a free color consultation. I thought that was a clever way to imply that he needed a new look. But he was just so flattered that she would want to do his hair that he said he would call for an appointment on his next day off.

When we got to the parking lot, I thanked Isabella for her help. She apologized for the crankiness of her grandmother and said she hoped that attitude wasn't genetic. And then she said she was looking forward to seeing me the following week as she glanced specifically at my roots.

CHAPTER 9

WHEN I GOT INTO MY car, I noticed I had two messages on my phone. One was from my sister, Frances. She was working in Ireland for a month, but she told her boss that she must be back for the Black Squirrel Ball. She works for a bank and travels often, and I don't really know what she does. I think it has something to do with IT, but it could be finance related.

Frances seems to enjoy her work and travel, but she's home for every holiday or special family event. She's another strong part of my support system.

In her message, she told me that she made sure my brother, Mark, would be at the ball. I had already assumed he would be. He lives in town and owns his own business. He is a welder and metal fabricator and is always busy, but during the winter he plows and makes sure Mr. Z's driveway is always clear after winter storms.

The other message was from Jonathan. He said that he was coming home for the weekend but that he had some work to do and needed to be close to his Blackberry in case something came up.

He gave me the time that his train would arrive and said he would see me then.

I guessed that meant I had to pick him up.

It would be good to see him. I missed him when he was away, but I thought I might even miss him when he was around, too, because he was so tied to that stupid Blackberry. I never knew accounting could be so demanding.

By the time I had listened to my two voice mails, I was already through town. Traffic is usually a killer in town due to the constant construction projects, but I must have timed the lights and school buses just right.

I drove toward the North End bridge and took a right onto Meadow

Street. This street must have been much nicer years ago before people moved out to drone-looking houses on the lots with no trees. Meadow Street now has houses on it with storefronts built in and an old hotel that has been converted to small apartments.

Gareth and his partner own a tire shop and gas station on the corner of Meadow and Mechanic Streets. I thought a $2,500 sponsorship was a big chunk of change for them. There must be some markup on tires.

I drove in and parked along the right side of the building. I was hoping that the mechanics in the bays on the left side of the building wouldn't notice my bald tires the way Isabella eyed my roots. When I received my final paycheck from Peaceland Park, I figured I'd take a few bucks and buy a used set of tires from Gareth—only if I didn't land a dream job where I could afford a new car. After that walk home last night with him, I wouldn't mind him giving something of mine a balance and rotation—it might as well be my car.

My car was a 2000 Mercury Cougar that I loved when I first bought it and hated within about three weeks. It was sporty and had a bunch of space in the back with the long hatchback, but the seats dug right into my lumbar so painfully that I couldn't drive it for more than forty-five minutes without needing a massage or a hot shower.

I walked into the waiting room/office of the 1950s style service station and saw Gareth sitting behind what looked like the back end of a 1950s-era Thunderbird. He made a desk out of half a car, and he had an old carburetor sitting on the right side with the guts of a lamp sticking out of the top.

"Hey there, what's rolling in the tire business?" I asked, amused with my pun. There were two cars up on lifts in the garage stalls and four cars parked on the left side of the building. They could be done, or they could be waiting for new tires, but they were definitely business going on the books.

"Couldn't be better. Seems as though the city is slow to fix the late spring storm potholes, and I have a bunch of bent rims to replace and bubbles to fix. Nice to see you again so soon." His eyes looked even bluer in the fluorescent light reflecting off the white walls.

As I looked around the room, I couldn't get over how clean everything was. It was like he met the sanitary requirements of a hospital.

"Who does your cleaning? This place is spotless." I peered out the office door to the shop and noticed everything in its place on the work benches by each stall.

"When I bought the place, my mother told me that she would help me out if I kept the place as clean as she kept her operating room." Gareth's mom is a nurse at the local hospital. Thank goodness, I've never had to encounter her at her workplace, but she is awfully nice and always looks meticulous.

"When I have new guys start here, they hate it, but then they realize how much business we get and how little time they have to waste trying to find stuff, and they get over it pretty quickly. I think people like to come in here knowing that they won't have to smell grease and get grimy."

"Wow—what else have you promised to your mother? She has some pull."

There was a one-cup coffee pot and a small 1950s retro refrigerator with a sign that said, "Help Yourself."

"Especially when she's an investor," he said. "But business is so good I'm gonna pay her back two years earlier than I planned."

While I was being enthralled by his entrepreneurialism, I almost forgot the reason I stopped by.

"Here is the sponsorship package I mentioned last night. If you can e-mail me a logo, I'll add it to our publicity," I said, pulling one of the 8½ x 11 inch pocket folders I had in my red leather Coach briefcase that my former colleagues gave me as a good luck present.

"I was telling my partner that you want new people to go to the ball, and he had a good idea—we'll have a contest. We'll put all the customer receipts from June and July in a hat, and at the beginning of August, we'll draw five names to win two tickets to the Black Squirrel Ball. That way, we'll get new people to the ball."

"But then you will be giving away all your tickets. What about you and Bill?"

Bill had been his best friend since they played flag football in grammar school. Bill went to Ohio State on a football scholarship and tore his ACL in the final game of the year and lost his chance for an NFL career. Good thing he was pretty smart and got a degree in English literature, too. It wasn't exactly what you needed to run a tire shop, but he was always good for cocktail party conversation. A few months earlier I was at a Chamber of Commerce dinner, and he was educating the group of small business owners at our table about how significantly the industrial revolution influenced Dickens and then segued smoothly to the subject of good tire maintenance.

"I'm going to sit with my family, and Bill is going to sit with his soon to be in-laws. They're going to be in town early for the Labor Day nuptials, so he figured he would buy a few tickets to show the fancy Boston blue bloods how the locals party." He chuckled a bit to himself and shook his head. Bill was marrying a very nice girl who came from a very snooty family in the eastern part of the state. Gareth told me that it was Bill's goal in life to educate them on how simple people live.

"So I noticed that your tires are a bit worn," he said as nonchalantly as any man could tell you that you had spinach in your teeth.

After eight years, I think the tires would be bald by now, but the car was on the other side of the parking lot behind a pickup truck that had pulled in after me. "Wow—you have some eagle eyes if you can see them from here," I said. Not only are those eyes pools of Hawaiian waters, but with sight like Superman.

"I'm good, but not that good," he said. "I noticed them in the driveway last night. You can take my jeep to your meeting in Springfield, and you'll have new tires on by the time you get back."

"Thanks, but tires aren't in my budget right now. I need to be a little more frugal for a few months, but when I get my final check from the ball, I'll be back."

"I'm not letting you drive that car with those tires. Your brother would kill me." Mark and Gareth share some customers, especially when Gareth had a customer with a custom car rebuild that needed some specialized welding. And, plus, my brother wouldn't kill him, but I have been avoiding both him and my father in my car so they wouldn't give me a hard time. "You can pay me when you get the money."

"I couldn't do that," I said, but I could tell from his determined look that I wasn't getting out of there without new tires. "How about you throw on a set of used tires, and I'll pay by credit card." By the time the bill comes in I'll have some money from the Black Squirrel Ball committee, and I'll just pay it off in two installments, I thought.

"I have a set that will be just right, and I won't take your credit card. You can pay me when you get the money," he said. It wasn't a subject of negotiating. "Here are my keys. I can put the top up if you don't want to get your hairdo messed up before your big meeting."

"I'll be fine. My hair isn't much of a 'do' to get messed," I said as he tossed the keys, and then I walked out to his red 2007 Jeep Wrangler with chrome wheels and the black top rolled back.

As I drove east on Route 20, I had to stop at every red light, and it took me a bit longer than my previous morning commute. It probably didn't help that I used to travel the same route at 6:30 a.m. compared to midday.

I got to Springfield in about thirty minutes—I was being extra cautious with Gareth's Jeep since I hadn't driven a stick shift in a few years. Usually, I would have just parked my car on the street and loaded the meter with change, but because I was driving Gareth's Jeep, I decided to splurge on the $4 hourly rate in the business tower parking lot. I was trying to keep even the smallest expenses to a minimum, but I also didn't want to have my biggest sponsor's car stolen.

After I parked and walked a block down Court Street, I entered the atrium of the building and went up in the elevator to the eleventh floor. I was greeted by a lovely, very young receptionist in a conservatively cut dark red suit who could double as a Bud Light model in a bikini at spring break. She said that Tom's earlier appointment was cancelled and that I could go right into his office.

I walked down the hall to a huge corner office that had Tom's name on the door, but he wasn't there. I paused and looked back to the receptionist. She gave me a nod and a hand gesture that it was OK to go in. I wasn't sure where to sit—on the couch by the wall might look too casual. If I took a seat at the conference room table, what if I took his seat? And if I sat in one of the wingback chairs in front of his desk, I would feel a little too formal. I'm not a close friend, but I did work with him in the past so I wanted to use that to my advantage.

Just as I was in the middle of this internal debate, Tom walked in. "Samantha, how are you?" He was really loud and walked very fast. Everything about him seemed so pronounced and over-the-top and yet genuine at the same time. He reached out his hand and gave me a kiss on the cheek. He was wearing a blue and white seersucker suit with a light yellow shirt and no tie. He was the Cape Cod version of summer casual.

"I'm just fine, Tom. And I appreciate you seeing me on such short notice."

He gestured for me to sit at the conference table. He sat on one side, and I sat on the opposite side. I probably could have sat in any chair—but he did have everything in its place, and it was best to wait and let him find his own.

We started off the meeting by asking about each other's family. He had two children—a boy and a girl. The girl was older and was looking forward to starting high school in the fall. The boy would be starting middle school and was looking forward to playing the trumpet in the jazz band.

"I thought you were climbing the corporate ladder, taking that big company by storm, and then I heard that you are organizing the Black Squirrel Ball. Do you think this is the best career move?" He sounded more like a parent than a former co-worker at that point, but he is a financial advisor; his job is to help people plan for their financial future.

"I just felt like I was losing my identity, and I had very little interest in anything I was working on. This opportunity came up, and I jumped at the chance. I have savings, very little debt, and a good jump start on my retirement planning. I figured I could afford to take a little detour for a couple of months with a pay cut to get my head clear and help Peaceland Park with their biggest fund-raiser." I sounded quite like the assertive and well-thought-out young professional, but I could tell that my speech was a bit fast. Hopefully, he didn't sense my nervousness.

"Well, I wish you all the best. And Peaceland Park is lucky to have you. I only have about fifteen minutes, so I don't mind if you cut to the chase. Considering you are between jobs, I'm guessing you don't need your financial plan updated—right?" he said.

"You are exactly right. However, I do need to think about combining my two 401(k)s, so this won't be my last visit to see you this summer."

I told him about the ball—the date, the band, the $100,000 goal, and how I hoped he and his firm could support the endeavor.

He said he would gladly support the ball at the $5,000 level, and if I sent him some posters, he would post them in the community boards at the Longmeadow grocery stores and post office. "We need to get some of the east of the river people to support this west of the river establishment. I don't know why people think Westfield is a world away. My wife is in a book club with a bunch of Longmeadow women who think nothing of driving to West Hartford for lunch, but won't go to Westfield for a garden tour. It drives me crazy," he said with a bit of rage in his voice.

Longmeadow is the town that all the local real estate agents send relocating executives to when they move into the Springfield area. I was once told it was the town of "long mortgages" because the houses were so much more expensive and the taxes were so high, but it is considered the most prestigious town in the area by many.

He continued his minor rant by saying that all the people at his table would not be from Westfield in an effort to help spread the word on how nice the park is and get future donors, too.

"I'm also working with Dax LaFluer on a slide show to showcase the history of Peaceland Park. Do you have any old pictures I could borrow?" I asked.

"I don't have too many, but my brother had more. I worked there in the late 1970s and early 1980s, but he was sixteen years older than me and worked there from 1966 to 1972—through his college years. He worked at Formula 333 in the research and development department during the day and also at night as a driver for the sales conference attendees."

"Do you think you could introduce me to him?"

"I wish I could, but he died from heart attack four years ago. His wife died two years later, and I just cleaned out their house with their one son last year. I have a bunch of boxes that I haven't had a chance to go through. It's about time I do something good with that stuff."

"Anything you can find would be great. We might not use everything in the slide show, but Dax is trying to fill up his retirement days by collecting all the information he can to develop a comprehensive history on the park."

"I'll go through the boxes this weekend. It will be a good project for the kids to help me with, and I'll call you next week to pick up anything I find of interest."

Then he asked who else I had for sponsors. I told him that the committee was going to all their favorites, and we had about $15,000 committed from five previous sponsors. I also mentioned our new sponsor this year, All Around Tires. He looked like he recognized Gareth's name. Tom wouldn't confirm if he had Gareth as a client due to confidentiality issues, but I had a funny feeling that Gareth was well insured and had a solid financial plan.

"I just met with Lucinda Marino, who lent me her archives. I hope to pull some names out of her old newsletters and newspaper clippings. And Dax and Esther are going to visit with Mr. Suarez next week, so we hope he will support the ball."

"Isn't that a bit of a long shot, considering he hasn't been back to Peaceland Park since his wife died?" I was surprised that he mentioned this to me, as he was just a toddler when Mrs. Suarez died.

"I didn't know that many people knew of Mrs. Suarez's death. How do you know about her?" I asked.

"My brother worked with Mr. Suarez and he very much influenced his career choice of becoming a chemistry professor. When Mr. Suarez's wife died, he pretty much lost it. I remember my brother telling me that he once worked for a man who had a nervous breakdown over his wife's death."

"So Mr. Suarez was institutionalized, and that's why he left town?" I felt like Inspector Clouseau stating a very likely conclusion.

"I'm not sure if that was speculation or the truth. All I know is that Mr. Suarez, according to my brother, was distraught about Mrs. Suarez's death, and my brother never believed it was an accident."

"Funny you should say that. I was having dinner with Dax and Esther last night, and I got the same gist from Dax, too. However, he may have been a bit closer to the situation—he actually was the one to find Mrs. Suarez the day after the very first Black Squirrel Ball. How awful that must have been," I said as I shook my head from side to side in dismay.

He looked down at his watch and the receptionist announced over his phone that his next appointment was there.

"I'm sorry I have to give you the bum's rush, but if I want to write you a check for $5,000 that won't bounce, I need to get back to work."

I thanked him for his time. I was a bit disappointed that he didn't offer $10,000, and it was so quick that I didn't have a chance to counter the $5,000 offer, but he did say he would provide me some help on fund-raising via publicity and getting new people to come to the event. He said that he would also send a fund-raising letter on behalf of Peaceland Park to his guests after the ball.

I walked down the hall with Tom to the receptionist's desk, where she had parking validation for the garage waiting for me. He gave me a quick hug good-bye and reminded me to send him at least five posters for him to hang in Longmeadow.

"And I'll also mention the ball to Mr. Suarez. I see him from time to time, and, although I doubt he will come to the event, he will probably sponsor a table or two for the workers at the park. He always was very impressed by how well manicured Peaceland Park was, and what a good job the landscapers did keeping it up."

I bet he has Mr. Suarez as a client too, but I didn't want to ask. It really shouldn't matter to me why he keeps in touch with Mr. Suarez—but if Tom could help land a big donation that would be great.

As I got into the elevator, I remembered that the committee decided at the last meeting not to print posters this year in an effort to reduce expenses. "Oh well," I thought, "I'd have to whip something up out of my pay and send them along to Tom. I wasn't going to let my biggest donor down. I needed him to lead me to the next biggest donor."

I got into Gareth's Jeep and enjoyed the ride back to Westfield. It seemed like I hit every red light again, but it did give me more practice with the clutch and brake, and it was nice to be out enjoying the sunshine. I turned on the CD player and was surprised to hear a great mix of Tom Petty, Rusted Root, and oddly enough—Neil Diamond's "Sweet Caroline." It's funny the things you learn about people by their choice of music.

When I got back to All Around Tires, not only did my car have new—not used—tires, but new rims, too. The black car looked all tricked out with a set of black matt painted rims and Pirelli high performance all season tires. This set-up was going to run me about $1,400. I was hoping more for $200.

I walked into the office with the weight of a new set of bills on my shoulders that I just couldn't handle right now. Before he even turned around to say hello, I blurted "Gareth, I appreciate your efforts, but I really can't afford those."

I also really couldn't get over how good the clunker looked. He also had it washed and a few of the little scratches buffed out.

"It really was nothing. A guy ordered these tires a year ago, gave me 30 percent down in cash and then left town. I haven't heard from him, and our policy is to wait six months before we return the product. These were a custom order so I couldn't return them. You only have to pay the difference between my cost and the 30 percent down."

"What if he comes back?" I asked.

"By the time he comes back in seven to ten years, his tires and rims will be the last worry on his mind."

Something didn't feel right about taking advantage of a criminal's bad luck.

"And don't feel guilty. The guy had it coming," he said with a defiant look right into my eyes.

Maybe he could read my mind.

"So how was your big meeting?" he asked in an effort to change the subject. "You look like it didn't go as well as you hoped." I was still staring at my totally cool looking yet uncomfortable car and wondering if it was right to take advantage of a felon who would never enjoy the tires and rims.

If I could only look at it and didn't have to drive it, it would be my best car ever.

I turned toward Gareth and breathed in new air with an optimistic attitude all the way down to my toes.

"The meeting went pretty well. Tom asked me about other sponsors, and I was pleased to tell him that All Around Tires joined the list this year. I was hoping for ten, but he committed to five and some help with future fund-raising."

"Seventy-five hundred in one day—not bad for a day's work," he said and gave me a quick fist bump.

"And I have a trunk full of pictures and memorabilia from Lucinda Marino that I need to scan tonight."

"Oh—that's what those boxes were?"

"Yah," I said with a lilt of panic in my voice. "What happened to the boxes?"

"Nothing. I was going to play a trick on you and say that we got hydraulic oil all over them, but you would probably have had a heart attack considering the stuff belongs to Mrs. Marino," he said with a chuckle.

Mrs. Marino has always been known as a big meanie throughout town.

"She used to give out stale lollipops from the bank drive-up for Halloween candy," he said.

"She didn't work at the bank; she worked at Formula 333," I said.

"That's my point. She would get lollipops all year long from the bank drive-up, and then give them out at Halloween. She was mean and cheap."

"Well, she was generous to lend me her boxes of pictures. And before I realized how generous she was with four of those huge boxes, I promised to have them back to her tomorrow morning, so I better get going and start my long night of scanning."

I took another look at my car and smiled. I never knew my car could look so cool—but if anyone could make it happen, it was Gareth.

CHAPTER 10

"HEEEEYYY," I HEARD FROM MY kitchen door. It was my dad with one of his drive-by visits. He had a remarkably Fonzy-type greeting for a fifty-plus-year-old man.

Dad wasn't a large man, but he wasn't small either. With white hair and light blue eyes, he was about five feet eleven with a full build. His belly showed off his love for ice cream, but his overall body shape exemplified that he was not afraid of manual labor.

My apartment is on the way from his work garage to my parent's house, so I was frequented with impromptu visits. I tried to get him to follow the "Please call first" rule, but with Jonathan out of town more than ever, there was little risk for any interruptions. Plus, it was nice to have him visit.

"Come in," I yelled from the living room. I had set up the room as an office since I was working from home now. It took me almost an hour to connect the scanner I had bought for Jonathan's birthday present, which was about a month away. I decided I'd think of something else—maybe a new tie would be thoughtful enough considering the way things were going between us.

"What are you doing?" he asked, looking at the mess I had created. The room was pretty tight, and I had every square inch of the carpet covered with the scanner box, Styrofoam from the scanner, and Lucinda's boxes of photos. I was in the middle of a mess, and I needed to make progress quickly.

"I have all this stuff from Lucinda Marino, and I promised to have it scanned and back to her tomorrow. I'm going to be up all night," I said with a pathetic look of hopelessness.

He sat down on the chair that was covered with the scanner's manual, shook his head, and let out a deep sigh.

"I was going home for dinner, but I can ask your mother to bring it here, and we could help," he said. Usually my mom is the one to come up with brilliant solutions when I got into an administrative pinch. Dad is the one to get speeding tickets fixed. They both have their strong suits.

"I am starting to get cranky from hunger—anything would be great. Here's the phone." I threw him my cell phone. He looked at it like it was a toy and then tossed it back to me.

I dialed and tossed the phone back to him. He told her to pack up dinner and come over—that we were in the middle of a project and needed some food for fuel.

"What'd she say?" I asked.

"She sounded a little annoyed, but she'll be here in a while. How about I set the table so when she gets here, we can dig right in?"

He must have been pretty hungry himself, since he wasn't usually the domestic type to set a table.

"OK—I'll try to get a process down so she can hand me a picture, I can scan it, and you can tell me what it is and what time period it's from. This will actually save me a lot of time because I may not have to go back and meet with Lucinda to go through what is what. She scares the shit out of me."

"She scares the shit out of everyone. But she loved your grandfather. He would always pick her flowers and bring them to her in the dark basement switchboard office with no windows. She was across from the mailroom, and no one would visit her except Grandpa," he said.

"Did he really visit her or was it that he had to walk by her every day to get to his office?"

"It was a little bit of both. He figured it was better to keep her happy than have her as an enemy. She liked to listen in on conversations," he said. I guess people could do that years ago—before the advancement of digital recorded lines and privacy rules in the workplace.

He had the table set and was sitting waiting for dinner to arrive. I'm not sure how he got it done since I don't think he had ever been in my kitchen drawers or cabinets before. Mom arrived within a half hour, and we were sitting down enjoying London broil, salad, and baked potatoes.

My mom is always well put-together. She has a flair for clothes and likes to demonstrate her sale-buying ability at the mall close to her office in Connecticut. That night, she was wearing jeans with different colored sparkles along the legs and a purple top. She's convinced that if she doesn't look like an old lady, then she isn't an old lady. I would agree with her on that point.

"So, how much do you have to do tonight?" my mom asked as she looked into the crammed living room.

"All of it. I told Lucinda I'd have everything back tomorrow. There wasn't much space in her room, so I didn't think she'd have this much. Whenever we opened her closet, I thought a furry blue monster was going to jump out at us."

"She would be one person I would guess who would have a monster in their closet. She knows about everyone's monsters in their closets," my dad said.

"Lucinda was always nice to me. She was terrible to your Aunt Reggie, but when I worked for Mr. Brown in the human resources department, she was always helping me out," my mom said.

"She didn't like Reggie because Lucinda didn't get a job back in the sixties that Reggie did get. Lucy—as Grandpa called her—never forgot that. And she liked to help you because she liked to get her hands on the personnel files. She was a busybody."

"Well, it was good that you didn't tell Lucinda that Reggie is on the committee. She might not have let you borrow this stuff," my mom said as she started clearing the table and putting dishes in the sink. I figured I'd just let them sit there for the time being and put them in the dishwasher later. She's a dishwasher virgin and refuses to learn how to work one.

"What have you found so far?" she asked.

"I have gone through a bunch of newsletters and sales contests from Formula 333 and newspaper articles from the last ten years, but I want to get to the old stuff. Ready to get started?"

I had my mom hand me pictures, then I scanned them and gave them back to her so we would keep everything in order. We numbered each picture while my dad looked over the photo to give his best guess as to what it was, who was in it, and about what year it was taken.

Some of the pictures were easy—like the Carillon Tower dedication with the newspaper article from 1950. The One Acre Lawn construction was one of the first projects—so that was right after Grandpa started, in the early to mid-1940s.

And some had dates on them. I was amazed by how many people Dad remembered. There were pictures of kitchen workers who worked on the sales conference picnics, landscapers who took care of the grounds, and also people from the Formula 333 office.

Then we got to some pictures of the first Black Squirrel Ball. There was even a newspaper picture of Mom and Dad dancing. They looked like they were at their high school prom.

"Remember this?" Mom asked him. He was wearing a white jacket and dark pants. "He wore a pink carnation, and I wore my senior prom dress—it was light pink with a tulle skirt and iridescent sequins through the top. I loved that dress." She was describing it like it she just worn it yesterday.

When I unfolded the newspaper, I noticed the obituaries were on the back page. Paulita Suarez's obituary was there.

Paulita Suarez, 30, wife of Raul Suarez

She was a top salesperson at Formula 333 for the past four years. Daughter of Orlando and Maria Garcia of Mexico City, Mexico, she moved to Westfield with her husband in 1964 when he joined the Teaching College as a chemistry professor and associate of Formula 333. Private funeral services will take place on Wednesday morning at St. Mary's Church.

That was it. Nothing else. No cause of death. No details on the funeral services. No nothing.

"Hmmh. This is interesting. I've been hearing more and more about this woman, but this is a boring obituary," I said.

"That was so awful that I never wanted to talk about it to anyone—even you," Mom said. She turned toward my dad, touched his arm, and said, "I can still remember your father coming into the kitchen at the old house and crying uncontrollably. I never saw him that upset before or after."

"I never knew that," he said. "I knew he was pretty stirred up by their finding Mrs. Suarez in the park dead, but I didn't know he showed how he felt to anyone. I was with him later the evening of the day she was found—I drove him and Mr. Suarez to the funeral home to meet the priest and make the arrangements, and he was cool as a cucumber."

"All I remember was him coming into the house all upset looking for your mother, saying, 'Pauli's dead—we found Pauli dead in the waterfall,' over and over. I went out on the porch with your brother Joe so we didn't hear what was going on, and your mother was able to calm him down. In about a half an hour after he came in, we were sitting down at the kitchen table having a lunch of ham sandwiches, and then the police showed up to question your father."

"I didn't know that either. Why did they question him, if it was an accident?" he asked rhetorically.

My mom continued, "I'm not sure they knew it was an accident at first. Think about it—why was she in the waterfall? They thought she fell through the fence, but those fences were built so well. How could she fall through? It just never made any sense to me."

My dad agreed that it was a little odd that Pauli fell through the fence—since the grounds were always in pristine condition—especially at the time of the Black Squirrel Ball. "It couldn't have been that the fence was weak because everything was just so. Grandpa walked that park every day, and if there was anything out of place, it was fixed immediately, especially if it had to do with safety."

"Do you think Grandpa thought he was partly responsible for her death, and that was why he was so upset—since they thought it was an accident?" my mom asked.

"Maybe, but it wasn't his fault at all!" He was pretty forceful with his words—pronouncing each one with syncopated rhythm. "There was no way it was his fault, and no one thought it was."

I reached over to him and touched his hand. "Dad, I know that, and you know that, but how could Mrs. Suarez have gotten into the waterfall? It seems to me that she was pushed. The fences were stable, but if someone was pushed with great force, she might have fallen over it. Do you remember if the whole fence was broken or was it just the top?"

"I don't remember. I do know that Dax was with Grandpa that morning, and I bet he would know." I noticed his eyes were glassy with tears building up.

"Dad, why are you upset?"

"It never added up to me—how she died. Everyone said it was an accident, and no one was to blame, but it just never seemed right. And no one ever said anything about it. I do remember seeing him place flowers by the waterfall the night of the Black Squirrel Ball the year before he died. I was about twenty feet away, but I could tell that he was crying. I never asked him why he was upset, or why he put the flowers there, but I figured it out. That was about ten years after she died, and he still wanted to make sure her memory was celebrated."

There was a silence among the three of us that seemed to last an hour. It was probably only ten seconds.

"Do you think she could have been murdered?" my mom asked.

"I've thought of it from time to time over the years. My father told me right after Mrs. Suarez's funeral that Mr. Suarez wanted the investigation to continue, but the police didn't find anything so they deemed it an accident. I remember the investigation was pretty quick."

"Did they do an autopsy?" I asked.

"I have no idea. I was only about eighteen and didn't ask too many questions," my dad said.

"Do you remember if the funeral was within a few days? If so, then they probably didn't do an autopsy—it would have taken awhile," I said.

"I remember going to the funeral services, and there wasn't a casket. Now that I think about it, she was cremated, so, no, I don't think there was an autopsy," he said.

My dad had a perplexed look on his face, like he was trying to think of an answer to a crossword puzzle.

"I don't know what happened, but you got me thinking," he said. "I never thought it was an accident, but I didn't think it was my business to ask."

I knew from experience with my dad that his tone of voice and the determined look on his face expressed that he thought it was his business now, and that he would get to the bottom of it.

CHAPTER 11

THANKS TO MY PARENTS' HELP, I was able to get through all of Lucinda's photos and scan them in time to return them the next day. I snuck in and out with Jerry's help, and I only had to leave a note for Mrs. Marino. I was lucky to escape that social challenge.

The weekend flew by. I picked Jonathan up at the train station on Friday afternoon, and he needed to run errands. He had to take his car, which he left at his parents' house while he traveled, to be inspected before 4:00 p.m., drop it off for an oil change, and go visit his grandmother at the assisted living center.

I ended up spending my weekend carting him around, and before I dropped him off at the train station on Sunday night, he "reminded me" to pick up his car at the mechanic's.

Unfortunately, the most intimate moment of the weekend was the bit of time when we were waiting to meet his parents for breakfast after church. He didn't want to stay at my place because he didn't want to inconvenience Mr. Z—which made no sense at all since Jonathan had stayed with me plenty of times before—and he suggested that I not stay at his place because his aunt was in town and needed a place to stay. She wouldn't have approved of us sleeping together with her in the guestroom next door.

So for more than forty-eight hours, I was his chauffer and Girl Friday.

At Sunday breakfast, I tried to get him to commit to coming to the ball, but he said it was almost three months away, and he could only plan day by day with the project he was working on. However, his parents signed up for a table. They said that they would get all their neighbors to join them who hadn't attended before. Finally—some new people to add to the invitation list.

Jonathan's mother had a figure at sixty that I wished I had now, so when she asked me what she should wear, I told her to "show it off." Her husband grinned, grabbed her hand, and gave it a kiss. I didn't get more than a kiss on the cheek from Jonathan all weekend—and that was at the train station when he was leaving.

On Monday, I had to make a bunch of calls, set up a meeting with the caterer and Aunt Reggie, meet with the printer in the afternoon to review the invitations, and also see how much twenty posters would cost—if I needed five for Tom's Longmeadow crusade, I could find a few places to hang fifteen more. The printer was donating the invitations, but I didn't want to take advantage of his generosity.

I spent the day in the apartment, overlooking the backyard which is connected to Peaceland Park. From my bedroom, I could see the top of the large fountain. At night it was so cool to see the lights turn different colors. I usually used the fountain shutting down as a sign that it was time to go to bed.

This section of the park was designed by a landscaper out of Boston. All the trees were so different and beautiful, from the cherries to the evergreens and maples. And the benches under the trees were the favorite spot for young lovers to hold hands or for mothers resting on their daily walks with their strollers.

I still remember sitting on a bench under a maple tree the night before my senior prom—but not with my date. Someone else asked if he could take me for a drive, and I thought nothing of it. I was a bit naïve back then. We went, had a nice time together, and saw each other in school the next week. That was it—nothing after.

As I was recalling that innocent interlude, I couldn't remember his name. If I did, I would have added him to the invitation list and asked him to make a donation. I needed all the names I could get.

I had my kitchen set up as Black Squirrel Ball Central. My project plan was updated and posted on the refrigerator, and my invitation list was on gigantic stickies lining the walls.

Our goal this year was to attract $40,000 in corporate sponsors—which would account for about 120 attendees—and sell one hundred tickets at $150 each. They'd get dinner tickets and a DVD copy of the slide show that hadn't yet been made, with additional publicity depending on the size of the donation, and sell another one hundred tickets at $100 each for $10,000. That still left us with a gap of $35,000 of individual donors to attract. If Mr. Suarez was good for $35,000 or more, we would be fine, but I couldn't put all my eggs in one basket. I needed to find a few more high rollers or else this would be my one and only fund-raising consulting job and my future job prospects would be nil.

I was going to meet with Mike and another former co-worker, Sarah, for lunch that day. I felt very tense as I entered the office building of my former employer. It was like I was Pavlov's dog, but instead of eating the meat when I heard a bell, my blood pressure started to race when I entered the parking lot.

Sarah and I were lunch buddies for two years. She was the friend who gave me the OSHA analogy for the toxic situation I was working in. She was a bit more immune to the political crap that I was being subjected to—she was older and nearing retirement, so she cared less about the bureaucracy than I did.

As I entered the visitors' lot, the friendly security guard was surprised to see me in jeans and a blouse after encountering me in suits everyday for years while I worked there. I told her who I was going to meet, and she raised the thick metal gate and wrote down my license plate as I slowly entered. I never knew the company held that many secrets that we needed such high levels of security.

Mike and Sarah were both waiting for me at the visitors' entrance. I left in such a rush a couple of weeks ago that they didn't feel they gave me the proper send-off. However, since both were pretty busy this week preparing for the annual sales conference, they only had time to meet me in the cafeteria.

"So how is the best ball coordinator doing today?" Sarah asked. She had a very singsong voice that could be amusing or irritating—depending on the amount of caffeine you did or didn't consume in the morning.

"I'm doing pretty well," I said, and I was. My blood pressure settled down a bit, and I was really excited to see both of them.

"You look great. I can say that now because you can't send me to HR, but you really look fantastic." Mike actually moved his eyes up and down over me. I had on a pair of Calvin Klein jeans, a peacock blue peasant blouse with a necklace and earring set made of blue dichroic glass, and a great pair of taupe high heels. I love that jewelry set—I bought it for myself a few years ago in a little shop in Kennebunkport, Maine, on my first overnight trip with Jonathan.

Mike's once-over sort of made me feel a little like a piece of meat, and yet I didn't mind at all. He was a happily married man, and he was just giving me a compliment. It was better than any compliment Jonathan gave me the past weekend—if he had given me any at all.

"I do feel better. It's amazing what a week's worth of good night's sleeping, going to the gym again, and not having to wear high heels every day can do for your psyche." But I do love those taupe heels. I just can't wear them every day.

"You have to tell me about this Black Squirrel Ball, and I definitely want to be on the invitation list. I can't imagine a bunch of people getting dressed up to celebrate a rodent," Sarah said.

"The Black Squirrel is not just any rodent; it's the mascot of Peaceland Park and even of Westfield." I continued by telling them the story of how the black squirrel got out of its cage so many years ago.

"The same black squirrel that got out of its cage is the mascot today? That must be some squirrel!" Sarah exclaimed with an infectious laugh that we all joined.

"No, silly. It isn't the same rodent. The species is the mascot, not one particular critter."

"Not only am I coordinating the event, but we're also coordinating a slide show history of Peaceland Park." I filled them in on the slide show and the combined history of Formula 333 and the park.

Sarah asked, "Do you think you'll make your $100,000 goal? How much have they raised in the past."

When I told them that the goal was more than double any past ball fund-raising goals, both of them dropped their jaws.

"Did you go from the oven straight to the deep fryer?" Mike asked, referring to going from one stressful employment experience to another.

"No, we're going after more corporate sponsors this year—which I already have two new sponsors—and we're trying to get a big $50,000 personal donation from a former Formula 333 executive."

"Is it a long shot?" Sarah asked.

"I'm not sure. There's a bit of intrigue around this man because he hasn't been back to Peaceland Park since his wife died there the night of the first Black Squirrel Ball forty years ago."

"Sounds like a long shot to me," she said.

"This man who is getting the archives together—his name is Dax—and his wife Esther, have stayed in touch with the potential donor, and they're visiting with him this week. Hopefully they can convince him to come and make the donation in his wife's memory. It would be a big deal for the park. However, I can't count the money until I see the check, so I'm trying to come up with a list of other prospects—smaller, of course—who can donate $5,000 to $10,000 each."

"When do you need to have all the money committed by?" Sarah asked.

"I feel like we should have 75 percent of the sponsorship and 50 percent of the tickets sold one month from the date of the event. The rest of the tickets will sell right up until the day before, but it would be great to have everything in place for August 1st. That would give us the last three weeks to focus on logistics and general publicity, but that's very unlikely," I said.

"Are you going?" Sarah asked Mike.

"And miss the most coveted event for black squirrels?" he asked her sarcastically. "Of course I'm going. And I bought six tickets for the whole family to go. Oh, I almost forgot—here is my check. Nine hundred dollars, right?" he asked me.

"That's if you want one DVD per couple and seats closer to the band and dance floor," I said. "Otherwise, it would be $600."

"Oh—I already wrote the check for $900. You can keep two DVDs—we only need one per family," Mike said.

"You can give it for a Christmas present. Maybe you have a few team members who are from Westfield who would love to have it," I said.

"Good idea. So, are you going?" he asked Sarah.

"You bet. I'm just not sure if we need four tickets or a whole table. We usually get together with four other couples around that time of year for an annual gathering, and I think this would be the perfect event. I'll have to get back to you with the final count, but it'll be before July 15th, for sure," she said.

"Well, this was certainly a profitable lunch. I feel like I should have picked up the tab," I said as we were cleaning up our trays and walking to the stacked conveyer belt to the dishwashing station.

We wished each other well and said we should get together for lunch soon; although I had a feeling I wouldn't see them until the end of August.

CHAPTER 12

THE PRIOR WEEK, AUNT REGGIE and Esther both asked if we could cancel the Friday morning meeting and just catch up the following Tuesday with everyone. Aunt Reggie's knees were bothering her, and Esther had a morning commitment at the Rosary Sodality that might run a bit long.

In the meantime, I had gone through all of Lucinda's scanned photos again. Lucinda had very few captions or dates, so I was still clueless about most of what she had.

There were a few of my grandfather as Santa Claus going through Formula 333's offices that I hadn't seen before. There were also some formal pictures taken at a formal dance. It looked like it was at the park, but I didn't recognize any of the people.

The photos were in black and white, but there was one that reminded me of Dax's description of Pauli Suarez. I brought the disc and my laptop to the Tuesday meeting to ask Frank, Aunt Reggie, and Esther if they recognized anyone.

"Hello, everyone," I said as I entered the meeting room. I thought I was five minutes early, but everyone looked like they were waiting anxiously for me.

"Am I late?" I asked.

"No, but we're all interested to hear about your meeting with Tom Marfucci last week," Frank said. It was nice to see Frank excited in a positive way. Usually he is ready to blow a gasket in a negative way.

"Sooooo. How did it go?" Doree asked.

"It went fairly well. He was pretty quick, and before I could ask him for $10,000, he told me how he was going to provide a $5,000 sponsorship and that all his guests will be from Longmeadow because he wants us to ask them for donations in conjunction with the ball. He was so committed to the

$5,000 and excited to be supporting the ball for the first time that I thought I would risk that donation if I went for more," I explained.

"I knew you'd strike out," Frank said.

"She didn't strike out," Aunt Reggie said in a very supportive manner. "She just hit a foul ball, that's all."

"Considering he never gave before, I added him to the corporate sponsorship list, and went to visit him on my own, I see it as $5,000 and potential for more that we didn't have last week." I was a bit ticked off that Frank could be so negative about new-found money and potential for more. I didn't think it was a foul ball. I would like to think of it more as a strong double with a runner advancing to third.

"Frank, have you come up with any more potential sponsors that we didn't have last week?" I asked with the least sarcastic tone I could come up with considering my impatience with him.

"I told you once and I'm not telling you again, everyone I know is already on the list and will come again this year as they have come every year in the past."

"I have a few new names. Being new in town has its benefits because everyone wants to do business with us," Doree said. "The landscaper said he would buy two tickets, the real estate agent who sold us our house said she would buy a table, and the car dealership where I bought my new 6-series BMW convertible will be a $2,500 sponsor."

"Way to go, Doree," I said. That's at least another $4,200. With my new $5,000 from Tom Marfucci and another $2,500 from All Around Tire, these additions, and if we really can count on about 75 percent of the past attendees, I projected that we were at about $25,000 in corporate sponsors, and with the projected $25,000 in ticket sales, we were at $50,000 total.

We were half way there.

"Now that Dax is retired, we keep getting invited to all these retirement planning and estate planning dinners by the local insurance agents. They're trying to sell these crazy products to 'protect your investment with no down side,' which we don't believe, but we go for the meal, and I also talk to each one of the presenters to ask them to buy tickets. Here are three new names from the last week," Esther said.

"You went to three of those presentations in the past week? Doesn't it get old?" I asked.

"We only went to one, but we sat with these three lovely widows in their eighties who both remember going to the annual balls in the early days, and they want to go to this one."

"If they're still alive by then," said Frank under his breath.

"They have more life in their little fingers than you do in your whole body," Esther quipped. She had a look that said she wasn't taking any more of his attitude today.

I told everyone that I was meeting with Police Chief Cerrazo later that day, and with Violet tomorrow.

"Aren't you spending too much time on spending money and not enough on raising the money?" Frank interrogated.

"As I was saying, I also have a few names and photos I'd like to review with all of you from Lucinda's archives." I really hoped he would lose his voice for the rest of the summer.

We reviewed the names, and even Frank remembered one man from his early sales days at Formula 333. "So you'll follow up with Chad Howard and get him to commit to a table?" Aunt Reggie asked in a way that Frank knew he had to say yes.

He rolled his eyes, said yes, and then wrote a note to himself in his Black n' Red notebook. His handwriting wasn't more than a scribble.

I continued to scan through the photos, and Aunt Reggie and Esther remembered quite a few people. Each of them added three or four people to their list to call.

Then we got to the picture I thought might be Pauli.

"Oh—how beautiful she was. Not only that night in her ball gown, but she had a natural beauty about her. That Pauli was something else," Esther said.

"I remember when I worked in the kitchen, she was especially nice to me—actually she was nice to everyone," Aunt Reggie said.

"She used to call everyone señorita or señor, and her voice was so soothing. It was as smooth as the wonderful flan dessert she showed us how to make when the sales reps from Puerto Rico would come to town," Aunt Reggie continued.

"And the young men certainly liked her. I remember a number of the college boys who would drive the executives and sales reps during the annual conferences. They all would cut cards to see who would win to bring her home."

"Frank, weren't you a driver back then? Did you ever win?" Esther asked.

Frank was more agitated than usual when we started talking about Pauli.

"I thought we were trying to add names to our lists of potential donors. She isn't going to give us anything. She's dead," he said more abruptly than any other time I'd heard him attempt to squelch a conversation.

"It's a shame about her death. I just don't understand how it could have been an accident. My dad was telling me that she fell through the fence by the top of the waterfall. She must have had some force to go through that—especially at the time of the Black Squirrel Ball since everything was in its best shape in Peaceland Park," I said.

Frank said, "I can add a few more people to my list. I noticed the fellow in the kitchen picture—he is my brother's neighbor—and the woman next to him is his sister." I don't know what got into him, but he wanted to keep moving on the invitation list. I certainly didn't want to curb his sudden enthusiasm.

"And isn't that fellow in the picture with the fountain—collecting the coins—isn't he a relative of yours, Reggie?" Frank asked.

"He is, but he's been dead for twenty years. That was Uncle Freddy. His kids are already on the list. I'm not positive if they'll be coming, but I'll call them to warm them up a bit," Aunt Reggie said.

She continued by telling a story about how Uncle Freddy was in charge of the lawns, and he once treated the grass with weed killer near the newly planted pansy garden. The wind picked up, and the flowers all died within three days. His buddy, Ed Kolmulki, was in charge of the flowers and was almost in tears when he showed up to a full bed of dead flowers. She said that my grandfather simply told him, "Then, go plant new flowers." We all chuckled at the ironic common sense of the story.

"And Dax and I are going to visit Mr. Suarez next week. We have plans to take him some pictures and ask if we can borrow his. I bet his has some really good stuff," Esther said. "Sam, do you want to join us?"

"You bet!" I said. I love to go on research adventures. Plus, I had to go—we needed to get a good-size donation out of Mr. Suarez.

She told me that they were leaving early in the morning on Tuesday, and it would take us about two hours to get to his home on the Connecticut shore.

"It's some place. Wait until you see the view of Long Island Sound from his home. It's like you're looking at a huge photograph that takes up his entire wall—but it's just a wall of windows looking out on the real thing," Esther said. "Dax called this morning and Mr. Suarez said he would get his and Pauli's boxes of pictures and memorabilia out of storage for us to go through with him. Sam, you should bring that computer thing of yours, too, so we can show him all the pictures we already have."

"I'll remember to take out the picture of Pauli so I don't upset him," I said.

"Yeah, you don't want to upset him. You want him to write a big check," Frank said.

We continued the meeting, discussing the next few weeks' worth of tasks, including meeting with the caterer, the florist, and the police chief. Aunt

Reggie would be joining me for the caterer, Doree for the florist, and I was going to go meet with Police Chief Cerrazo on my own.

I thought it would be best to go on my own since I wanted to talk more about the first Black Squirrel Ball than the upcoming event.

CHAPTER 13

It seemed like everywhere I went, I was being asked questions about the ball: church, the post office, and even the grocery store. Now that I wasn't just going to Walmart once a month to stock up on necessities late on a Saturday night and eating takeout pizza and Chinese food, I was actually visiting and seeing people I hadn't seen in ages. And they all wanted an invitation to the ball.

I was certainly making a name for myself with this event, and that was good because I needed to make sure it was a success. If it didn't turn out well, I'd be hopelessly jobless.

Within the week we had added twenty more people to the invitation list, which brought us to four hundred. That didn't mean all of those people would be coming, but since many had attended in the past or specifically requested to be added, I thought we had a good chance of reaching our goal of 250 tickets.

I was getting a little nervous about the meeting with Mr. Suarez later in the week. If we don't get a HUGE contribution from him, I might be back to square one—for the ball and any future job prospects.

As I was getting ready for another day of around-the-town errands and meetings, I was looking out the back window of my bedroom and saw a couple on the park bench under the maple tree.

And then I remembered the name of the kid who I went for a walk with the night before the prom. It was Chris Morozick. I think his mother still lives in town. I added her to the invitation list.

As I left the apartment, Mr. Z yelled out, "Hey there, good lookin'. Where did you get those wheels? Do I need to raise your rent if you have that kind of money to burn?"

"No—do *not* raise my rent! I'm just scraping by since I took on this assignment," I said.

"Then why did you piss your money away on those fancy wheels?" Mr. Z asked.

"Gareth was supposed to replace my bald tires with a good set of used tires, and this is what he had on the car when I returned," I said. The car looked a little meaner than before. I knew it was horribly uncomfortable due to the pointed lumbar support, but the exterior made it look a little like a stealthmobile. "He insisted on making sure I was safe, and this is what he had. He made it fit the budget."

I gave Mr. Z a wave and got into the car. It did look good on the outside, but the inside could use a little care. I had a few extra granola bar wrappers in the door pockets, about twenty spare Subway napkins in the console, file folders of miscellaneous subjects from my old job spewed on the floor, and my golf clubs and two pairs of golf shoes in the hatchback. "All this stuff has got to get cleaned out," I thought. I'm so organized in many ways, and then I let my car get the best of me.

As I drove down Western Avenue, I noticed how lovely a day it was and took a glance in my rearview mirror at myself. I looked better than I had in a while. It had been a while since I had a series of full night's sleep, going to the gym on a regular basis, and now that I was seeing family and friends more regularly, I was eating better. If I couldn't make money at this gig, at least I didn't have bags under my eyes and look like a miserable rat.

I passed the hospital and City Hall and then took a left onto Washington Street. With it being such a nice day, there were about five or six little old ladies sitting on the bench near the Washington Street apartments—the housing for the elderly. They looked like they were soaking up the sunshine. I parked on the street, fed the meter—and wondered how many people actually chance not feeding the meter right in front of the police station—and entered the police station lobby.

And who, to my surprise, was there, but my dad.

"What are you doing here?"

"I'm here to sit in on your meeting with the chief," he said.

I was a bit confused. This wasn't the first time I've met the police chief, and this wasn't the first time I'd had to coordinate traffic and public safety issues, so I was a bit put off that my dad thought I needed backup.

He must have noticed the annoyance on my face because he quickly said, "It's not that I don't think you can handle what you need to do with the traffic plans, but I thought we could ask Jake about Pauli's death."

"Dad, this is not the time to bring up an investigation that he was involved with forty years ago. I need to ask him to donate police time to the event," I pleaded.

"Oh—I didn't think it would be a big deal. Plus, I've been thinking about this more, and I want to figure out what really happened to Mrs. Saurez. After looking through that stuff the other night, I realized that Grandpa was never right after she died. I want to get to the bottom of this for his memory, too," he said.

"Well, I guess we'll have to make it not be such a big deal since you are here." I sighed and then took a deep breath. It's not my favorite task to tell my dad what to do, but here was my attempt. "I need to get through my list of questions first, and then you can ask questions about Pauli, but don't get the chief annoyed. I really need him to make sure we don't have the traffic problems the ball had last year."

All of a sudden, Jake Cerrazo, the police chief, came up to the dark brown wood-looking Formica countertop and nearly scared the bejezus out of me. "Hey there, Cummings family. I thought I was just going to have the pleasure of meeting with Sam, but I get the dad, too."

The chief was a very talkative character—it seemed like you just had to wind him up and let him go. I don't think I've ever seen him with his mouth closed or quiet. He gave my dad and me a handshake over the counter and gestured toward the doorway to the offices. As soon as we met up, he started telling a story about how the two of them first met at Abner Gibbs School in the second grade, then how he used to work for my grandfather at Peaceland Park as a security guard and a driver for Formula 333 when he was a teenager and into college, and before I knew it, he was describing the Pauli Suarez investigation.

I gave my dad a quick glare, and he just shrugged his shoulders and gave me a very quick Cheshire cat grin. My dad must have called the chief.

The chief told us how he never really understood how they could have deemed the death an accident, and over the years he had collected information about Mr. and Mrs. Suarez. When someone would mention something, he would write it in his notes. Nothing ever jumped out at him, but he always thought it was a murder. I was sitting there so dumbfounded that he had started on this subject that I almost missed it when he said that she was known to be flirtatious with the young men of Formula 333 and Peaceland Park, and that many had crushes on her. He also mentioned that some of the older men in the company were jealous of her success at such a young age and being a woman.

He must have breathed through his ears, because he never stopped talking about Pauli for twenty-five minutes. He told us how they found her body lying across the top of the waterfall, how her necklace was found a few rock levels down, and how the medical examiner proclaimed her death a drowning. Jake remembered seeing a gash on her head when they lifted her body from the water; but years later, when he was privy to the medical report, that wasn't noted in the file.

Finally, I thought I could get a word in when my dad asked, "Did you ask the medical examiner?"

"I couldn't. By the time I joined the police force a few years later, Dr. Roberts had died. I asked Dax once if he remembered the gash, and he said yes. Dax told me that he would never forget the details of Pauli's injuries. She had a black eye, the gash, and red marks on her neck—like she was strangled."

"Do you think someone tried to steal her necklace off her neck, and that's how she got the marks?" I asked.

"No, the necklace was made with one large stone in the front, but the chain portion was very thin. And it wouldn't have made that type of mark on her neck. Now, after more years of police work than I'd like to count, I think someone tried to strangle her and somehow she ended up in the waterfall. It wasn't an accident, but I don't know who did it or why."

All of a sudden he got quiet and put his head down a bit and looked out his window at a view of the cruisers' parking lot. "Mrs. Suarez was something else. Spirited, ambitious, and, yes, a bit touchy-feely with the young men, but she was so in love with Mr. Suarez. It truly broke my heart that he had to leave town to try to mellow the harsh memories of his lost love. And to think how hard it was on your grandfather."

"He was depressed for months—maybe even years. He certainly put on a good face, but he would never walk by that waterfall without stopping to say a prayer. I remember walking with him once while he was giving a tour to a group of master gardeners from the Boston area, and he stopped right there and looked up at the waterfall, whispered something to himself—probably the Hail Mary—made the sign of the cross and snapped right back into the tour. A few people looked a little perplexed, but no one said a word. They just looked up at the waterfall and made the sign of the cross, too."

At that moment I realized that my dad, the chief, and anyone else we needed to rope into this situation had to help solve this decades-old mystery. Something horrible happened to Mrs. Suarez, but it also affected Grandpa. Solving the case now wouldn't help him live a happier life, but maybe he would rest a little more peacefully.

After almost an hour of the chief talking about a bunch of slightly unrelated things, my dad gave me a glance and then looked at the clock. We had to talk about the ball. I had to be at the caterers to meet Aunt Reggie in twenty minutes, and it was ten minutes away. Trying to stop the chief was like trying to get into the fastest session of double dutch. And then my dad cleared his throat a bit.

"Would you like a glass of water?" The chief asked my dad.

"No, thanks. I'm all set, but I think Sam needs to ask you a few questions about the ball."

So my dad was helpful on my quest after all. I shouldn't have been so hard on him in the lobby, but I had to get this straightened out, or we would have traffic snafus throughout Westfield.

"Oh—yeah. That's why you wanted to meet with me, right? The Black Squirrel Ball. Oh my—it will be the fortieth anniversary this year! Wow. Do you know that the first ball was my first date with my late wife Adele?"

I was in for it now. There went my ten-minute drive to the caterers. He would start up about Adele, and there was no stopping him.

"God rest her soul." His wife had passed away from colon cancer just a few months ago. I noticed him glance to her picture on his desk. It was at his son's college graduation.

"I'm not sure if I'll attend the ball this year, but I do want you and the committee to know that you have my and the department's full support." He continued with details about the traffic plans, similar to what is used for the nearby college's annual graduation exercises. He explained that the recent commencement ran without a hitch due to the deployment of traffic cops, along with communications being sent to the area residents advising them to utilize alternate routes to cut down on their wait time. He said it worked like a charm, and as a resident of the neighborhood most impacted, I was much appreciative of the reverse 911 recorded call I had received from the chief himself to inform me when to avoid Western Avenue during the first weekend in May.

He also said that he knew a number of officers would be in attendance, and he offered for the department to pay for their tickets if they went in their dress uniforms, agreed not to partake in alcoholic beverages, and served as additional security for the evening. They would be expected to arrive thirty minutes early and stay until I gave them the go-ahead to leave. He also requested that I spread them around—with their friends or family. Then they could easily get in and out of the seating area to help cover the large traffic crowd at the beginning and the end of the night and also enjoy themselves a bit during the dinner and dancing.

And then the chief's phone rang. At that point, I had fifteen minutes before my next appointment with Aunt Reggie. She says that being late is a sign of arrogance, but I couldn't just get up and walk away from the police chief after he had offered more than I expected for the ball and had also provided so much information on Pauli's death. This was like hitting the jackpot.

He looked a little startled by the number on the caller ID, and picked up the phone with a stern "Chief Cerrazo" as a greeting. He cupped the receiver and asked that we excuse him; he needed to attend to an emergency right away.

Dad and I quickly stood up as if we had buzzers under our butts, quietly shook the chief's hand, and gave him a polite wave. In a matter of minutes, he went from complete chatter bug to solemn widower to focused public safety officer and traffic coordinator, and then to firm leader to whomever was on the other end of the phone.

Dad and I retraced our steps through the blue cinderblock hallways and out to the lobby and down the steps. Neither one of us said a word until our feet hit the sidewalk, and then we both looked at each other. "Can you believe it—he doesn't think Pauli's death was an accident either?" I said.

"Yeah, and he told us so much, I don't think I caught it all. Can we meet up later and go over what he said?" he asked.

"Sure. I have to meet Aunt Reggie in a few minutes at the caterers and then run a few errands. I'll easily be home by 6:00 p.m. I even have chicken salad that I made earlier today that we can have for dinner," I said. "Why don't you mention it to Mom, and see if she can make it."

"She's getting her hair done tonight, so I think she's tied up, but I'll see you about six-thirty." He leaned over for me to give him a kiss on the cheek and started walking to his car. He looked like he just added a fifty-pound bag of potatoes to his back compared to when I saw him walk into the police station.

I knew Dad knew Pauli and Mr. Suarez, but I couldn't figure out why he would be this absorbed by the subject of her death. If she was murdered, the culprit should pay the price, but why was he looking so burdened by what we just heard?

I thought that maybe it was hearing how much of a burden Mrs. Suarez's death was on Grandpa. First it was my grandfather who had this cross to bear, and now it was my father.

We needed to get to the bottom of this for everyone's sake—Mr. Suarez, my grandfather, my dad, and the chief, too.

I checked my watch and noticed that I had eight minutes to get to the caterer. I spun the car around in a U-turn, took a quick left and then right onto South Maple Street and hoped I wouldn't hit any lights on my way to Southwick. I used to work with the woman who owns the catering company with her husband. I was glad the committee chose the Route 10 Bistro before I joined because I would have wanted to give them the business, but I'm not sure they're the lowest price.

They certainly provide a good value and make sure everything is just as their clients want it—so that means you have to pay a few extra dollars per person. As I cruised South down 10 and 202, I was going over all the things Chief Cerrazo said about Pauli's death. I was glad I was going to meet up with Dad later—he probably would have caught onto a few things I didn't, and we could write some notes.

All of a sudden, I realized I was turning into a sleuth. Either that or a very nosey fund-raiser. But the more I knew about Mrs. Suarez, the better prepared I would be for the meeting with Mr. Suarez. And that's the difference between a fund-raiser who simply asks for money and gets lucky, and someone who builds relationships with patrons who will partner with organizations for the long term.

Learning as much as possible about Mr. and Mrs. Suarez was very important so I could raise as much money as possible and turn this short-term assignment into a career stepping-stone.

I turned into Route 10 Bistro's parking lot and noticed that Aunt Reggie's car wasn't there. I may have beaten her. And then I thought, "Was I supposed to pick her up?" As soon as I started to panic that I had forgotten her, she parked right next to me and gave me a big wave and smile. Phew! Not only would I have been arrogant with my tardiness, but I would've been downright goofy for forgetting to pick her up.

"I hit every light from the north side of town and then got stuck behind some tractor for the last mile," she said. I must have just missed the tractor. Lucky me.

We went into the bar area, and Ella was waiting there for us with Artie. She takes care of all the logistics and business details, and he takes care of the food. They had dishes of appetizers, entrees, and desserts for us to try. Again, lucky me! When I mentioned the chicken salad sandwiches to Dad, I realized I hadn't eaten for hours, and I was getting a little woozy from low blood sugar.

"You look great," Ella said with a little bit of disbelief in her voice.

"I think I should say thank you," I said, "but you sound so surprised."

"Well, I don't remember the last time I saw you look this good—well rested and you have great color in your cheeks—and I can't believe you took a job that requires you to deal with Frank O'Connor. He is such a pain in the ass," she said and rolled her eyes, and then she quickly apologized to Aunt Reggie for swearing.

"Don't worry about me. I've known Frank since we were kids. I've known he was a pain in the ass well before you were even born," Aunt Reggie responded.

Artie said, "Ella, that's not very nice to talk about our customers that way. He may be a pain, but he eats here a few nights a week. And it's because of him that we have the ball this year."

"Frank eats here? No offense, but he is squeakier than an old screen door and you don't offer early bird specials. How do you get him to let the moths out of his wallet?" Aunt Reggie asked.

"We make him special meals to keep him on his diet, and he has his own table over there." Artie pointed to the last table in the bar. "He's lost twenty-five pounds since his last heart attack. He calls a day ahead of time and tells us what type of fish, chicken, or pasta he would like, and we make sure we have it ready for him. I even try to whip him up a heart healthy dessert once in a while to offset his scotch intake."

"Does he come alone?" I asked.

"He usually comes by himself or sometimes with his neighbor, Barney," Ella said.

"Hmm, well, I guess we need to thank Frank for bringing us all together for the ball. There's good in everyone," I said, trying to convince myself that in this example it was true.

We started tasting six different appetizers, including endive with boursin cheese, Moroccan meatballs with spiced chutney, figs with prosciutto, chicken satay skewers, a variety of brushetta, including olive, pesto, and tomato, and also a spicy spring roll. We agreed that we would skip the endive (too strong), the spring roll (too spicy), and meatballs (we decided on bison wellingtons), and we decided to have seven passed hors d'oeuvres—after all, seven is a lucky number.

Then we tasted the entrée choices. We were going to have one entrée with both "surf" and "turf." We liked the tender seared scallops instead of the stuffed shrimp. And then we had three options for beef: beef tips burgundy, prime rib, or tenderloin of beef. Artie had prepared all of them for us to compare.

"I can't believe how tender this is. This is the best tenderloin I've ever tasted," Aunt Reggie said. If I wasn't mistaken, I think she even got a little flushed as she was eating from her sample plate.

"Well, I haven't had that kind of response from a woman in quite some time," Artie said, while looking at Ella with his eyebrows raised. "I think we have a winner with the tenderloin."

"We'll serve the scallops and beef with green beans—which will be in season and super sweet at the end of August—and roasted red potatoes. The salads will be plated and at the tables ahead of time, with covers to ensure no little bugs begin their dinner before the guests do, and fresh rolls will be provided by the bakery in Russell at no charge," Ella said in a methodical voice as if this part of her job was very precise. She was so organized that I think she may be genetically linked to our family.

"You got the bakery folks to donate to the ball? I should call them and ask them if they would like a few tickets as a trade," I said.

"You can, but don't be disappointed. I don't think they go to parties like this," Artie said. The bakery is run by a religious family, and those women can make a loaf of cinnamon raisin bread like no other holy women I ever met.

"That will cut down the price one dollar per person. I know it isn't much, but I figured every bit helped. We just switched over to them rather than baking ourselves, and it's working out much better for us. Plus, they give us the two-day-old cinnamon raisin bread that we use for our bread pudding," he said.

"So how is the ball coming? Do you have enough sponsors?" Ella asked. Her voice seemed to change tones—like she just switched from professional event planner to interested and gossipy friend.

"Sam is leaving no stone unturned, and she has already closed a few asks that we wouldn't have had a chance of getting without her, so I think it's going well," Aunt Reggie said. She's always the voice of optimism.

"I would like to have had another $10,000 in corporate sponsors committed by now, but I've been working on the invitation list so we can get them out next week. I needed to have the dinner choices for the printer tomorrow—so now I can pass along this information. I just hope I don't screw up spelling or proofing," I said.

It took us just about an hour to get through the appetizers and entrees. Artie had suggested that we serve one of my favorite desserts—individual blueberry pudding cakes with locally made vanilla ice cream from Brown's Dairy in Granville.

I think it quickly became Aunt Reggie's favorite dessert too, because she ate the entire sample. For such a tiny woman with a usual emphasis on not overeating—or, rather, not eating more than what a four-year-old would eat—she certainly packed a punch today.

Ella printed us a few copies of the final menu, e-mailed it to the printer for me while we were together so that I wouldn't make a mistake on anything, and I signed the contract. I'm not sure if I really had the authority to sign anything, but since the only person who would throw a stink was Frank, and he had recommended the Route 10 Bistro in the first place, I figured it was a chance I could take and ask for forgiveness later if necessary.

We said our good-byes and agreed to meet up again at least three weeks prior to the event for an on-site walkthrough.

CHAPTER 14

I HEARD MY MOM TALKING with Mr. Z before she knocked on the door.

"Hi, Mom, come in. I didn't know you were coming, too. Dad said you had a hair appointment," I said.

"I did—can't you tell?" I guess it did look a little poofier than it was the other night. She had her makeup all done up, too.

"Are you trying to get a date with that look?" I asked.

She just had her brownish-gray wavy hair trimmed and blown dry. "No, I like to have my makeup just right when I get my hair done. It's a lot of work to look good when you're my age, but I don't like to think of the alternative."

My parents are in their late fifties, and except for the high blood pressure medication, they're both in pretty good shape. My dad could lose a few pounds, but he keeps active. My mom goes to the gym at least three times a week and is very proud of her balance and flexibility. She says that will help prevent her from falling and breaking a hip.

"Dad told me that you had an interesting meeting with the chief today. He said that Jake's mouth was going so fast that he didn't think Jake was breathing."

And then my dad came through the kitchen door. He had a box of files and pictures with him.

"What's all that?" my mom asked.

"I went to the library this afternoon and sweet-talked some old bag into helping me look up all the newspaper articles about Pauli's death."

"Nice talk, Dad. How would you like it if we referred to you as an old buzzard?" I asked.

"Sometimes it's true, so I guess I can't mind. Plus, this lady was all hunched over and raggedy looking. I wasn't sure if she worked there or lived in the basement." My mom and I just rolled our eyes at him.

"I thought there weren't many articles in the paper—that the park and police kept the investigation kind of quiet," I said.

My dad went on to explain that there weren't any articles, but that the reference librarian helped him access the medical examiner's reports.

"How did you get those? I didn't think those were public records," my mom said.

"I didn't either, and in some cities they aren't, but when the medical examiner died, he had a bunch of cases in progress and some he deemed as 'suspicious.' The lady told me that the doctor's wife found these files in his office almost ten years after his death and donated them to the library, but that no one had gone through them since, and that was almost twenty years ago."

Dad went on to say that the reference librarian had never seen the files before, but when she did an internal search on the name Suarez, this box reference came up. One of the high school volunteers happened to be taking something downstairs at the same time my father showed up, so she suggested the volunteer look around and see if it was easily found. Within a few minutes, the young boy was heaving a twenty-five-pound box of papers and pictures up the stairs, and Dad and his new friend were going through everything.

He continued to tell us how the librarian remembered being a young girl when Pauli was found dead and that all the kids in school were talking about how they didn't want to go to Peaceland Park past dark, or they might wind up dead too.

"So the kids thought she was murdered back then?" I asked.

"Not really. They all just got spooked about someone dying in the park. The librarian lady grew up over off of Franklin Street, so she went to school with kids who lived right next to the park, and the kids must have exaggerated the story by the time they started school a couple of weeks later," he said.

"Or maybe those kids knew the truth." We all looked at each other in a solemn pause after my mom said this.

We quietly split up the files and folders and each read what we had. It was like we were all in school, quickly trying to finish a final exam—trying to be thorough but also trying to race the clock. We wanted to know if the answers to our questions were in this box.

How did she die? Was it from drowning like Dax said, or was it strangulation like the chief said? Was there an autopsy even though she was cremated? Who was involved in the investigation, and who made the call to close the case?

And although we probably wouldn't find out in the medical examiner's files, I was already thinking of more questions. Were there any suspects? Did she have any enemies? Were any of those young men the chief mentioned

Mrs. Suarez flirting with more so—like a jealous lover? What could be the motive?

And then my heart stopped.

Was it that Mr. Suarez was really distraught and heartbroken, and that's why he left town, or was it that he was guilt stricken because he caused his wife to die somehow?

After about a half an hour of quiet, we each started to review what we had learned.

Dad read the medical report. I'm glad I didn't get that part of the file since it had pictures.

I couldn't believe that this stuff was in the library. There must have been some type of privacy policies broken. But then again, there weren't many rules about personal information in the 1960s and 1970s.

The medical examiner made notes that although her lungs were filled with water and drowning was the final cause of death, she did have ligature marks on her neck that may have been the result of a strangulation attempt and the gash on her head was about a half inch deep. He noted that he did not do a full autopsy since the police chief wanted to close the file very quickly and have the medical examiner release the body to the family right away to be cremated.

The medical examiner's comments made it clear that he was pressured by the police chief to rush the investigation, even though he requested that the police chief discuss the mysterious facts with the family.

My mom's section of the box pertained to medical journal articles regarding strangulation techniques and also various types of head trauma. The articles ranged in date from August 1968 to November 1975.

I had the man's diaries. I couldn't believe the details he included. I skipped through most of the books to find the time period near the first Black Squirrel Ball.

The entry on August 25, 1968, was:

I had to examine a lovely young woman's death today. It seems to me very odd, but everyone else involved has come to the conclusion that it was an accident. I spoke with Police Chief O'Malley about my obvious suspicion, and I pleaded with him to persuade the family to allow me to complete a full autopsy. He was reluctant—actually that is an understatement. He was adamant that he would not mention my suspicions to the family, and I may not speak to them directly. He said that it would be too painful, and it would be best to go with the first assumptions by all of those involved and deem it an accident. Even the state police didn't want to pursue more details of the investigation.

I feel as though I should report this to my state supervisor, but he is at Cape Cod on vacation and not reachable until next week—which will be too late.

I did take scalp, skin, and nail samples from the victim before turning her body over to the mortician. If other physical evidence is collected along with these samples, maybe the investigation can be reopened at a later date. I hope these samples will be able to prove something in the future.

I plan to send the samples to my instructor and mentor, Professor Anderson. Hopefully, he will understand my concerns and run the proper tests.

I read that to my parents and then continued with another section from a few months later.

I received the results back from Professor Anderson regarding the Peaceland Park victim. He agreed that there appeared to have been a struggle because the neck tissue had signs of abrasions that could be caused by friction similar to or resulting from strangulation. He also agreed from my report that the cause of death was drowning, but that the gash in the head was from a sharp, irregularly shaped mineral-based weapon—like a rock.

After receiving word of his findings, I went to Peaceland Park to get a closer look at the scene of the victim's death and compared it to the photographs taken the day she was found. There was a rock in the waterfall that had a protruding sharp point that, although it could not have been used as a weapon, could have caused the gash to her head if she struck it with sufficient force when she fell into the waterfall.

I had to gingerly climb over the fence that protected park-goers from harm's way with the waterfall. As I climbed over the fence, I noticed that one section was painted with a different shade of brown compared to the other sections. This was where the victim must have fallen through, where the fence had broken and had been repaired.

I noticed that all the fence sections, this new one and the older ones, were all very sturdy. I leaned against the fence with all my body weight and it didn't budge a bit.

It is very hard to believe that the victim could have accidentally fallen through this fence, and if she climbed through it like I did today for some reason and slipped, the fence wouldn't have been broken as it was.

I went back to the office and looked through the photographs again. I'm not a police detective or a forensic expert, but I do know enough in my gut to realize that this was no accident.

I wish I could speak to the victim's family, but the chief forbade me to do so. If I go against his instructions, he could have me fired. He wields a great deal of power in this part of the state and no one goes against him.

"So he thought it was a murder, and yet Chief O'Malley and the state police didn't let him investigate further." My mom said, "I thought the medical examiner had the last say on investigations and releasing a body in a case like this."

"He would have, if he wasn't dealing with Chief O'Malley," my dad said. He mentioned that the chief back then was a little squirrely and liked to control the town with an iron fist. "The mayor and the district attorney didn't have anything on him—he did whatever he wanted whenever he wanted."

"Is this Chief O'Malley related to Jonathan?" I asked.

"Yup. He was Jonathan's grandfather. And he thought he ruled the town," my dad said.

"Why do you think he would just sweep this under the rug? If Mom heard Grandpa say that he thought it seemed odd, Dax told us he thought it wasn't an accident, and now we know from the medical examiner's diary and notes that Chief O'Malley actually didn't want to suggest an autopsy to Mr. Suarez, there must have been something going on," I said.

"It was a different time back then, and Peaceland Park was the star of Westfield—the brightest star by far. It was before the college was big, and it was pretty much the only reason people came to Westfield from out of town. Maybe Chief O'Malley thought if there was a murder in the park, the visitor count would be greatly reduced," my dad said. "Or maybe he was paid off or holding this against someone."

From Dad's dramatic pause before his last sentence and the deliberate way he said it, I could tell that Dad thought that the past police chief was responsible for some type of cover-up.

"So what should we do with what we've found?" my mom asked.

We all agreed that my dad would bring the copies of the files to Chief Cerazzo first thing tomorrow morning, and that we wouldn't say anything to anyone else. If the case could be reopened, it was up to the current police chief, not us.

"What about your new friend at the library, Dad? You don't think she'll tell anyone?"

"I doubt she has anyone to tell. She wasn't wearing a wedding ring, and somehow it came up in conversation that her only sister died in a car accident when they were teenagers. I'm guessing I may have been the only person she has talked to in weeks," he said. "She went on and on about how it was good to have someone to talk to."

"You might have more than a new friend—you might have a new girlfriend!" my mom said with a little sarcastic jab to my dad's ribs.

After we packed up the files, they thanked me for dinner, and then they left. My gourmet creation of chicken salad with celery and craisin' sandwiches and salt and pepper potato chips had hit the spot, but we had hardly noticed.

CHAPTER 15

IT WAS NICE TO JUST sit and let my mind wander for a while. I was under the hair dryer at Isabella's and reading *In Touch* magazine. In just twenty minutes, I was up to date on the best and worst dressed in music, TV, and movie stardom, who was marrying whom, and who had divorced whom to marry someone else. I probably could have spent that time making a list of something or another for the ball, but it was nice to just veg out and let my mind go for a bit.

"OK, you're cooked." Isabella said as she flipped up the dryer and led me to the sink. As I sank back into the sink, I started to tell her about the latest twist of the ball plans. I didn't know if I had a date.

"Jonathan doesn't know if he can make it back that weekend." I rolled my eyes and made a squinchy face with my mouth and nose. I probably looked like one of those wrinkly dogs.

"What do you mean, he doesn't know if he can get here?" she asked indignantly. She was definitely a fiery red-headed Italian woman. "You barely see him with his travels, and he can't make the effort to come home for your biggest weekend of the year?"

"Are you coming?" I asked, trying to change the subject without making a big deal of Jonathan not coming to the ball. I was getting to the point with Jonathan that I didn't care much anymore. If he did come, that would be fine; but I would be pretty busy entertaining the big donors, making sure the sponsors were getting the attention they deserved, and honoring Dax's service and hard work to Peaceland Park.

"Yah, Salvatore is going to be here, too." Sal is Isabella's husband, but they aren't "really married" yet. They met a few years ago, fell in love, and had a long-distance relationship between Italy and western Massachusetts.

They were married in Italy last fall, but he just got the go-ahead to come into the country.

I gave her a big grin and almost jumped out of my seat, shampoo and all. "You mean, I'm finally going to meet the mystery husband?"

"You bet. He doesn't quite get why we're going to a party for a squirrel—I think my Italian translation is missing something—but he'll understand when we get there. He's supposed to get here that week, so this will be our first big social event."

She went on to tell me that her grandmother wants the family to go to the ball to celebrate her civil marriage. Even though Lucinda Marino can be a mean old bat, she loves her family and wants them to be happy.

"I can't wait to be there with Sal, my parents, Grandma, and my brother and sister. We're all looking forward to it more than I can express." She had a glimmer—a real sparkly twinkle in her eyes like no precious gem I've ever seen. I was excited for her, too.

We continued to chat about Salvatore, her future "formal" wedding plans, and the ball.

I was successful in avoiding the Jonathan conversation and enjoyed getting a new "enhancement" as I call my coloring experiences.

When I got in the car, I checked my voice mail for messages. There was just one from my dad: "Did you hear from Jake? I haven't. Call me."

My dad dropped the files off at Chief Cerrazo's office the day after we went through them, but neither Dad nor I had heard from the chief, and that was a few days ago. I thought it was a bit odd since the chief was so interested in Pauli's death, but he hadn't called to say that he had found anything or even that he had read through the files.

I really wanted the chief to call to tell us something. I had high hopes that the files included something that proved Pauli's death was solvable. I thought, "Wouldn't it be great to go meet Mr. Suarez this week and have Chief Cerrazo with us to tell him that the Cummings family solved his wife's mysterious death? He would have to donate money to the ball. He would donate so much that we would exceed our goal and gain tons of publicity for Peaceland Park, and then I would be highly sought after for future work."

Before I had a chance to dial my dad, my cell phone rang. I didn't quite come out of my elaborate daydream until I read the caller ID. It was not Chief Cerrazo or my father—it was Jonathan.

"Hey, honey. How are you?" he asked. Just when I was thinking I didn't care if he came for the ball, I felt like I should try again to get him to come.

"Great. I just had my hair done, and Isabella's husband is coming to the ball. I finally get to meet the mystery man," I said. I went on to tell him how the ball arrangements were coming. About three minutes into my babbling, I realized that he wasn't on the line.

The phone rang again. It was Jonathan again.

"What was the last thing you heard?" I asked.

"Something about a mystery man," he said with a bit of sarcasm. I could tell that he didn't really want to hear about my hair, my hairdresser, or her new overseas husband.

"So, since I already told a dead air phone about my day, how about you tell me why you called."

"I have a great opportunity, but I wanted to talk to you about it first." He went on to tell me how he was offered an assignment in Miami, Florida. He would be leading a team in a pretty high profile audit that was a result of an FBI investigation in a regional investment firm. He said that this could be his big break to get a longer-term assignment where he wouldn't have to travel anymore.

Yeah. I bet that he won't have to travel anymore. I'll believe that when I see it.

I wanted to say, "Go—when are you going to have this opportunity again? You should go and build your career while you are young." After all, it wasn't like my career was really going anywhere. I couldn't hack the politics and bureaucratic bullshit, and I'm planning a party in honor of a fluffy-tailed rodent.

I kept thinking to myself, "It's not like we ever see each other anyway. It is easier to just keep quiet and let him make his own decision without any influence from me." But I also wanted to tell him "no, don't go" or "why do you have to ask me—you should know that I want you to come home."

"It sounds like a good opportunity, and you should do what makes you happy," I said. There, I said it. I told him to go with no regrets.

"I told them that if I did go to Miami that I had to be back home for the first weekend in September," Jonathan said.

"What's the first weekend in September?" I asked. I couldn't believe that his only request was to be home for some reason that I was clueless about. Not the ball, not my birthday in mid-September—not any special reason I was part of.

"It's your ball, silly. I want to be there to support you," he said with at least a smidge of sincerity.

"You know what? You can go to Miami or go wherever you want for that matter, and don't bother coming back the beginning of September," I said, and I hung up on him. I couldn't believe that he had called to basically ask my permission—or ask at least for my input, or just to try to make me feel better, when he didn't even have the date right. This is all I've been talking about for weeks, and he hadn't even gotten the date right!

For a CPA, he's not very good with his numbers, and I wasn't going to settle for mediocrity in my career or my love life.

So much for my great new hairdo, a boyfriend who I thought cared at least a little bit about me, and the career-making opportunity that I was hoping for with Mrs. Suarez's death solved.

Reality had hit. It hit me pretty hard, and I started to cry as I was driving home.

CHAPTER 16

I DECIDED TO START THE next day with a good attitude. No one has the opportunity to impact my positive thoughts more than me. I wasn't going to think about Jonathan and how he obviously didn't care about me. I got up early, went to the gym, and started the day with a spring in my step.

Although I was still fuming a little about Jonathan, I was going to do my best to focus on the positive, and today was a full day. I had a meeting with Violet and Doree to confirm the table settings and lighting decorations for the ball, along with continuing to work on the slide show.

The meeting with Doree wasn't until about 11 a.m., so after I went to the gym, I went back to the apartment to take care of a few things.

As I entered the side door, I saw something scamper across the kitchen floor. It wasn't a mouse, and it wasn't a cat, but it was something very fuzzy and fluffy—about the size of my slipper from end to end. I quickly closed the door and looked from the steps into the room to see if it was going to move again.

I was peering into the window with my hands cupping the sides of my face around my eyes.

"Did you lock yourself out?" Mr. Z asked.

I nearly jumped out of my underwear.

"Where did you come from? You were so quiet; you scared me half to death."

"I was trained in the war—slithering around foxholes was my specialty," he said. I didn't know he was in World War II, but I decided to question him later and ask him for help on the fur ball in my kitchen now.

"I'm not locked out. I just came back from the gym, and when I walked through the door, I noticed a dark fuzzy thing run across the floor. I came out on the steps to see if it would come out from under the counter," I said.

"Did you see what color it was? How big was it? Did it lump along or slide? What do you think it was?" He sounded like he had each question in his head way before he had the previous one answered.

I took a deep breath and then started to answer the inquisition. "It looked like it was black, and it was very fuzzy—bigger than a mouse, but not as big as a cat."

"It's a skunk," he said with great confidence.

Oh, God. A skunk is in my house. A skunk. A smelly, fuzzy critter in a confined unusual place.

I'm doomed.

And then I said, "How do you know it's a skunk?"

"I saw one lingering around the backyard throughout the past few days. I think it got in from your dryer vent," he said.

"My dryer vent?" I exclaimed. "How could it get in through my dryer vent?"

"Well, I noticed last week that the dryer vent cover over there on the side of the house was loose, but I forgot to mention it to you, and I haven't had a chance to fix it," he said in a very calm manner. His southern accent certainly helps put you at ease, but this is not a time to be at ease. That little critter could be stinking up my whole apartment, including the pictures and records I borrowed from Dax and Peaceland Park.

"Mr. Z, you mean to tell me that you noticed that stinky thing in the past few days, and you didn't fix the dryer vent that enters your house?" I was fuming. I know he is a sweet man, but his lack of assertiveness both annoyed and disappointed me. I wouldn't have dreamt of not helping him or taking action on fixing something for him. I was upset, but I had to remain calm under the circumstances.

"OK, let's just think this through. I could take a moving blanket from the garage, ease in slowly, and then scoop it up in the blanket and startle the critter by hitting him against the wall," I said.

"Are you crazy? That fumigator is going to spray you so hard, your grandchildren are going to be born needing a tomato juice bath," he said. "Let's just call animal control and get them here. Everything should be just fine." He patted my hand with one of his and put the other on my shoulder. He did have a calming effect on me. So he may not have been proactive to prevent the skunk from entering my home, but he'd take care of getting it out.

"I'm going to sit here and keep an eye on the dryer vent while you go in your house and call animal control. Maybe he'll realize he invaded a place he shouldn't be and find his way out," I said.

Mr. Z went around the house to make the call, and I went into the garage for some duct tape. I sat vigilant in his yard chair, staring at the dryer vent and willing the black and white to come out. If it came out on its own, I'd wait until it was out of spraying distance and reattach the dryer vent with the tape.

After about an eternity and a half, which is the equivalent of five minutes in skunk surveillance time, Mr. Z came back.

"I've got good news and bad news. Which do you want first?" he asked.

"Give me the bad news first. I can't see how anything could be much worse than my home needing new wallboard, flooring, and furniture, and then replacing my entire wardrobe," I said.

"Well, the animal control officer is not available for three hours," he said in a deliberately slow and singsong-ey voice "because she's trying to get three raccoons out of a storm drain. However, the Westfield police called the assistant animal control officer to come and help. She will be here in an hour."

"An hour? She'll be here in an hour? I'm held hostage in the back yard for an hour? I have to get ready for appointments. I think my idea of going in there with a blanket is now an option again." I was determined not to have the skunk take over my life. I needed to get ready for a big day—not sit in the sun and wait.

"It's important that we remain patient and not react too rashly. This woman is a professional and has experience in successfully coercing skunks out of places they shouldn't be," he said. "Why don't I get us some orange juice, and we can watch the dryer vent together." He walked toward his door.

I just shook my head and put my face into my hands. And then I quickly realized I couldn't sulk; I might miss the skunk coming out of the dryer vent. And then I remembered the door on the second floor that connected my apartment with Mr. Z's house. "Wait—what if I go through your house to my apartment and close him off from the top of the stairs?" I suggested.

I could go into his apartment, go through that door, and then at least put something in the way of the stairs so it couldn't get into my bedroom or closet.

He looked at me like he really didn't want to have to tell me something. "Sam, that would be a great idea if we knew for sure the skunk wasn't upstairs already. But let's think of it this way—he is at least contained to your apartment. If he is upstairs and near that door, he could get by you and get into my house. Then we're both doomed. Now, we have at least contained our assailant." He talked like he was discussing an enemy of war. And then he continued toward his door for the orange juice.

He returned with a pitcher of juice and two glasses, plus some cheese slices. "I thought this might lure the skunk out," he said as he showed me the chunks of stinky cheese.

He moved a small garden table near the dryer vent and placed the cheese on it. I hoped the skunk had a strong sense of smell to find the cheese—which doesn't make any sense since they can cause such a stink.

After almost forty-five minutes, the assistant animal control officer drove into the driveway. I would have thought it was a police car from afar, but the hood had a paw print on it that could have been imprinted by a ginormous-sized dog. She had a big toothy smile, was only about five feet two, but was about 180 pounds.

"Hello, I'm Olga. I understand you have a skunky in the house?"

A skunky? She called it by a "pet name." I was thinking "this is the enemy, an evil little critter than can wreak havoc on my life," and she's making it sound like a cuddly companion. No matter what she said, she was my only hope to keep my house from needing to be exorcised with bleach, so I had to let the professional do what she does best and wait until it exited the house before judging.

"It's in my kitchen—or at least it was about an hour and a half ago. Do you think there could be more than one?"

"No, these guys are lonely. They don't travel in packs," she said. "Well, I better get in there and get the little guy out. When I go in, I'm going to leave the door open. If he wants to get out, and if he forgot how he got in, the breeze from the open door will be his road map on how to get out."

She was a pleasant enough woman, but she sort of smelled like chewing tobacco and manure. I wanted to ask her to wipe her feet just in case she stepped in something at her last animal eviction this morning, but then I realized a little manure on the kitchen floor was the least of my potential problems today.

Olga didn't have any weapons or tools on her belt or attached to her multipocketed pants. She just went to my door, opened it quietly, and then maneuvered her way in. I stayed back a few feet from the steps. So did Mr. Z. I think we both figured, "Why smell like skunk if the perpetrator got angry or scared?"

We could hear her very clearly. She was saying, "Here little skunky. Come on out so you can go home," and, "Oh, you must be so scared in here. Don't you want to go home?" I kept thinking he was invading my space, and she was more worried about him being scared and wanting to go home than him spraying her. On the other hand, she was the professional in this situation, and I had to have faith.

"Do you want me to get my wife's old rosary beads? You are whispering Hail Marys and prayers to St. Francis as fast as an auctioneer," Mr. Z said to me. During the whole time of sitting watching the dryer vent, not moving, and waiting for Olga, I was praying that the skunk would leave as calmly and nicely as he broke in.

"Oh, there you are. Are you all snuggly on that afghan?" I heard her say from the living room.

Just then, a silent siren went off in my head. The afghan that my grandmother made for me when I was a baby was in the living room. Yes, I still have an afghan that's more than twenty-five years old, and I do use it all the time. It's one of my favorite tangible items that I own, if not the most cherished, and that stinking fur ball is taking a nap on it. This is war. When she gets that thing out here, he won't know what hit him!

"Oh, there, there little skunky. Are you taking a nap on that nice warm blanket? I know, you must have been very scared in here." She was talking in a baby voice, like cooing an infant to sleep. As this was all registering in my head, I could hear quick yet quiet footsteps come toward the door. This brave heroine picked up the dosing skunk and was carrying it out of the apartment.

And she had it wrapped in my blanket. My cherished, priceless blanket.

Olga continued down the steps and out toward the back part of the lawn. Meanwhile, Mr. Z attached the dryer vent with so much duct tape, you would think he was trying to keep a gas line airtight.

She cautiously placed the sleeping skunk on the ground—still in my blanket—and then started to walk back towards us.

"There—you're all set. Skunky is out, safe and sound."

I was burning. My face was red, and if I could have pushed steam out my ears like on those cartoons in the 1960s, I would have. That skunk HAD to get off my blanket, and he had to move now. I could not take the chance of him directly spraying what I slept with on a regular basis. How could I get to sleep tonight?

"He HAS to get off that blanket. It's an heirloom and cannot be replaced," I said. I wasn't about to tell her, at twenty-five-plus years of age, that I had an emotional attachment to a blanket. That would be embarrassing.

True, but embarrassing.

"Oh, once he wakes up, he'll waddle off, and you can take it. As long as he doesn't get startled, he won't spray, and your blankie will be safe."

"It's not a blankie ..." I started to say, when her cell phone went off to a tune of the trumpeter starting a horse race.

And then it happened. It was like a slow motion silent movie.

Skunky propped up on all fours, looked straight at us, turned quickly in the other direction, and raised his tail.

Like a mother bear looking after her cherished cub, I ran for my blanket—not thinking through the consequences of what could happen next.

And then it REALLY happened.

CHAPTER 17

CONSIDERING I WAS EYE TO eye with the skunk's pucker hole when he sprayed, I didn't think I did such a bad job getting the smell off of me.

In my rage to save my blanket, which I thankfully did, I grabbed it with my left hand and it went up in the air with the skunk, and I got hit with a full blast. Well actually, the skunk may have been turned upside down at the time that he sprayed, so I may have just gotten the overcast mist, but when it happened, I felt slimed.

Olga wrote me a warning for animal endangerment. She said my actions were rash and unnecessary, but she also realized I was in an emotional rage, so she didn't write me a ticket; however, she said if I ever encountered a skunk like that again, I could get charged.

By the time we were done, it was only about an hour before I had to meet Violet and Doree.

Mr. Z had a case of tomato juice, and he quickly got it all for me. I was a bit surprised he had that much, but he does like his Bloody Marys after church on Sundays.

I poured it all into my tub and washed my hair with it. I think it really worked. Then I took a water-based shower and washed my hair again three more times.

Skunky didn't leave even a trace of stink in the apartment. Thankfully, my clothes and furniture were all safe. It must have been all the prayers I was saying so fast.

I quickly got into a white pantsuit and was looking for shoes in my closet when the phone rang.

"So, you had a visitor this morning?" It was my dad.

"How did you hear?"

News travels fast through my family, but I didn't even tell anyone. And Mr. Z and I agreed to keep this little episode to ourselves.

"The police scanner was on this morning, and the garage flies heard about a skunk invasion on Western Avenue. When I got back from the registry, they were laughing about it. And then I heard the animal control officer call into the station saying that the skunk had left the building, and I heard your address," he said.

"Dad, it was one of the most terrifying experiences, and I'll tell you all about it later, but I have to run now. It took me about a half hour to get the stink out of my hair, and I'm going to be late for my meeting with the florist."

"You got sprayed?" He asked as he was laughing. He didn't even try to hold it back. "You must stink to high heaven!"

"I don't—I smell very nice now, but I have to go. I'll fill you in on the details later." And then I hung up.

I bet he'll have all his details from Olga pretty soon, I thought. He can track down the particulars on the most obscure happenings in town. Too bad he wasn't a detective on the case of Pauli Suarez years ago. I bet he would have found out everything that happened.

In all the foulness of the morning, I forgot all about Mrs. Suarez. I wondered if Chief Cerazzo had reviewed our findings.

I was so caught up in saving my precious blanket and home from being stunk up that I forgot what we were focusing on—solving Mrs. Suarez's death once and for all.

After putting finishing touches on my makeup and hair, I went out to the car. Mr. Z was waiting for me. He was working on his prize-winning roses.

"How'd everything go? How do you smell?" he asked, trying to sniff me for information like a hound dog. However, in fairness to him, he did look very concerned.

"I don't think I'm putrid—just a little hint of skunk. I guess the better person to judge would be you," I said. "What do you think?" I moved closer to him so he could get a good whiff of my hair.

"Not bad. You definitely have a tinge of skunkiness to you, but here—take this." He picked a beautiful rose and put it in my suit lapel. "That should overpower any lingering trace of the varmint."

It was a beautiful flower and was quite fragrant. I wasn't sure if I could stand the potency of it, but it certainly was less offensive than the alternative.

"Thanks, Mr. Z. I appreciate your wanting me to 'smell like a rose' in spite of my rash behavior earlier."

"Sam, I would have done the same thing," he said as he went to give me a hug and then gagged a bit when he got closer.

"Well, I guess you shouldn't try to get any dates for a few days, but from about three feet away, you smell just fine," he said and patted me on the back as if to encourage me to move along.

Doree and I were meeting Violet at her home studio. She had a shop in the center of town, but she said she'd rather meet with special events coordinators at her studio so she wouldn't be interrupted.

She lived out past Peaceland Park—almost in Southwick on the Westfield line. As I drove in, I was amazed by the glorious rose bushes in a rainbow of colors with a field of white begonias under all of them that bordered both sides of the paved driveway. Violet and Doree were in the front yard looking at the daylilies.

Violet was definitely a free-spirited looking person. She had wildly curly shoulder length dirty blond hair with purple wire-rimmed glasses. She was average height and weight and wore a multicolored flowered dress with green sandals that matched.

"Good morning, ladies." I had to really put on an act to be somewhat cheery, between my disappointing exchange with Jonathan last night and the events of this morning. "Violet, I don't think I've ever seen such a lovely combination as roses and begonias."

"It helps keep the weeds down and the beetles from the roses," she said. "It looks nice, but best of all its low maintenance and helps keep the yield up on the roses. I use them in my bouquets at the shop, so I try to get as many out of each bush as possible."

"I am sorry I am a bit late. I had an emergency this morning that caused me to be a bit delayed."

"I heard about your skunk encounter," Doree said. "I saw your dad at the post office, and he mentioned that you got sprayed."

"When did you see him? I just talked to him a few minutes ago." I guess news really travels fast.

"I saw him about a half an hour ago. He said that he heard on the police scanner that you were sprayed and that you were written a warning from the animal control officer because you threw the animal," she said.

"That wasn't exactly how it happened, and I hope you don't mind, but it was all a bit traumatic. I don't want to talk about it. I'd rather focus on something more uplifting—like our floral arrangements and lighting for the Black Squirrel Ball," I said.

Violet got the hint to change the subject and said, "Well, let's go out back to the deck, and I can show you some samples."

As I walked around the house on the flagstone path, I felt like I was in an annex of the rose garden at Peaceland Park. Violet's garden was formal and rigid, with the beddings being angled away from the path. And then we walked through an old iron trellis and gate, and the theme changed dramatically. It was much more whimsical and free flowing with herbs and perennials in raised, stone-lined, curvy planting beds. I looked down and was greeted by a little metal frog painted the same bright color of a yellow and orange marigold that bounced around a bit with the breeze, and then the birdbath was an old ceramic mixing bowl affixed to a pitchfork.

"Violet, I love your backyard garden. It's so much fun," I said.

"Look over there at the vegetable garden. The beans and tomato plants are tied up to a series of wires that are outstretched from the body of an oversized purple spider," Doree said.

"This garden is more my style. My husband made these flower beds for me the year before he died. I didn't have too much time to get them to this point until the kids got to college—I was chasing after one going to soccer or another going to dance class. Now that they're working at the shop in the summer, I can take more time to enjoy gardening rather than make a living at it," Violet said. "I was becoming a hostage to the shop—trying to get as much as possible out of every minute so that I could pay the bills, save for college tuition, and still have a little left over for retirement."

We sat down on the deck. Violet had the deck set up like an outdoor living room, with two couches and two chairs around a large tiled coffee table. The couches had colorful cushions and throw pillows of orange, yellow, teal, and royal blue.

Violet offered us glasses of raspberry lemonade and sugar cookies, and I quickly sipped half of the beverage down. It was a perfect combination of sweet and tart, made from scratch with the sugar not quite dissolved and plenty of fresh pulp. While I was admiring the thirst-quenching liquid, Doree was taken by the coffee table.

"What a beautiful table," Doree said.

"Thank you. I made it with tiles that my son crafted during his summer abroad program last year in Mexico. He's a sculpting student at Skidmore College, and he had the opportunity to apprentice in a tile manufacturing plant. He learned all about the process of firing and glazing," she said. "I'm not quite sure how he'll earn a living from these skills, but he's a good kid."

"And he's quite talented. I remember seeing tiles like these when my husband and I traveled to Mexico a few years ago. The intricate designs like these are only made by very skilled artisans," Doree said.

I wasn't sure what Doree had done in the past, but I thought Aunt Reggie told me she was an art museum curator. Or maybe she was a teacher at an art museum. Sometimes Aunt Reggie confuses the details.

"Do you have an art collection?" Violet said.

"No, my husband and I are not collectors. We truly believe in supporting the arts via membership at area museums," Doree said. "We would rather donate funds to a museum where others can also enjoy beautiful things than hoard them for ourselves."

"Do you have a background of working for an art museum?" I asked. Since I didn't know the details, it was as good a time as any to find out.

"I have a degree in Latin American humanities, and I've volunteered as a docent in art museums throughout my married life," she said. "I'm very fortunate that I don't have to work—with my husband being so successful," she said with a classist air about her that I hadn't noticed before. "So I match my interests and talents with the community's needs. That's why I volunteered to help with the Black Squirrel Ball. I'm a great organizer, and my husband said that the committee needed someone like me to get things in line."

All of the sudden I felt like the rage against the skunk was nothing like the rage of insults I'd like to spray on her. Organized? She's organized? What does she have to organize except her workouts, book club meetings, and grocery lists? I had to remind myself that Aunt Reggie also thought the group needed organization—but that's why she suggested the committee hire me.

"And now we have you," Doree said in a tone that combined jealousy with antagonism and a small roll of the eyes.

"Is there something you are trying to say to Sam?" Violet asked. I'm glad she interjected because I was going to ask the same thing—but with a definite tone to it.

"No, why would you think that?" Doree asked. She really seemed surprised by Violet's question.

"Because you just insinuated that Sam took your place of organizing the ball, and you seem like your nose is out of joint over it—that's why," Violet said.

"If I took a role or responsibility you thought was yours, I do apologize," I said sincerely. "But as I understand it, from when you joined the committee to when I was hired, not much took place. I don't think I took much away from you."

She started to tear up. We must have touched a nerve.

"I am glad the committee decided to hire you. I was just hoping that I could really own something and make it mine. All these years of marriage, I've been my husband's support and companion, but it has never been the other way around. I wanted to show him that I could have a vital role in our community—other than showing snot-nosed school kids around a local art museum." She was not only tearing up, but she was sniffling and getting a very red nose.

"Doree, we don't know you very well, and you are new to town. Heading up an event like the fortieth anniversary Black Squirrel Ball is something that a professional with local ties needs to manage," Violet said. I had only met Violet a few times, but I guess she knew my family and the event well enough that she made the connection of my strengths with the ball committee's weaknesses.

She continued, "You shouldn't be so hard on yourself. It sounds like you have been a very good wife to your industrious husband, and we'll certainly use your artistic eye with the floral arrangements and lighting."

Violet really turned that around quickly. She got up and went into the kitchen and came back with a box of tissues.

"Now, dab your eyes a bit, blow your nose, and start telling me your ideas," Violet said.

When she got up to go to the kitchen, I noticed a number of arrangements that were similar to what she described to me on the phone. However, I was guessing that she wanted Doree to feel more part of the process than I did—which is fine because an unhappy volunteer doesn't stick around too much longer, and I did really need all the help I could get.

"I thought you had some ideas already—based on pictures from the first Black Squirrel Ball?" Doree asked.

"I do, and I do have a few samples, but I'd like to hear what you have to add before I show you the demos. If you think my son the starving college student is a true artisan, then I need to gather all your good ideas," Violet said. Way to turn an extremely awkward moment into a great opportunity!

Doree told us how she thought we should use bright and festive colors rather than plain white to accent the beautiful colors of Peaceland Parl. Violet suggested that we pick some flowers from the yard in the colors Doree was thinking and make some other samples to compare to the ones on the table.

We split up to gather our flowers and then we convened on the deck. We followed Violet into the kitchen to gather the three beautiful all-white and green arrangements. I am a fan of simplicity, so it was going to be hard for me to be convinced that the colorful versions would be better.

Violet instructed us each to take out half the white flowers and replace with similar size and structured colored flowers, trying to get an equal mix of the red, orange, and yellow.

We then took a few minutes and quietly looked over the three cheerful displays. No one said a word, but I hoped they were thinking what I was thinking. Each of these looked like you could add a smiley face balloon to the vase and make the most ailing hospital patient come back to life.

These were not ball arrangements.

"I think simple white is best," Doree said. Oh, thank God. Thank goodness she had the sense to know when she's wrong. "I appreciate you both entertaining my idea, but I think the professional knows best, and Violet's original mock-ups were much more elegant."

Violet said. "I'm glad we tried this test. We might have been pleasantly surprised. It could have gone either way."

"But do you think the white ones are the right scale?" Violet asked. "Do you think they are too small?"

"The tables will be sixty inches round—which is bigger than this coffee table, and they look a little skimpy for this size. I think the arrangements should be about one third higher. Too high will be a distraction to the table and no one will be able to see the band," Doree said.

"Or the slide show," I interrupted.

"You're having a slide show? Of what?" Violet asked.

"If you can keep a secret," I paused as she nodded with wide eyes. "We're having a slide show of Peaceland Park's history, but it will also have a special ending to honor Dax's retirement."

"That's a great idea," Violet said. "I was just cleaning through a few boxes for the church's Second Time Around Sale, and I found some pictures from when I worked there."

"What did you do?" Doree asked.

"I was a kitchen worker when I was a teenager," she said. "I remember working during the summer at the conferences. I worked with Sam's grandmother. We sure worked long days—but it was fun. We would go in about noon on Sunday—after church, of course—and then go back and work all day on Monday, Tuesday, and Wednesday until the visitors went home."

"I'll go get the pictures now," Violet said, and went into the house—leaving me with Doree—who I wasn't sure was off her rocker or jealous of me and my low-paying job.

"I'm sorry that I got all weird before. I'm on hormone pills—trying to get pregnant—and I sometimes go off the deep end. My husband thought joining this committee would keep me busy while we wait until the next injection date," Doree said.

Even if she was drugged up, at least I found out she was more off her rocker than jealous of me.

"I'm sorry that you aren't feeling yourself. I'm sure it's a very difficult time for you and your husband," I said in my most concerned voice. I really didn't want to know anything more.

"It's been years of trying—we got married in our early twenties, and we still haven't conceived. Every time I'm a half day late with my period, I hope that this is the time we're going to have a baby," she continued. "I can't start a new job, knowing that I want to become pregnant and quit as soon as I give birth—that just isn't right—so I volunteer to keep busy in between treatments."

No matter how much I wanted her to stop, she continued on about how her husband's job change had more to do with moving closer to the Yale Medical fertility clinic than joining Formula 333. Where they lived before, the fertility clinic was subpar and the staff was not friendly. She did extensive research and found that Yale was one of the top facilities in the country for *in vitro* births. After about five more minutes of details regarding ovaries, egg count, sperm specimens, and hormone shots, Violet came back with two photo albums.

"Here are the photos I found. I have some good ones—even a few of your father and Dax when they were teenagers," she said to me.

We all sat on one couch with Violet in the middle and Doree and me on either side. I found it odd that Doree was so interested, since she didn't know anyone in the pictures, but then I realized that I might not recognize many people from forty years prior either, and yet I was intrigued.

"I have a bunch of pictures of the kitchen workers. It looks like we took a group shot at least every year," she said. Each photo was labeled with the date and sometimes those in the picture.

"I also have some from the conferences. Sam, look at this one of your grandfather, in a horse and buggy. He would take the 'city folk,' as he called them, for a ride around Peaceland Park," she said as she was pointing to a photo. He looked just the way I remembered. He was a jovial man with a big round head with happy eyes and a smile that took up most of his face. You could tell who in town was part of the Cummings clan by their smile. It was distinctively friendly.

"And here is an aerial picture of the Carillon Tower on the day of the dedication. These must have been my husband's photos—I don't remember these," she said. She continued to describe photos of the rose gardens and lily pond, and then she stopped cold. Her face turned white and stonelike.

"Are you OK, Violet? You look like you've seen a ghost," Doree said and reached for Violet's hand.

She shook her head a bit and frowned her lips, and then said, "It was such a shame that a nice lady like Pauli died so tragically."

"Is that a picture of Mrs. Suarez?" Doree asked. I already knew who it was from the pictures I saw with Dax and my parents. She really was stunning.

"Yes, that's my friend Pauli," Violet said sadly. "She was a few years older than me, but she was always especially nice to me when I worked in the kitchen. She would come in first thing in the morning to check on how things were going. We used to joke that we wondered what she would do if things weren't under control, because she wasn't the kitchen type."

She continued, "But she was quite the saleswoman. For all her husband's inventions, she could sell them like crazy. And all the other salespeople really admired her tenacity. She was something else," she said as she shook her head in dismay.

"I just never did understand how she could have accidentally fallen through that fence into the waterfall. Those handrails were inspected on a regular basis," Violet said. She described how my grandfather was a stickler for safety. She told us he was such a nice man, and they all had fun at work, but that he always wanted everyone to be safe—whether by wearing safety goggles when the boys were trimming brush or when the ladies were using the meat slicer in the kitchen. Safety was paramount.

"Then if everyone knew that the fence was safe, and she couldn't have weighed more than 110 pounds, why did the police deem it an accident?" Doree asked.

While listening, I did everything I could to hold back and not blurt out, "I have evidence that it may not have been an accident." But I couldn't. Mom, Dad, and I agreed we wouldn't tell anyone. It was in Chief Cerrazo's hands now, and we had faith in him that the truth would come out.

"I just don't know why the police would have come to that conclusion. It never made any sense to any of us. We were all devastated by the decision to call off the investigation just after a couple of days," Violet said. "None of us stayed late without being in a group and with a watchman. Your grandfather instituted that rule the night after the first Black Squirrel Ball," she said, looking at me. "He wasn't going to have any accidents like that happen ever again. And to his credit, no one has ever been seriously injured in Peaceland Park since. Oh, sure, there have been plenty of skinned knees and sprained ankles, but nothing like Pauli Suarez's fall into the waterfall."

I decided to get a little brave. Doree started the questioning. I figured I could continue—but it would have to be delicate. "Do you think she was murdered?"

"I do," Violet said solemnly. "Pauli was very successful, and although she was liked by many, she was also envied by others. There were a few of the middle management men who didn't like that she got more attention from the executives. And there were also the other salespeople who could never compete with Pauli—she was the best and no one would ever be better. Unless she was gone."

"I remember hearing two women from Puerto Rico talking about her one night. They were speaking Spanish, and they didn't realize that a young girl from western Massachusetts would be able to understand what they were saying. They described Pauli as a conniving bitch and said that she didn't deserve any of the attention she received."

"Do you think they killed her?" Doree asked. She isn't so bad after all, I thought—she jumps in before I do and asks the questions that could be considered too nosey.

"No. They were mean but not vengeful. They were just jealous and spiteful," Violet said. She flipped another page in the photo album and a piece of notepaper fell out. Doree and I both read it over Violet's shoulder. It said:

Bobby,

I will meet you by the waterfall after the ball. My husband will be at the Executives' after-party and I will need you to drive me home.

Sincerely,

Mrs. Suarez

"Oh, my. Oh, my!" Violet exclaimed. "I've never seen this before in my life." She threw the note across the table.

"My husband, Bobby, was a driver for the company when he was a teenager and then through college. In the summers, he would drive a van back and forth to Springfield with the salespeople, but during the school year, he would drive the executives to the airport or to Boston and New York City for meetings. I never knew he drove Pauli. He never told me about driving her."

She was starting to breathe erratically, and I was worried that she might hyperventilate or pass out. This was an interesting twist to the puzzle. Maybe Bobby Dorion was the last to see Pauli alive, or worse, maybe Bobby killed her.

"I don't know what to do. This could be a piece of the puzzle of how Pauli died and why Bobby stood me up after the ball that night," she said.

"He stood you up?" I asked.

"Yes, we both worked that night—I was in the kitchen and he was helping with security, or at least that's what he told me—and after the ball, everyone was getting together by the river for a bonfire. He never showed up. I had to get a ride home from one of my girlfriends," she said.

"The next morning he called to apologize and tell me that something came up that was out of his control, but I never questioned it. He was always so prompt and diligent that I figured if he had to work late then that's what happened," she said.

"I think you should share this with Chief Cerazzo. He'll know what to do with this," I said. This could be a clue in solving the mystery.

"How about we pack these pictures and the note up, and I'll drive you down to the police station?" I offered.

"I wish I could join you, but I have to meet my husband for an appointment this afternoon," Doree said. She gave me a wink. I guessed that was supposed to mean that there was a baby-making deadline or task involved. I was glad she didn't give any more details, and I was especially glad she didn't want to come along. The fewer people who know about this note, the better.

"Let me just get my purse, and let's go right away," Violet said.

Doree and I brought the mangled, colorful, flower-filled vases into Violet's kitchen.

She whispered, "Do you think her husband was the killer?"

"I only knew of Bobby from my father's stories. He was a nice, quiet man, who was an engineer at the utility company. He died from cancer when his children were very young, and Violet raised them on her own. I don't think he had a reason to kill Pauli, but I do think this note may help the police piece some old evidence together," I said. "We'll just have to hand this over to Chief Cerazzo and see what he will do."

"I can't wait to tell my husband that we may be part of solving a forty-year-old murder mystery. Maybe this volunteer thing will turn into something extraordinary, just as I had hoped."

At that moment, I realized that I really didn't like this woman so much. She was thinking that she might be part of solving a murder only because she was sitting next to someone who found an old note. Doree didn't deserve any credit for finding the note, and yet she thought she was Sherlock Holmes.

Then Violet walked into the room and stopped me from thinking about this woman being a selfish scammer.

"Ready?" I asked.

"Ready as I'll ever be," she sighed.

"Do you want to call the kids?" Her two college-aged kids worked at the flower shop, which is within two or three blocks of the police station. Her son was in graduate school for art, and her daughter was in business school. Violet hoped that one or both would take over the business in the future.

"No, there's no need for them to worry about something their father was involved in years before they were born," she said.

Doree leaned over and gave Violet a squeeze and told her to take care of herself. Violet rolled her eyes so only I could see as she accepted Doree's hug and thanked her for the flower arrangement suggestions.

CHAPTER 18

WE ALL WALKED OUT OF the house toward the driveway. Doree got into her new 6-series convertible, which I had been drooling over since the first time I saw it after a committee meeting. Violet and I got into my black clunker with the awesome tires and rims. As soon as we closed the doors, Violet started to clear her throat, and she opened the window, leaning a bit so part of her head was out the window.

"Is something wrong, Violet?" I realized that was a silly question. Of course something was wrong; her teenage sweetheart and deceased husband may have been involved in a murder forty years ago.

"Sam, I appreciate you driving me to the police station, but can you open your sunroof and your window. It smells like that skunk crawled into your car," she said as her eyes started watering.

"I thought there might be a hint of that smell in my hair still. It must have gotten stuck in the car on my ride over and then percolated in the sun while I was at your house," I said. I was so embarrassed.

"Would you like me to take you back home, and I'll follow you?" We were almost half way there, but I didn't want her to get sick. She looked like her stomach was turning and her complexion was as pale as the white flowers she arranged.

"No, we're almost there, and I can go to the shop to help close up after we're done with Chief Cerazzo," she said as she was carefully breathing through her mouth and not her nose.

We drove the rest of the way down Granville Road, onto Court Street, and took a left onto Washington Street in silence.

We got out of the car, and as we walked up the steps, I noticed something move in the shrubs along the building. I let out a yelp.

"What was that?" I asked and grabbed ahold of Violet's arm.

105

"I think it was a chipmunk or a squirrel," she said as she rubbed my hand and disconnected my arm from hers. "Geez—that skunk really did a job on you—not just your smell, but your nerves, too."

We continued walking up the stairs and into the reception area. Violet asked for Chief Cerazzo. She told the officer on duty that it was not an emergency, but she had information about a murder case that the chief should have. The officer didn't wait to hear the end of the sentence. Once she said murder case, he took off with a high-step pace toward Chief Cerrazo's office.

In less than thirty seconds, Chief Cerazzo jogged out of the hallway into the reception area and looked a bit perplexed to see Violet and me with information about a murder case.

He squinted his eyes and cocked his head to the left, and said, "Helloooo, Violet. Hello, Sam—or should I call you the skunk assailant?" he said with a chuckle.

"It isn't funny, and I've received my written warning for my action of self-defense. There's no need for further police action or teasing," I said. "I brought Violet down to show you something we found today while we were looking through old photos from Peaceland Park."

"Can we go to your office, Chief?" Violet asked.

"Of course we can, and, please, call me Jake," he said, extending his hand to shake hers in a less formal way than I would have expected.

"Thank you, Jake," Violet responded.

We walked down the hallways just as I did the day the Chief and I discussed the traffic and security for the ball, except this time, he took us into a room that had a large mirror on one side.

He was taking us to an interrogation room. I must not have hidden my look of concern, because Chief said, "I'm not interrogating you, but I'd like to record our conversation, and I can do so from this room. Here are papers to sign. Do you mind, ladies?" Violet and I both shrugged our shoulders and nodded and then reached for the pens provided. Since we weren't involved in Pauli's death, I didn't see a reason why not to sign the releases. And she must have felt the same way.

"Please, have a seat. Can I get you some water or coffee?" All of a sudden I remembered a *Law and Order* episode when an offer for a drink turned into a way to get a DNA sample with consent.

"No, thank you, we're all set." I answered for both of us. Violet looked at me with a bewildered face, but she went along.

"Please show me what you found," the chief said.

Violet reached into her handbag and took out the note. The chief read it out loud so the recording mechanism could pick it up. Violet than described how Bobby stood her up that night and apologized the next day, and she didn't think anything of it. She also told the chief how Bobby drove for Formula 333, but she never remembered him driving Mrs. Suarez.

Then she started to weep. She pulled a handkerchief out of her bag. It was a lovely laced piece that didn't seem to be of much use for her tears since it was so delicate. Chief Cerazzo pulled out a box of tissues from the credenza behind him.

"My husband was a great man. We fell in love when we were so young, and we stuck by each other until we married. He continued through graduate school while I lived with my parents, and when he was done, he got a great job with the utility company. By then, we were in our late twenties, and he had already been exposed to so much radiation that the doctors suggested it was best that we not have children. He had a vasectomy and within three weeks, I was pregnant," she said.

"Violet, why are you telling me all of this?" the chief asked. I was also wondering if this was the baby-making story day. I heard about Doree's trials and tribulations and now this.

"I'm telling you this because Bobby didn't keep any secrets. He told his family that he was having the vasectomy because he didn't want his mother to expect grandchildren from us. The doctors back then thought the level of radiation exposure he had during his graduate school internships might have a deforming impact on children, and we agreed that we didn't want to be selfish and bring ill children into the world. He told everyone about the vasectomy; he was embarrassed, but he wanted his co-workers to understand the importance of safety at work."

She continued, "And then I got pregnant. He wanted everyone to know these children were his, and it must have been that God wanted us to be parents—no matter what the outcome. Seven months later, I gave birth to the two healthy—yet premature—babies, and there were no effects of the radiation to them."

"A few years later, when he was diagnosed with cancer, it was radiation that kept him alive for a few more months than the oncologists thought could be possible," she said. "He wanted everyone to know about his disease and that he probably contracted liver cancer from his exposure to radiation in graduate school."

"My husband didn't keep secrets," she said emphatically. "He wasn't a murderer."

"Violet," the chief said in a very soothing voice as he reached out to her hand that was not clutching the handkerchief, "I don't think Bobby was a murderer. I worked with him at the park, and I was with him that night.

We had to drive a few drunk guests home in their cars, and so he and I were jockeying cars back and forth together."

"Oh, thank God," she said as she let out a gallon of air. "I didn't think he could be a murderer, but I don't know what to make of this note."

"This note is interesting, but I recall that Pat O'Connor suggested to Bobby that he take Mrs. Suarez home so that Bobby and I could drive the guests home. Pat usually drove the company cars, and he couldn't drive a stick shift. One of the executives had a four-speed 1965 Mustang convertible that Pat would have embarrassed himself in. Bobby and I grew up driving tractors so it was a treat to drive that souped up fancy car. I remember Bobby and me flipping a coin to see who had to drive the park truck behind the car, and who got to drive the car. I won. That was one of my favorite rides ever!"

From what I learned recently, Pat was the nicer brother of the Pat and Frank twosome. He was an active member of the Irish Club's parade and float committee for years until he recently had a stroke and now lives at the nursing home where Lucinda is also a resident. Pat was recently honored by the Irish Club for his hard work and dedication. I heard all about the festivity from my friend Jerry. Jerry escorted him from the nursing home to the event since Frank couldn't wrangle Pat's wheelchair—or, better stated, Frank couldn't be bothered to help his dear brother. Jerry thought it would be fun to dress as the Lucky Charms leprechaun for a St. Patrick's Day celebration, and Pat was delighted to have such an enthusiastic caregiver.

Pat and Frank got their jobs with Peaceland Park and Formula 333 because of their father, George. George joined the company when he was just in his twenties and worked his way up to chief financial officer before retiring when he was in his sixties. He and Grandpa were on the same bowling team for many of those years.

Nepotism was not a bad word in the 1960s and 1970s like it is in corporate America today; it was just the way of doing business. I remember my dad telling me how Pat was a real hard worker and Frank was a moocher, trying to get everyone else to do his work, so Grandpa gave him the night shift cleaning duties, but he gave Pat the better assignments, like driving guests and executives in the company Lincoln.

Chief Cerrazo continued, "What makes this interesting is that I don't think anyone knew that Pat was supposed to meet Mrs. Suarez except the three of us—me, Bobby, and Pat. I don't recall anyone asking us, and I don't remember telling anyone. If it wasn't for you finding this note, that fact may have never been remembered."

"What are you going to do?" I asked. I was hanging on every word they had just said. I felt like I was not part of the conversation, but that I was looking through a cloud seeing the two of them exchange their details from decades prior with such clarity that it seemed it just happened.

"I'm going to take some time to go through the information your father dropped off the other day. I've been so busy I haven't had a chance to even peek at anything," he said.

"If you'd like, I can give you the highlights in just a few minutes," I said.

"Yes, that would be helpful," the chief said.

I went on to describe the medical examiner's notes and thoughts—how he didn't think it was an accident and that Mrs. Suarez was murdered. Both Violet and Chief Cerrazo hung onto every word for a few minutes, and then the chief stopped me.

"Who else knows about this information?" he asked.

"Violet and I know about the note—and Doree Bowers, a volunteer for the committee—and my mom and dad know about the medical examiner's information, but that's it. No one else. Why?" I asked.

"I need to get to this Doree woman and ensure that she doesn't tell a soul about the note," the chief said very sternly. He called a lieutenant in and gave him instructions to find her car in town and escort her to his office as soon as possible.

"Chief, I know where she is and I have her cell phone number. I think it would be best if you call her rather than pull her over. I don't think she's in the best emotional state," I said. "Or if you'd like, I could call her and ask her to meet me here as soon as possible. That may reduce the odd nature of the request."

"Good idea, Sam, that way there will be someone here she knows," he said.

"So are you done with me?" Violet asked.

Chief Cerrazo turned his attention to Violet, "Yes, thank you for coming down so quickly and sharing this note with me. I'll go through the files Sam's dad left; I'll try to cut Doree off the chase before she tells anyone anything—we don't want this to leak out before we have more information. And I think we need to question Pat. Plus, if this was a murder, the suspect could still be living in town."

"But Mr. O'Connor just had a stroke, and he isn't well. I saw him the other day at the nursing home when I was visiting Lucinda Marino," I said.

"You visited Lucinda? You are a brave young lady, Samantha Cummings," Chief Cerrazo said.

"She was actually helpful and quite pleasant—in her curt and forceful way."

"I'll have to talk to him one way or another. I have an aunt there. I'll stop in later today and see if I can catch a word with him," the chief said. "Pat doesn't seem like the murdering type any more than Bobby, but we need to get to the bottom of this."

We said our good-byes. Violet insisted on walking to the flower shop. She said she wanted to enjoy the fresh air.

CHAPTER 19

As I DROVE HOME WITH the sunroof and windows open to get the lingering smell out, I called Doree and left her a message to call me right away.

Although I didn't think I needed it, I showered again and washed my hair three more times. After drying my hair, I noticed my cell phone had a message on it. It was Doree. She returned my call, and she needed to speak to me right away, too. She must have called while I was in the shower.

As I dialed the number, I was thinking it was a bit peculiar that *she* needed to speak to *me* so quickly since I was the one who called her first. After all, I was going to see her in a couple of days at the next committee meeting, and it wasn't like she was working on any critical Black Squirrel Ball assignments.

I dialed and barely heard a ring when she picked up.

"Doree, it's Sam. I'm returning your call."

"I'm so glad you called so soon. I told Mike the story about the note, and he thought we should go to the press about the note. Even if Bobby wasn't the murderer, Mike wouldn't want it to look like anyone was hiding anything."

I thought her husband Mike was a little theatrical. He may be the CFO of Formula 333—which is the largest supporter of Peaceland Park—but to go to the media at this point would be melodramatic and the last thing anyone should do.

"Oh—I hope you didn't do anything," I said.

I explained it was imperative that she—and now her husband, too—go and speak with Chief Cerrazo immediately.

"We're at the pharmacy, filling up my prenatal vitamin prescription and my husband's folic acid prescription. Even though we're going for *in vitro* treatments, you never know if the swimmers will get there on their own with a little extra help."

That was, again, more information than I needed to hear.

"The chief asked that I meet you at the police station. I'll leave right away," I said.

I left without finishing my makeup. I skipped out the door and down the steps and called the chief from the car to tell him Doree, her husband, and I were on our way.

I followed a similar route down Western Avenue and Court Street, like I did with Violet earlier today, except this time I was slowed down by two ambulances as they neared the emergency room entrance of the hospital. For a community hospital, two ambulances at once was unusual—unless there was a car accident. Maybe the prayers I said for my silly skunk incident could have a carryover effect for those in greater need of prayers.

When I arrived at the police station, I saw Doree's car. I joined her and her husband in the lobby, and then the same lieutenant who was supposed to track Doree down led us to the chief's office. We didn't go into the interrogation room this time.

"Please, have a seat," the chief said as he gestured to the chairs he had around a conference table in his office.

"I'm sorry that you had to come here on such short notice, but I do appreciate your cooperation."

He continued, "Doree, as you know, and as I believe you have shared with your husband, Violet found a note that may have some connection to Mrs. Suarez's mysterious death forty years ago."

The chief reviewed the importance of this "case"—which is not what he called the "situation" earlier today—making it clear that he was personally dedicated to tracking down the latest clues and reviewing the files from the late 1960s.

"I was working at the park that night, and I am equally puzzled by the conclusion that Mrs. Suarez's death was deemed an accident. It wasn't until Violet and Sam provided this note from Violet's late husband that I thought we may have a lead to reopen the case."

"So you think it was Bobby who killed her?"

"No, I don't think it was Bobby. Matter of fact—I know it wasn't him because I was with him. I do know who was supposed to fill in for him taking Mrs. Suarez home, and I'll be researching that lead tonight," he said as he tapped his pencil on the desk to emphasize what he was saying to show his adamant feelings about the subject.

"Who is it?" Mike asked.

"For the sake of the credibility of this investigation, which I've decided to reopen, I cannot tell you any details," the chief said. "And I ask that you do not speak to anyone about this. Mrs. Suarez's memory depends on you."

He usually spoke very quickly and with great force, but in just the last few hours, I noticed that he was quite deliberate in his word choice and facial features. That last statement had pauses in between words, and he looked Doree and Mike dead in the eye.

"As I mentioned before, I thank you for coming down on such short notice," he said and stood up. He escorted us all to the reception area, and Doree and Mike left the police station. I said I needed to retrieve something I left in the chief's office and went back in.

The chief was still in the reception area, and he looked surprised to see me. He was so formal and "by the book" when he escorted us out, and then when I walked in, he was chitchatting about the Red Sox scores from the night before.

"Chief, I had a couple other questions for you. Can we chat just a few more minutes?"

We went back to his office, and on the way I mentioned that I wanted to know how the visit with Patrick O'Connor went.

"Oh—I can't believe I forgot to tell you. He was out for a walk with your crazy high school friend Jerry when I went to visit him, so I didn't even get a chance to talk to him," he said. "And since I went in, I did have to visit my aunt so she didn't find out I was there and didn't visit—which turned into a thirty-minute monologue about the horrible food and a match of gin rummy where she whipped my butt, and I lost $7."

He told me that he planned to go back the next day, but that he didn't want to call ahead so that he didn't raise any suspicions.

So I left again, and this time for real. The more time I spent with the chief, the more I was impressed by his way of being pragmatic, friendly, and forceful—all at the appropriate time.

When I got into the car, I checked my voice mail and there was a message from Tom Marfucci.

"Sam, please call me as soon as possible. I found something most interesting in my brother's files that you need to see right away," he said in his rushed yet methodical voice.

I rushed home, hoping to not hit too much five o'clock traffic going up Western Avenue, rushed into the driveway, and came to a dead stop at my stairs. There was a case of tomato juice waiting for me with a note:

Heard you had a stinky day. Hope this helps you smell like a rose.

Drop your car off tomorrow, and I'll have it cleaned so it doesn't reek of skunk anymore.

Gareth

Seems like word got around town pretty quickly. I never thought a case of tomato juice could be such a thoughtful gift. Plus, he must have read my mind about getting the car detailed. This guy is all right!

I lugged the case of Campbell's into the kitchen and left it on the floor. Then I called Tom's assistant to set up an appointment. I had his posters ready, and I would deliver those and pick up the mystery find all in one trip. How efficient!

The whole skunk experience reminded me of a stinky story about my grandfather. There used to be a big manure and compost pile where the lily pond is at the park now. He slipped and fell into the manure pile, and he smelled so bad that the guys put him on the back of a truck to bring him home to shower and change.

I certainly didn't smell that bad, but that night I soaked in the tomato juice and washed my hair a few more times, and then I went to bed. I figured it couldn't hurt to make sure all the stink was off of me for good.

I checked my messages as I was towel drying my hair, and there was one from Jerry. I must have missed it while I was saturated in the red stuff.

"Hello!" he sang in a high-pitched voice. Sometimes I think he just tries to impersonate a drunk, loud Englishwoman. "I hope you haven't wasted your time sitting in a bathtub full of perfectly good Bloody Mary mix. It won't work. You need to make up a remedy that we use at the nursing home to neutralize odors. Call me."

I was too pooped to call Jerry for yet another stink-reducing remedy. A day of warding off skunks and trying to solve a murder mystery was exhausting.

CHAPTER 20

THE NEXT MORNING, I RETURNED Jerry's call, leaving him a message, too. I could only imagine what smell-reducing remedy he had in mind. However, I thought I was almost "unscented" at that point so I just called him back to be polite.

I also called Gareth's shop to make arrangements to have the car detailed. It was rainy, so I couldn't just let it air dry. He said he wasn't going to be in by the time I dropped it off, but I could use their loaner car for the day.

After getting ready, I traversed through Westfield from my apartment on the west side through downtown and down by the river. Construction caused a couple of detours that led me down some bumpy side streets.

I dropped my car off at Gareth's, and his partner handed over the keys to their loaner—a brand new Ford Escape Hybrid. I wondered if I could get a piece of this action—the tire business seemed pretty good. I couldn't get over how nice and smooth the ride was and how comfortable the driver's seat was compared to my back-breaking car.

Since I was just running in and out quickly to Tom's office, I parked the loaner on the street. The parking garage was about a block away from Tom's office building, and it was raining buckets by the time I got to Springfield. I tried to bolt from the car to the door, but the sidewalk was as slick as an ice rink, and I slipped and fell into a big puddle.

"Just great," I thought. I was trying to make a good impression, and instead I was going to look like a drowned rat.

I was wearing a dark pantsuit, so I had hoped Tom wouldn't notice that I was soaked.

As I walked through the front door, the security guard was trying not to laugh at me. "Some spill you took out there, huh?" he asked as he was holding back a chuckle.

115

"Don't you think you should put a 'caution when wet' safety cone out there, or are you going to wait until an old lady breaks a hip?" I asked with as much attitude as there was water on the sidewalk.

"I'm not responsible for the sidewalk," he said quickly.

"Nice—just let it be someone else's job, right? Well then, whose job is it, so I can call them on that radio you have right next to your left hand?" I spurted out. It really gets me beefed when people refuse to do what's right because it isn't "their job."

"OK, lady. I'll call the maintenance guy now."

"Thank you. Thank you very much." I smiled sarcastically and walked toward the elevator.

I'm not sure if I was glad the elevator was mirrored so that I could try to fix my waterlogged outfit or terrified because I could see that I looked worse than I imagined. I was happy that I had the elevator to myself so no one else saw me try to groom myself.

I had just enough time to smooth out my jacket when the elevator dinged on the eleventh floor. I stepped out and slowly walked to Tom's office; I noticed that my shoes were squeaking from being so wet.

"Hey there, young lady. Come in here and have a cup of coffee. I was on a conference call looking out the window and almost coughed up a lung when I saw you fall," Tom said when I walked through the door, and he handed me a cup of coffee and led me to his office. So much for trying to be discreet about my wet and wild ride.

"I only have a few minutes before my next meeting, so I'm just going to get to the point," he said as he handed me an envelope.

"Go ahead, open it up," he said.

I opened the envelope and almost threw up. It was a typewritten note that said:

Mr. Suarez,

I strongly suggest you leave town immediately if you want to keep your dear Paulita happy and alive. You are a greedy foreigner and should get on a boat and go back to Mexico.

"How did your brother get this?" I asked.

"I don't know how he got it," he said with a horribly perplexed look on his face. "I went through all his boxes, and in between a stack of *Popular Mechanic* magazines, I found this."

He went on to tell me that he didn't find anything of interest about Formula 333, Peaceland Park, or Mr. Suarez.

"I think these magazines were Mr. Suarez's because they had a Formula 333 mailing address on them. I'm not sure if Mr. Suarez gave my brother this note, or even if my brother ever knew he had it."

"Tom, may I take this and share it with Jake Cerrazo, the Westfield police chief? I can't tell you the details, but I think this will be helpful to him."

"Sure. Should I call Mr. Suarez and tell him what I found?" he asked.

I said, "I think you should leave it to the chief only because he can fill Mr. Suarez in on a few other items all at the same time."

I continued to tell Tom that there had been some other things found lately relating to Paulita and Raul Suarez, and it would be best to keep things under wraps until the chief could piece everything together for Mr. Suarez.

I thanked him for his time and handed him the posters.

"Do you want to send me a dry set?" he asked with a chuckle.

"They didn't get wet. I had them wrapped and sealed just in case I had to walk from the parking garage—or in my case, take a bath on the corner of Court and Main Streets in Springfield."

He smiled and shook his head in a small bit of amazement. "You always plan ahead," he said.

I got up to leave and noticed that I left a wet spot on his chair from my drenched clothes.

If only I had planned ahead to avoid puddles.

CHAPTER 21

OVER THE WEEKEND, I MADE some progress on the slide show. It was a rainy couple of days, and I just kept scanning, dating, and sorting pictures in the boxes from Dax.

But then the sun was shining, and it was Monday morning—a whole new week, hopefully without any stinky skunks or rainy days.

I absolutely love Mondays. Some people think I'm crazy, but it's the best opportunity to make the week as productive as possible. If you have a lousy Monday, your chance for a successful week diminishes by 20 percent.

As I was getting ready that morning, I thought that it was going to be pretty hard to keep a poker face when I was with Esther and Dax all day driving to visit Mr. Suarez.

Chief Cerazzo was even more convinced that Pauli was murdered, and probably by someone she and Mr. Suarez knew, based on the note Tom found.

I walked to Esther and Dax's house and they were ready to go. She had snacks packed and a cooler of drinks. Dax drove their four-door automatic with both feet—one foot on the gas and the other foot on the brake. It was like stop and go all the way, even though we were on the secondary roads. It took us about three hours to get to Mr. Suarez's house on the Connecticut shore. If I had driven, it would have taken half that.

Esther told me that she and Dax would visit from time to time, and she warned me that it was a beautiful home but it felt cold—like it was a beacon of loneliness.

"Did Mr. Suarez own this house when Mrs. Suarez was alive?" I asked in between queasiness spells in the back seat of the car.

"Yes. He had just bought it the summer she died," Dax said. "He purchased it right before Memorial Day and took her to see it after the closing. He wanted her to have the summer to decorate it, and they had big plans to have a party on Labor Day weekend."

"I remember not only being disappointed that Mrs. Suarez died because it was so sad, but also because our extra work was cut," Dax said. "The boys would go down on the weekends and have painting projects or pull out shrubs. She had very specific instructions every Friday, and we were to get it all done before Sunday afternoon."

"Who would go help?" I asked.

Dax said, "Oh, it was me, and some of the older guys—like Walter and Mugsy. Sometimes your father would come or your Uncle Joe would come—he was quite a painter even in his early teenage years."

"Mrs. Suarez loved the gardening work that Mugsy would do. I remember that he laid out a bed of perennials in the shape of a heart, and she was so excited that she told all the women in the office back in Westfield how Mugsy was the best gardener. She really took a shine to him and his work."

"Where would you stay when you went down there?" I asked. I wanted to hear more about Mugsy and the other workers—maybe someone was jilted about unpaid work or something upsetting and had threatened Mrs. Suarez. Maybe there was something here that could have a connection with her death.

"We would stay overnight in the room above the garage. It was one big room with bunk beds, and we would work hard all day, then Mr. Suarez would cook us a nice big dinner, and we would play cards into the wee hours of the night," Dax said.

"I bet that's not all you did," Esther said.

"Ey—you know me too well. We would also drink a few beers, and when your father and Uncle Joe came along, they would always bring their guitars, and we would sing and laugh," he said while smiling brightly with his eyes.

"Mrs. Suarez would wake us up early on Sunday morning and insist that we go to church; then we worked until about noon, had lunch, and packed up to go back to Westfield," Dax reminisced. "We all liked to go because we had the chance to get out of town and also make a few extra bucks. Mr. and Mrs. Suarez paid really well," he said, emphasizing *really*.

"But then once Mrs. Suarez passed away, Mr. Suarez wasn't motivated to have the projects completed, and he waited many years to do any more work on the house. I think there are still rooms that aren't furnished," he said.

By the time we were at this point in the story, we were driving down the trap rock drive toward the Cape Cod style home. It had weathered shingles and a gray roof, with pink beach roses lining the driveway.

"It even looks a little sad—the way the windows on the top floor are so narrow and the porch doesn't have any chairs on it," Esther said.

It was a nice enough house, but she had a point. As nice as it was, it didn't give you the feeling like you were going to enter a happy home. Not a haunted house—but you had an indifferent feeling.

I also had a case of nausea that was only going to be cured with a carbonated beverage and some fresh air. Thank goodness for Esther's cooler and the ocean breeze.

I quickly took a few sips before we got out of the car and walked up to the front door. Dax rang the doorbell, and we all waited.

A man with jet black hair and green eyes came to the door. He looked like he had the face and stature of a seventy-year-old man with the tan of a Ken doll. Mr. Suarez must have loved the sun. His skin was almost as brown as Esther's leather handbag.

"Good morning. It's so nice to see you all. Please come in," Mr. Suarez said. "And you must be Samantha Cummings? It's a pleasure to meet you."

"You can call me Sam. It's nice to meet you, too." I was suddenly worried that the nausea may have not been cured by the soda and fresh air. My hands were clammy, and my ears were getting hot.

"Are you OK? You look a little peaked," he said. "I've set up some refreshments and snacks on the deck. Let's get you some fresh air."

As Mr. Suarez led the way, Esther was holding his arm and helping him a bit. He seemed jovial and spirited enough, but a little unsteady as he opened the door and shook my hand. I was a bit self-conscious that the first time I met the man, there was a chance I could have barfed on his shoes.

Dax and Esther suggested that I talk about the ball and all the plans we have, but that they ask for the donation instead of me. I thought that was a perfect plan because the fewer "asks" I had to do, the less nervous I would be.

They knew him, and they knew how to read his body language and responsiveness. Our goal was $50,000, but we didn't want to go home with less than $25,000. I wasn't sure how we would get by with only $25,000, but I didn't want to think about it then. I just needed to get outside so I would stop feeling like I was on a rocky sailboat on the verge of hurling my breakfast.

As we walked through the home, I noticed a couple of pictures of him and Mrs. Suarez and some awards of recognition from Formula 333 and civic organizations. I also noticed a picture of him, my grandfather, and a few other managers and executives whom I had recognized from Lucinda's photos.

It was nice to see that he was still nostalgic about the past and his life in Westfield, Massachusetts.

Mr. Suarez said, "Here we are—let's all enjoy the sunshine."

He pulled a chair out for Esther, and Dax did the same for me. It was nice to see such chivalry and good manners; of course, you would expect it from men of their generations. I sat across from Mr. Suarez, and Dax and Esther sat across from one another at the beautiful weathered teak table set.

He had a pitcher of iced tea and lemon drop and shortbread cookies on a beautiful silver tray. I couldn't wait to start the sugar rush!

Dax and Esther asked about his extended family and his hobbies. He was an avid golfer and sailor, despite his lack of balance. They exchanged some stories about people they both knew in Westfield.

Mr. Suarez said, "Sam, I remember a story about your grandfather that still gets me to chuckle."

He continued, "It was when Formula 333 was growing by leaps and bounds, and we had just opened the annex facility in Granby, Connecticut. Mr. Brown was new to company as the VP of human resources, and he was told to review everyone's jobs and develop a list of people who were superfluous and could be reassigned. There seemed to be too many chiefs and not enough indians."

I didn't notice until he started telling this story that he did have a bit of an accent. After all, he was born and raised in Mexico. Every once in a while, I would miss a word or two, but then catch on to the gist.

"Well, your grandfather's name was on the list, and Mr. Smith went right through the roof," he gestured with his hand in a thumbs-up sign and moved his arm vertically until his hand was over his head. "Mr. Smith called Mr. Brown and said, 'Why is Mr. Cummings's name on this list?' and Mr. Brown said because he couldn't figure out what he did."

"Mr. Smith said, 'Mr. Cummings does everything. He takes care of the kitchen workers, he looks after the maintenance crew, he oversees the landscapers, and he MCs the events at Peaceland Park. He knows how to get everything done.' So that was how your grandfather was taken off that list pretty darn quick."

Dax said, "Sam, it was a different time back then, but your grandfather could get just about anything done. He was a good trader."

"You mean a good tradesman? I thought he was a farmer?" I said with a confused look on my face.

"No, I mean your grandfather was a good trader. He knew how to trade anything for something and get a fair deal."

Dax went on to tell a story about how when he was a kid, he and the others would ride up to the reservoir once a week with my grandfather and rake up the pine needles, fill up trucks, and then spread the pine needles on the pathways through the park. "Your grandfather knew that the reservoir folks didn't mind, and it was a good way to keep the pathways nice and neat looking. We did it every week—so that once one group left Peaceland Park for a conference, the next group would see it in just as nice of a condition."

"I remember another story—about the time the Carillon Tower was dedicated. Mr. Smith called him and said he needed one hundred folding chairs for the dignitaries," Mr. Suarez said. "About ten thousand people attended, and the event shut down traffic throughout Westfield for miles." He was quite animated in his storytelling—using his eyes and hand gestures for dramatic effect.

"Peaceland Park had plenty of chairs, but not the nice white wooden chairs that Mr. Smith wanted for the speakers and special guests," he said. "So your grandfather went through the paper to see which funeral homes were busy that week and called the others to borrow their chairs. In just a few minutes, he had the one hundred chairs accounted for!"

We all laughed at that one. I could imagine my grandfather calling a funeral director and saying, "Since you aren't busy, I'm going to borrow these chairs for a day or so."

"I really miss those days. It was a good place, and there were good people. People helped one another," Mr. Suarez said. "I only wish times were like that again."

He looked a little sad all of a sudden, and his eyes got glassy. He looked down at his left hand and rotated his wedding ring around his finger.

"Sam, I'm guessing that Esther and Dax brought you down to meet me for a specific reason. What is it?" he asked, seeming like he was trying to change the subject from missing his wife and the times of years past. I was a bit startled by his abrupt change of topic, but I figured I had to go with the flow.

"Well, as Esther and Dax may have told you, I'm organizing the Black Squirrel Ball this year, and we'd like to make it the most memorable one ever." As I said that, I wished I could have shoved the words back into my mouth. What could be more memorable than the last time he saw his wife alive—forty years ago?

"I know how special of an event this is. I'm sure Esther and Dax—or your parents for that matter — told you that my beloved wife Pauli died the night of the first Black Squirrel Ball," he said soberly.

"They did, and I am very sorry for your loss. I understand that she was a successful woman, and from the pictures I've seen, she was a very beautiful lady as well," I said.

I wanted to tell him that the investigation was reopened. It might make him feel better. I was also thinking that I wanted to solve the mystery in memory of the grief my grandfather carried with him over the years for Mrs. Suarez's death.

"Mr. Suarez, we came here today to ask you to come and support the ball—in Pauli's memory," Esther said. "From what I understand from the stories I've heard from past committee members, she was an integral part of planning the first ball, and we're taking many of the ideas she had—for example, the tent setup and flower arrangements—from the first year's design."

"Mr. Suarez, we would really love if you would come and support the ball," I said.

He took a deep breath, lifted up his head to the blue sky, made a slight grimace, and said "Oh, Dios" with a loud and laborious sigh.

"I've not been back to Peaceland Park since that night. I can only imagine what has changed," he said.

"Many things have, but many things haven't. There still is the Carillon Tower, the Pavilions, the Rose Garden, and the One Acre Lawn," Dax said. "Of course, there's also the Angel of Independence statue, too."

"Oh—I remember the Angel of Independence statue," he said with a little chuckle. "I remember when it was unveiled and people gasped because the angel was topless!"

"It's a replica of the Angel of Independence in the Paseo de la Reforma from Mexico City," he said with his Mexican accent really coming out nicely as he pronounced the location of the original statue.

He took a long and labored inhale of ocean breeze air and said, "How about I think about it?" he asked as he grabbed one of each of Dax's and Esther's hands. "I just don't know about going back. It brings back such painful memories of Pauli's murder."

I really hoped my face didn't do what I think it did because I may have embarrassed myself. However, whether I did or not didn't matter much since Dax said, "Mr. Suarez, you know it was deemed an accident, don't you?"

Maybe the elderly gentleman was showing signs of senility, or maybe he was just speaking his mind.

"You can believe what the police told you, but I believe it was murder, and I won't rest until I find out who did it," he said.

There was an awkward silence that came over the table, and then I noticed a beautiful hummingbird land on the deck railing for a brief rest before darting off quickly. We all were drawn to the sight.

"Pauli loved hummingbirds. Every time I see one, I think of her," he said. His voice was a bit strained—like he started to choke up.

I excused myself from the table and went to the restroom. I couldn't sit there at the table with them any longer knowing that others also thought Mrs. Suarez's death was a murder but not know that the case was reopened.

Quietly, I called Chief Cerrazo. I was a bit surprised that he answered the phone on the first ring. I asked him if I could tell Mr. Suarez what we knew so far.

"Sam, you can tell him that we're looking into the case with a renewed interest," he said. "And is there any way you can get him to come back to Westfield? We could use his help with the investigation."

I returned to the deck, and it seemed that the spirit of the group had improved since I left. I only hoped that the chief's request wasn't going to cause Mr. Suarez to revert to his dismal state.

"When I left for the restroom, I also called Chief Cerrazo," I said.

"Jakey? That kid was all right with me," Mr. Suarez said. "He was the only driver who could drive a stick shift smoothly so you didn't spill your coffee when you were riding with him."

"He is the chief of police now and doing a fine job," said Esther.

I said, "Mr. Suarez, I wasn't going to tell you this just yet, because there's still more information to be researched, but we have found some information that may change the police's conclusions about your wife's death."

There was a silence that floated across all four of us. You couldn't hear anything—not the ocean, not the birds, not even any of the four of us breathing.

And then the silence was broken. "I knew it," he yelled as he jumped from his chair like a jack in the box at the moment the little crank hit the trigger to pop. "I knew her death wasn't an accident. It never made sense to me how she could have accidentally fallen through that railing and into the waterfall."

Dax and Esther looked equally surprised, but a little perplexed by the bomb I had just dropped.

"Mr. Suarez, I can't tell you much more, except that the chief would like to review the recent findings with you and that there's a renewed interest in this investigation," I said. "I realize this is short notice, and not what we were planning, but could you return to Westfield with us?"

"What have you been up to, Sam?" Dax asked.

I turned toward Dax, and I had a feeling that he was disappointed in me. His eyes wouldn't make contact with mine, and yet I could tell he was looking through me. I didn't share the information about the notes or the medical examiner's diary with him or Esther. There wasn't time. I didn't want to put them in danger if there was a murderer and if that person was still in town. I kept thinking of a number of excuses, but it was really that the chief told me not to.

"Dax, I'm sorry I didn't share this with you sooner. The chief instructed me not to share this information with anyone. He didn't want it to leak out, and he didn't want to put anyone in danger."

"I just can't believe that you may have found the reason why Mrs. Suarez died. I'm not disappointed in you, Sam," he said as he raised his chin ever so slightly and then looked straight into my eyes. He was blinking away the beginning of tears. I knew then that he was glad I may have found something to solve this forty-year-old mystery.

Mr. Suarez was in a gleeful stupor. He looked absolutely delighted. "Anything to find out what happened to my sweet Pauli," he said. "Give me a few minutes, and I'll be ready."

He left the table with a spring in his step. And then he stopped and looked toward me. "I don't know where this will lead, but I am sure glad you are involved, Sam. I just feel like we're going to get somewhere with this once and for all."

I felt goose bumps grow on my arms and neck, and my ears went hot again. I felt like I was going to faint. It was almost like a spirit had invaded my body and was trying to get out. I quickly took a big gulp of iced tea and let the cool drink soothe my warm tongue and throat.

He left the room, and I quickly told Esther and Dax a few highlights of the past few days, but added that it would be best for the chief to cover everything with them once we got back to Westfield and met with him the next day. They were both overwhelmed and a bit surprised and confused at what just transpired. They both peppered me with questions, and I tried my best to provide answers, but I stressed that it would be best for Chief Cerrazo to cover everything the following day.

Mr. Suarez returned to us in about ten minutes with two suitcases—big enough for someone to stay for a couple of weeks. He also had a wooden carved cane with a pewter handle. I couldn't see the details too clearly, but it looked like there were birds carved into the cane.

"Esther, I hope I can stay with you. I just threw things into the suitcases and then realized I need a place to lay my head," Mr. Suarez said. Esther told him that he was more than welcome, and she wouldn't have it any other way.

We all left in Dax's car, and I braced myself for another queasy ride in the car.

However, at that point, it wasn't just Dax's driving that was making me feel uneasy. Mr. Suarez had his hopes up that the cause of Mrs. Suarez's death was going to be revealed once and for all.

But what if we were wrong? And we didn't even get a chance to discuss sponsorship of the ball. It may sound horribly selfish of me, but we needed a donation from Mr. Suarez to make this year's ball more successful than any other.

CHAPTER 22

THE RIDE HOME WAS A bit less nauseating than the ride down, but it was also a bit livelier. Mr. Suarez insisted on playing car riding games. After the fourth time of playing the Alphabet name game and me starting with "A—my name is Amy, I come from Alabama, and I sell apples," I faked falling asleep.

I was mentally going over all the information we had found so far—the medical examiner's diaries, Bobby's note, and everyone's concerns that the police's investigation so many years before was rushed.

"Why? Why would they rush it? If Mr. Suarez really wanted Pauli cremated, he could have waited a few days if the police insisted on a more thorough autopsy," I thought.

And if Dax, Dad, or Grandpa thought the death was not accidental, why didn't they say something? Why did everyone just let their concerns go by the wayside?

The next day, I went to the gym in the morning and met up with my mom for a class. She and I stayed afterwards so I could catch her up on the details of the day before.

She was more than concerned after I told her about the note Violet found and that the chief wanted to see Mr. Suarez. "So, Mr. Suarez is in town? What if there's a murderer and the person still lives here. Aren't you in danger, Sam?"

"That's why it's so important that no one knows what is going on," I said. I wanted to ask her to pinky promise that she wouldn't tell anyone.

"I wish you hadn't told me anything. I'm glad that the police are looking into this, but now my stomach is in knots, and I feel like I'm going to throw up," she said. My mother is calm and cool when it comes to party planning, running extensive numbers of errands, and getting a dinner ready for thirty people, but keeping a secret of any type tends to get her a bit conflubagated. Her temperature rises, and her blood pressure increases.

"And to top it all off, I don't know how we're going to reach our $100,000 goal. With all the excitement about Mrs. Suarez's death and Mr. Suarez coming back with us, the idea of his sponsoring the ball never even came up," I said. "With the additional corporate sponsors we have attracted and the projected ticket sales, I think we are only at about of $50,000. That's dismal."

"Sam, you can't be thinking of that at a time like this," she said with a horribly disappointed look on her face. I supposed I should have been ashamed of myself, but whether Mrs. Suarez's death was an accident or a murder didn't change the fact that I needed to raise more money—and fast.

"I know you think I'm being selfish, but I have to think about the goal here. We need to raise much more money in the next couple of weeks, or this event is going to be a disastrous failure, and I'm not going to find another job," I said. I was about to go on that I would have to move away and start a new career, possibly doing PR for a rock radio station, where I had to wear skimpy clothes to get people to sign up for free T-shirts, when I noticed that we were being watched through the exercise class windows. My mom and I were facing each other at an angle and the mirrored walls were to the side of us so I could see our reflections and the outline of an older man peering in.

"Mom, I don't want to startle you more than I have already, but I think we're being watched," I said.

"I think the old hoot likes to check out the younger girls who stand closer to the back of the room and show off their tight butts," she said. "He is there almost every day."

"Mom, if he or anyone else heard this conversation, we could be in trouble. Let's go into the locker room and get out of here. Meet me at my apartment, and I'll fill you in on the rest," I said.

"I can't—I have to be at work early today," she responded. "I think it's best that I know only what I know for now, and that I put it out of my mind for today. You can call me later and fill me in on your meeting with the chief." She whispered all except the last word—which she mouthed in case that man was listening through the glass windows and doors.

We both left the gym a little uneasy about the last few minutes. My mother was not too thrilled to be in possession of more information than she had the other night when she and my father helped me go through the medical examiner's diaries, and I was not too thrilled because it hit me that I could be in the middle of solving a murder. And that murderer might still live in town.

I drove west on Route 20 and hit every red light. I had an eerie feeling that I was being followed, and I noticed a tan-colored Crown Victoria a few cars back that was weaving in and out of lanes advancing toward me. As I turned left onto the last part of Elm Street before I bore right onto Court Street, I quickly changed lanes and made a right onto Washington Street. If I was being followed, I was going to be followed to the police station.

But the Crown Vic continued up toward the hospital and didn't follow me as I turned. I zigzagged through some side streets and got back to the top of the hill at Court Street, where the hospital's emergency room entrance is, and I turned right toward Western Avenue without encountering that car again.

Even though I was a bit shaken, I pulled myself together enough to take a shower and get ready for another meeting with the chief. Doree had called with a few more leads on sponsors which I needed to follow up with, and Frank had left me a message that he had a new vendor who was interested in supporting the ball.

I had a strange feeling that a current vendor and a potential new vendor might be competing for a bid with a contribution to the event, but it wasn't my role to question Frank's motives.

After a couple of hours of phone calls, proposal printing, and running errands, I had another $10,000 of corporate sponsorships locked in and still a few other opportunities pending. We were only at about $60,000 at this point.

It was just a few minutes before 2:00 p.m. when I drove up to the police station. I skipped up the steps to the front door and was greeted by the sergeant on duty. He didn't even say hello—just pointed me toward Chief Cerrazo's office. I guessed he wasn't running for the "Personality of the Year" award.

The hallway walls were becoming much too familiar to me. I was hoping that the chief had Pauli's death solved once and for all, and we could live happily ever after. Between talking to my mom, thinking I was being followed by someone in a tan Crown Victoria, and that darn skunk smell still lingering around me, I was becoming increasingly anxious.

"Good afternoon, Sam. Come right in," the chief said as he stood to greet me and lead me to the conference table in his office.

"I'm beginning to feel like I'm a regular here."

"With the information you dug up on this case, I just might add you to the staff," he said with a slight chuckle.

"That's another potential job I can add to my list, because if I don't get back to raising money for this ball, I won't have anything to show for myself this summer, and I won't be able to get any other type of work," I said with a stone pan delivery.

"I wanted to meet with you first—before Esther, Dax, and Mr. Suarez come in. I think I have come to the same conclusion—with facts—that many had from their gut feelings for years." He stopped with such a dramatic pause I thought I was going to have to jump over a gully in the Grand Canyon to get to his ending.

"Pauli Saurez was definitely murdered," he said, shaking his head as if he didn't want to believe what he knew for years.

He continued to review the facts of the case, as he had from the early investigation: the diaries, the note, and his recollection of the evening.

He told me that there were testimonies from my grandfather, Dax, and others who worked at Peaceland Park who stated that the railing was built to withstand a force of five hundred pounds—about four times the weight of Mrs. Suarez. He also reviewed the medical examiner's diaries.

And then he went through his own notes from the tragic night. He showed me the diary that he had kept. I was so surprised—and yet, not surprised—that this man of such integrity and stature kept a notebook of his thoughts at such a young age.

"I didn't dream of becoming a public servant. I was intending to go to college and study English literature. I wanted to be a great novelist, and my high school composition teacher made us write journals on a regular basis. It's a habit I have to this day, and it pays off because I have a pretty bad memory, but my staff and family don't know because I can reference every day from the last fifty years!"

His tone shifted gears from lighthearted and conversational to very methodical. "Sam, I wanted to review this with you because I am absolutely stumped on who could have done this to Mrs. Suarez, and anyone could be a suspect. Anyone," he said, emphasizing each syllable in the last word spoken.

"I'll meet with Mr. Suarez, Dax, and Esther together, and then I'll meet with each individually, and we have started a list of 'people of interest.' Even though it is a bit unorthodox to work with nonlaw-enforcement personnel, I'm sharing this with you because you have become a great source of information, and I am a bit worried that if the murderer is still alive and still in town, you could be in danger."

Suddenly, I started to get a dry mouth and hot ears, and I thought I was going to faint. This was a feeling that was becoming too familiar to me. How could a simple fund-raising assignment result in me being scared for my life? This all seemed so intriguing—until the chief said that.

Just when my mouth started to get a little moisture into it, Dax, Esther, and Mr. Suarez came into the chief's office. They all looked especially chipper considering the topic they were about to review.

Once they sat down, the chief reviewed all the information that had been reviewed with me previously.

"Do you think we can still solve the murder? Do you think we can determine who killed my beloved Pauli?" Mr. Suarez pleaded.

"I just don't know, Mr. Suarez. It has been forty years since the incident, and much of the evidence has been destroyed," Chief Cerrazo said. He was becoming more and more solemn as the afternoon went on. It took him about an hour to review all the information and answer the threesome's questions. He looked drained, and yet Mr. Suarez looked especially perky.

"Mr. Suarez, I can only imagine that this is a very difficult situation for you to relive. Would you like to take a break before we start the next session?" the chief asked. He didn't want to come right out and state that Mr. Suarez and everyone else alive in 1969 was a suspect—or a "person of interest," in today's politically correct terminology.

"I haven't been this optimistic in years. I realize that nothing is going to bring my dear love back to me, but finding out how and possibly who caused her death will bring me peace that I have been longing for since that horrible night," Mr. Suarez said. He was distinctive in his voice, being very precise and assertive with each word. He folded his hands over one another and sat quite upright in his chair. I noticed at that time that he was much more alert and confident today than he was when he answered the door at his home barely twenty-four hours earlier. It was as if learning that he was right and that his wife didn't die as a result of an accident had lifted a heavy burden off his shoulders and allowed him to be more self-assured and less weary.

I wished my grandfather could have been there. Just knowing that he was right and Pauli's death was not an accident may have lifted his spirits, too.

The chief thanked me for my time and walked me out to the reception area for the others to see. He said he would call me if he learned anything new from his discussions with Mr. Suarez, Dax, or Esther, and that I should remain focused on raising money for the ball—not be consumed with solving this murder any longer.

I wanted to ask to sit in on the additional questioning, even if it was through the double-sided mirror. I wanted to know every detail. I couldn't just go back to my apartment knowing that Mr. Suarez and Dax were going to relive that horrible night again.

But I went home and left the investigating to the professionals.

CHAPTER 23

As I entered the apartment, Mr. Z was leaving. It was about 4:00 p.m., and he was dressed in a dapper polyester light blue suit with a vintage 1976 plaid shirt and white penny loafers.

"Hey there, good lookin'," he said with exuberance. "Why do you look so glum? Is this Black Squirrel thing getting you tuckered out?"

I told him that I just had a busy day, and that I was looking forward to a cold drink on the back patio.

"Well, you may be interested in sitting on the porch instead, because that pesky skunk keeps coming around," he said. "I've done a full inspection of your dryer vent and any other potential crevice or gap in this house, and we're air tight. There's no way he is getting in again."

I wasn't even that startled or put off that the skunk was still ruining my plans. I figured that I would resort to Plan B and put a movie on and sit in my favorite chair with my blanket and sulk. I just was in no mood to encounter that stinky critter again.

"I'm off to the potluck dinner at church. Those ladies from the retirement home down the street love my three-bean salad," he said as he raised a Pyrex glass bowl full of confetti colored beans and marinade. "My secret is the anchovies, but don't tell anyone. I hope to get a date for the ball out of this recipe for sure!"

He was such a chipper man. Even though he lived a somewhat lonely life without his wife for so many years, he always seemed to find joy in whatever he was doing at that moment.

I entered my apartment and heard the phone ringing. I couldn't find it, and I heard the answering machine go on. It was my father.

"Hey. I heard you were down at police headquarters today. Hope you aren't in any more animal cruelty trouble. Call me."

131

I didn't want to call him since I couldn't say anything. It's pretty hard not to tell anyone who doesn't know about the investigation, but since he and my mom had helped find some of the key clues, I didn't think I would be able to lie with conviction. I put off calling him back for a few hours—maybe the chief would call me with what he found out, I thought.

I got changed into some lounge pants and a T-shirt that was not of the most ladylike taste. It was from a crab house in North Carolina, and it had a crustacean on the back with the caption "I Pinch."

With a frozen dinner of mac and cheese and a cold glass of Coke, I nestled in for a good On Demand movie when the phone rang again. It was Mr. Z.

"I forgot to tell you that a package came for you today. It was hand delivered, and I had to sign for it. I think it's valuable. Go ahead and go through your door to my house—it's on my kitchen table. Sorry I got so caught up in my three-bean salad that I forgot to tell you." He went on to tell me that he was using one of those new-fangled cellular phones that he borrowed from Mrs. Swochak, who had received the phone from her daughter to use in emergencies. They agreed that a valuable delivery was an emergency.

I thanked him and then wrestled with the idea of leaving it for tomorrow. It was almost 6:00 p.m. by then, and there wasn't a word from the chief. Considering the circumstances, I didn't think no news was good news. I thought no news was bad. But what would be bad in this case—that someone I knew would be capable of murdering a lovely woman most people thought very highly of—or that this would be an unsolved mystery forever?

I just kept thinking of the pain and sorrow my grandfather had experienced, based on the stories Dax, the chief, and my mother told me. It always troubled me when a loved one was hurt, but this was years later, and I wondered if solving the murder now really would help Grandpa.

But since Mr. Z went to the trouble of calling me, I decided to go see what was so important. I trudged upstairs to the door that led from the end of my hallway into his house. Neither of us locked this door, as we agreed it would be best to use as an additional escape route in case of fire. As I opened the door from my subdued, bland-colored rental walls, I entered his sportsman-themed abode. Mr. Z was quite the hunter and fisherman in his day, and he had all the critters on wooden plaques to prove it.

In the hallway, I passed a deer, a moose, an elk, a swordfish, a 'possum, and a few squirrels—but not one was black. I felt that they were all looking at me with their glass brown eyes. It was almost like they were all related, since their eyes were so similar.

I went down his stairs to a more formal living room that looked like it had a woman's touch of decorating with floral drapes and a mauve couch, and then through the dining room that had a beautiful oak dining room set and buffet. In the corner, there was a mirrored-back china cabinet with lovely china and crystal.

The kitchen was through a pocket door, and it wasn't in the tidiest shape. From the look of the countertop and floor, Mr. Z must have had some trouble assembling his three-bean salad. I decided to be a good neighbor and clean it up a bit. The stickiness of the marinade would only bring out little black ants, and then the house would be infested. It seemed like I was being a good neighbor, but I was also selfish, as I only wanted to have the past encounter with the skunk for this week's critter activities.

After I spent a few minutes scrubbing the floor and counter, I noticed the package on the table. It was addressed to: Ms. Samantha Jane Cummings, Black Squirrel Ball Director with a typewritten label.

I opened the padded envelope, which was about nine inches by eleven inches, to find a black velvet box. It was jewelry.

Suddenly, I realized that Jonathan must have done something to try to make up for his insensitivity and stupidity. I'm not much of a jewelry girl, but it was a nice try to get on my good side.

Or maybe it was from Gareth. He arranged for rims to be installed on my car and sent me a case of tomato juice, so this could be a way for him to really make a statement. If the package was from him, I wouldn't even call Jonathan to break up—I'd let him figure it out on his own and call Gareth right away.

There was a typewritten note on plain white 8½ x 11 paper. It said:
The belle of the first ball wore a beautiful necklace in 1968.
You should wear one equally as beautiful.
If you live that long.

I opened the box to find a ruby and diamond necklace similar to what Mrs. Suarez wore on the night she died.

I was so freaked out; I didn't get a dry mouth or hot ears, but I started shaking. I darted around the kitchen into the den to find a phone.

I trembled and dialed—literally, since Mr. Z still had a rotary dial phone—911.

"911 emergencies. This line is recorded. What is your emergency?"

"Please connect me with Chief Cerazzo immediately."

"Ma'am, I need to know the emergency and your name. I can't just let anyone be connected to the police chief."

I was quickly irritated, and I realized I didn't want to be announced on the police scanner as receiving this package.

"My name is Samantha Cummings, and the police chief suggested I call him personally if I had any skunk trouble." I hoped the dispatcher wouldn't laugh me off the phone, but at least she would know that I was who I said I was.

"Ms. Cummings, I'll be glad to contact the Animal Control for you, since your little friend has revisited you, but I can't connect you to the chief for such a matter."

I was becoming more than irate. I couldn't exactly tell the dispatcher that I had new information on the murder investigation without it getting broadcast all over town. If she announced my skunk issue, I would only be laughed at—not possibly be in danger.

"I was in his office earlier today, and he told me that if I had any skunk problems again to call him personally. I wouldn't normally call him, except he told me to. Please give him this message to call me at home immediately," I pleaded.

And then I hung up. The worst thing that could happen was that I got charged for harassment or a prank, but then when the chief found out why I did it, he'd drop the charges.

I quickly grabbed the necklace and ran upstairs, past all the creepy stuffed animals, and into my apartment to wait for his call.

All I wanted to do was raise enough money to meet our large goal for the Black Squirrel Ball and move on to another, more permanent, job, and instead I got involved with a murder mystery and received a death threat.

The phone rang within minutes, and I didn't let it finish the first ring before I answered, "Chief? Is that you?"

"Sam, what are you talking about? Chief who? What indian are you talking to?"

It was Uncle Paul. He usually called me when the Red Sox were winning—especially when they were playing the Yankees, like they were tonight.

"Uncle Paul, I'm expecting a call from the police chief. I have to go." And I hung up. I had probably already said too much. I should have stayed on the phone with Uncle Paul and not alarmed him while I waited for the call from Chief Cerrazo.

The phone rang again. "Chief—thank God you called so quickly."

"Chief who?" It was Gareth.

"Hi, Gareth. I thought your number was the same as this guy I went to college with—we called him Chief." I had to lie. I couldn't let someone else know that I was waiting for the chief.

And then I heard a click on the other line. "Gareth—I'll have to call you back. Sorry." And I hung up on him. I didn't even find out why he called.

"Hello?" I answered. I wasn't going to make the same silly mistake three times in a row.

"Sam, this is Chief Cerrazo. What's going on? Why are you calling me about your silly skunk?"

"I'm sorry to seem like I'm playing a trick on you, Chief, but I received a package today, and I just opened it. I think you should come look at it."

"I'm not opening any package of skunk poop. I have to get through these notes from my sessions this afternoon with Mr. Suarez and Dax. I learned quite a bit."

"The package contains a necklace just like the one Mrs. Suarez wore forty years ago—ruby and diamonds—with a note that looks like a death threat."

"A what?" he asked.

"The note says I should wear the necklace enclosed to the ball," and then I paused before saying, "if I live that long."

"I'll be right there," he said, and then there was a dial tone.

The phone rang again. It was like Grand Central Station with so many phone calls.

"Sam, I heard on the scanner that the skunk is back." It was my dad. He was one of the many loyal police scanner listeners in Westfield who would be laughing about me now, rather than worried I was in danger.

"I'm fine. I probably shouldn't tell you this, but just in case something happens," I started.

And then he interrupted me. "Are you OK? What's going on? I'm coming right up there."

"Dad, I'm fine. I just received a package this afternoon that was a bit odd so I called the police chief, but I didn't know how else to get his attention without raising the attention of scanner groupies as well."

"I'm on my way." And then I heard another dial tone.

In less than ten minutes, both the chief and my dad were in my kitchen looking at the necklace and note.

"I don't like the looks of this. It is definitely a death threat. I'm going to put a watch on your house tonight, and then I need you to come to the station tomorrow morning and we'll come up with a list of everyone who knows you are the ball's director," the chief said.

"I think a police car in my driveway will draw some attention, don't you?" I asked.

"Can't you have the guy across the street pull some overtime?" my dad asked. I forgot that the man across the street from our driveway is a lieutenant, and he just switched from working nights to days.

"I think that's a good idea. I'll have a couple of the day guys stop by and give him a hand throughout the night," the chief said.

"And I don't know how we can narrow down who knows I'm coordinating the ball. I've been to all the area Chamber of Commerce breakfasts, the Rotary lunches, and the Westfield Women's Club meeting last week. Plus it was announced in a press release, and my name is on Peaceland Park's Web site. Everyone knows," I said with my head in my hands. This was turning from the best career move to the worst life event in just a few weeks.

The chief went on to tell both my dad and me what he learned in the afternoon. It seems that Pauli was not well liked by many in the company, as Violet had said.

Mr. Suarez told the chief that there were some saleswomen who were quite jealous of Mrs. Suarez's success, and that she had received many threatening notes telling her to stop working so hard and to leave town or else she would be harmed.

Dax also told the chief how some of the young women were not very nice behind Mrs. Suarez's back—saying nasty things about her ethnic background and that she was successful because she was a floozy.

He then stepped away from the kitchen and excused himself to the living room for a few minutes to make some calls.

"Are you going to be OK? You look white as a ghost—like someone erased all your freckles from your cheeks," my dad said. He wasn't the best at saying the right thing at the right time, but I knew he meant well.

I took a deep breath through my nose and let it out through my mouth. "I'm going to be OK. I just wish this case was solved so I could focus on the ball. I'm starting to get nervous that I made a wrong decision to take this job."

"Don't worry. This will work out, and the ball will go off without a hitch. How much are you up to so far?" I didn't want to tell my dad that we were off our goal. He liked the idea of the ball, but not the fund-raising. He thought the fund-raising part of the event—especially at these levels—took away from the spirit of the original ball, which was to raise just enough to cover the costs and a few little improvements every year.

"We're more than half way there, but I need a couple of big sponsors to get us over the hump. I had hoped Mr. Suarez would be our biggest donor, but after the past couple of days, I don't think his mind is on check writing—especially for Peaceland Park."

Just then, the chief reentered the room and picked up the box with the necklace to take with him.

"You're all set. The guys happened to have a poker game scheduled for tonight, so they moved the location, and they will be watching you from across the street. Come over here—you can see the lieutenant from his upstairs window," he said as he pointed to a second-floor window across the street.

"But if they're going to play poker, how are they going to watch me?" I asked with a pathetically selfish tone.

"They just got another player added, and they will all take turns," he said with a sheepish grin. "Now, if you'll excuse me, I have to run to the grocery store and pick up some chips and clam dip. Call me on my cell phone if anything comes up. I'll also tell the dispatcher to connect you to my private line if you call in to 911 without it going on the scanner."

He wrote his cell phone number on a page from his pocket notebook and handed it to me.

My dad asked if I wanted him to stay over, but I thought that may raise more suspicions. I didn't want whoever gave me the lovely necklace to think I was frightened. I needed to play it cool.

I walked both the chief and my dad to their cars and tried to be nonchalant about looking across the street. I could see a faint outline of a tall man in the second-story window. I kind of wished I was asked to play poker—at least I would be *with* the police officers instead of being their entertainment for the evening.

CHAPTER 24

ANOTHER SUNNY DAY. ANOTHER ADVENTURE at the gym. With working from home, I was noticing that I was snacking more and drinking more Coke. I thought that this work arrangement would get me to eat healthier, but instead I was eating like a bird—skipping the schedule of three meals a day, but snacking continuously.

After the gym, I went home a different route than usual. Instead of going all the way down East Main Street, I took a left onto Noble Avenue and then a right onto East Silver Street. I sometimes like to drive by the Slovak Hall to see if any of my relatives' cars or trucks are there. At this time of the morning, the parking lot was empty.

When I left for the gym, there were two extra cars in the driveway of my new approved protector across the street, and upon my return there were two new and different cars. I'm not sure if anyone followed me to the gym, but if so they did a good job because I lost the paranoia I had yesterday with that Crown Vic.

The committee meeting was at 9:00 a.m. and I was a bit nervous about discussing the fund-raising goal. Plus, how was I going to admit that we didn't ask Mr. Suarez for anything, and he was in town?

I called Esther to tell her I'd pick her up so we could get our stories straight. When I called, she suggested she pick me up so I didn't have to double back a few blocks to get her and then go in the opposite direction to Peaceland Park.

She picked me up at 8:45 a.m., and she looked especially pretty. Her hair was just done, and she even had a bright new shade of pink lipstick. She said she was doing a trial run with her "stylist" Ramon for the ball. I had heard of brides doing trial runs for up-dos, but I have never heard of a ball-goer going through such troubles.

"I'm a little too plain normally, so I have to get myself into the mode of dressing up, getting my hair done, and being a painted lady for such events," Esther said.

"Let's tell everyone that Mr. Suarez is considering how large of a gift to give—not say that we didn't ask yet," she continued.

"Because that is lying. We don't know if he is considering anything," I said. I was a bit surprised by Esther's willingness to stretch the truth.

"I just don't want to raise Frank's eyebrows," she said as she was rolling her eyes. She was driving just fine, but when she spoke to me, she would turn her head entirely in my direction and take her eyes off the road.

"But are we going to tell Frank and the others that Mr. Suarez is in town?" I asked. I was almost whining, but I just didn't want to deal with Frank. He could be such a pain in the ass, and I wasn't in the mood. I was thinking more and more about who could have maliciously hurt Mrs. Suarez, how Mr. Suarez was so pleased that his wife's death was finally being deemed as suspicious, and who sent me a death threat.

As I was thinking more about Mr. Suarez, I realized that Esther took the left turn into the parking lot from Western Avenue pretty tight—so much so that she was entering the exit. We almost took out the security guard in his energy-efficient golf cart.

"Oh, dear Jesus, where did that guy come from?" she said in such a surprised tone.

"He was on the right side of the road. Where were you going?" I asked as I grabbed for my seat belt and braced myself for another sudden jerk of the car. We didn't have to solve Pauli's death if we were goners ourselves.

She just shook her head and kept heading toward the area of the parking lot where we needed to go—near the walking paths to the rose gardens.

I slowly got out of the car and grabbed my red leather shoulder bag. It was a gift from some former co-workers at the social service agency at my first job, and every time I really took a minute to look at it, I thought of how great it was to work with a good, supportive team.

And then I snapped back to reality when Esther slammed her door shut. I would have to come up with a reason to walk home so I could avoid getting back in the car with Esther. One near-death experience per day was enough.

"OK, let's get this over with," she said as we started walking toward the pavilion where the meeting room was. We quietly walked down the flagstone paths that were first laid in the 1940s. It wasn't yet 9:00 a.m., but it was almost eighty-five degrees and so humid I was already sweating. We walked past the flower beds filled with tall red callas and low spreading alyssum, and then the rose beds. When we got to the fountain with its stone base and twenty-foot plume in the center, I thought of the story that Aunt Reggie told me and chuckled.

"Aunt Reggie told me that she got into her swimsuit and jumped in when she was little. She thought this was her personal swimming pool."

"Can you imagine her splashing around until your grandfather pulled her out and sent her home?" Esther said with her arms flailing in the air.

We both started to laugh, and we lost any tension about the harrowing ride over. It was nice to get back to a happy moment.

We continued walking down the path and then entered the gateway to the pavilion area where the tall pines and rhododendron bushes were lush and dark green. The bushes had already blossomed about a month earlier, but the green waxy leaves contrasting against the wispy pine needles welcomed us into the cool shade. As we walked a little further, a slight breeze came through.

"Now I know why Mr. Smith chose to have the summer sales picnics here—it's much nicer near the pavilion than out in the sun. It must be about five degrees cooler over here compared to the parking lot," I said.

"It's cooler in this area, and it certainly is nicer than the basement of the old headquarters in downtown Westfield. He thought that the sales teams would be inspired by nature. He said it gave them a nice balance from their everyday rat race of selling," Esther said.

We entered the meeting room, and Frank was already there. As I took one step into the door, I could sense the tension already.

"It's about time you got here. I was just about to leave," he said in such a tone that I thought he had vinegar in his coffee mug.

"It isn't even nine o'clock yet, why are you so antsy?" Esther asked.

"I have a job to get to, you know. It isn't like I live the life of retirement luxury or flexible work hours," he said as he shot jealous daggers from his eyes to both Esther and me.

Doree and Aunt Reggie entered just as he finished his mini-rant.

"How are you today, Frank?" Doree asked.

"Just rosy, Doree, I'm just rosy," he grumbled.

We went over the latest standings of the sponsorships first. I figured it was best to just cut to the chase—we weren't at our goal, and we still had a good deal of work to do, but it wasn't insurmountable based on our prospects.

Frank had his half glasses on at the end of his nose, looked up to Esther and me, and asked, "What about Mr. Suarez?"

"That's a good question, Frank. Mr. Suarez is considering how to best support Peaceland Park," Esther said. "He even came back with us so that he could spend some time with us. I trust that he will make a good decision." She just cut to the chase, too, and took him head on.

We reviewed the flower arrangements, the police support, the schedule for setup and takedown, and the final details for the menu in about thirty minutes. It was like everyone, not just Frank, wanted to get through the agenda and get somewhere else. I wanted to get back home and wait for a call from the chief. Doree had a hair appointment; Frank needed to get back to work, and I'm not sure where Aunt Reggie was going, but when we got to the last item on the agenda, she was the first to say good-bye.

I told Esther that I needed to take some measurements of the stage near the One Acre Lawn so I would just walk home. She walked out toward the parking lot with Doree, and I walked in the other direction.

In recent years, the ball was held in the Pavilion, but the committee thought we should "switch it up" and have it under a tent on the One Acre Lawn. The stage wasn't in the best condition, but a fresh coat of paint would make it look respectable.

I stepped onto the stage and turned around, realizing that I was the only one around. For a few seconds I just took in the sights and sounds.

"What a beautiful spot," I thought. The blue sky had a few thin, wispy clouds, the birds were chirping, and three black squirrels were chasing each other near the tree line.

Then my phone rang.

It was Jonathan. I hadn't talked to him since I hung up on him the other night, even though he had been calling and leaving pathetic voice mails.

I inhaled deeply, hit the green button on my cell phone, and said, "Hello."

"Hey there. I'm so glad you picked up. Sam, I'm sorry I screwed up the dates—but I have it straight now, and I wouldn't be anywhere except by your side at the ball." He sounded a bit whiny.

"Jonathan, you have a decision to make. You can either go to Miami and take the job you want or figure out a way we can have a relationship. You can't have both. You won't be happy, and I deserve better than a boyfriend that doesn't want to be with me. I love you and wish you the best, and now it's up to you."

I was pretty blunt, but my mouth got going, and it didn't stop.

"Wow—well I don't know what to say, but how about you come down to New York this weekend and we talk about it more? I do miss you, and I'd love to show you around the city."

He did sound like he was trying, but New York City in the middle of the summer was not my idea of fun. Hot, sticky, and that summer city smell of gas fumes and stinky garbage gets me nauseous.

"Jonathan, I do appreciate that you are trying to fix things between us, but I can't leave town now. I can't explain the details now, but more is going on than just the ball."

"What do you mean? Are you OK? Are your parents all right?" Jeepers. He was sounding like Mr. Z when the skunk was in my house—all questions and no time for answers.

I looked around to see if anyone was around to hear me. I knew that the chief told us not to tell anyone, but I felt Jonathan could be trusted.

"If I tell you something, will you promise not to tell anyone? Swear on your grandmother's grave?" Jonathan was a grandmomma's boy rather than a momma's boy, so I thought that tack would work better.

"Of course. Sam, you are worrying me. What is going on?"

"You can't tell a soul, but we think that Mrs. Suarez—the woman who died the night of the first Black Squirrel Ball—died as the result of foul play, not an accident."

"You mean she was murdered?" He gasped so loudly I think the squirrels and birds around me stopped to listen.

"Yes, but I can't get into all the details, because Chief Cerazzo is going through files and some information that we recently found."

"Who's we?" I wasn't sure if he sounded worried or jealous.

"My mom and dad found some old notes from the medical examiner. Violet found a note that led us to look into who was with Mrs. Suarez last, and we have learned that Pauli wasn't well liked by everyone she worked with." I stopped quickly when I heard something move behind my right shoulder.

"Sam—what's wrong?" Jonathan asked.

"Nothing. I thought someone was listening to me, but I must be just imagining it," I said. "Anyway, um, I really can't say anything more, but I hope the chief will have more information by this weekend. I just don't think I should leave town, because Mr. Suarez came back from the Connecticut shore with Esther and Dax and me yesterday. He has been briefed by the chief; plus, we need to still ask him for a sponsorship."

"Then I'm coming home."

He quickly went online while we were still on the phone and scheduled a train ticket to come home that night. "I don't want to wait to see you. We really need to talk, and I have a funny feeling about you and this murder mystery you have fallen into."

He told me that he loved me, and that he would see me later that night.

After I hung up, I continued on my measuring project and then started to walk home. I was excited to see Jonathan, and maybe this would be the night that things would become clear for him. I hoped he chose to stay in western Massachusetts with me. Why would he want to move to Miami? It's hot and sticky there almost the entire year. Ick. That's ten times worse than New York City in the summer.

As I walked toward home on Peaceland Park's pathways, I still had a feeling that I was being watched, so much so that I was going to call the security guard and ask him to bring me home in his golf cart, but then I thought I was just being paranoid. Plus, if someone was watching me, it was probably just one of Chief Cerrazo's guys making sure I got home safely.

With the temperature close to ninety degrees and way beyond humid by the time I entered the apartment, I was perspiring in places of my body where I didn't think I had sweat glands. When I was twelve years old, I used to pick blueberries for a woman who would say, "It's hotter than Hades." This was such a day. Why would Jonathan want to move to Miami when he could get a healthy dose of hot humidity here?

I was planning on spending the day scanning pictures, so I hopped upstairs to take a quick shower, and I cranked the air conditioning—I figured it would be cooled down by the time I de-sweated.

I looked out the front window and noticed two new cars across the street. I felt a combination of creepiness and also relaxed contentment knowing that I was being protected by Westfield's finest—or at least whoever showed up late for roll call this morning and was assigned to play babysitter instead of directing traffic through the latest bridge construction project. It seemed like the City of Westfield had one bridge undertaking or another for the last ten years, causing traffic chaos either on the north, south, or east sides of town.

After a nice cool shower and a day of scanning and categorizing photos, I checked the clock and realized Jonathan's train was just about to arrive in Springfield. He said he would meet me at my apartment rather than have me pick him up. I was sort of glad he was getting his own ride—especially since I lost track of time and would have left him waiting at the Springfield train station.

I was looking through my shoulder bag for my notes from today's meeting when I realized my notepad wasn't in there. I left it at the One Acre Lawn, and it had a list of names and phone numbers of prospects—not something I would want anyone to pick up.

It was still pretty hot out, at about 8:00 p.m., but at least there was a slight breeze and the sun was setting. It was a nice night for a walk or to sit outside and enjoy the fresh air. The sky wasn't dark yet, and the gate to the park was still open. I figured I could run over to the One Acre Lawn and be back in about twenty minutes—plenty of time before Jonathan would arrive from Springfield.

I looked across the street to the watching house and tried to make a signal with my head that I was going, but nothing happened. This whole being watched thing was overrated. I was going to be in a public park—what could happen to me?

But just in case something did happen, I wasn't going down easily.

I grabbed my SureFire flashlight, my pocket knife and a small can of hairspray—a ladies' version of defense spray—and threw it all in a small shoulder bag. I didn't want to look like a pushover, but I also didn't want to take out the butcher knife.

While I was in college in Florida, I took a self-defense class, and I remember the instructor telling us that we should walk tough and with purpose. She told us not to dawdle or look like you are on a "walk in the park"—even if you are on a walk in the park.

I took big steps and made sure I made a good amount of noise with my sneakers against the road. I would usually walk through the paths in the woods, but I wanted to stay out in the open. Out of the corner of my eye, I saw something move and jumped. Then I realized I had startled the teenage couple making out under the trees.

I took a left on the road, walking toward the Rose Garden through the large parking lot. I bet it was much nicer back in the day when it was all a big field and grandpa took visitors on horse and buggy rides. With more and more visitors coming to the park, the field was changed into an asphalt parking lot over time.

The Rose Garden fountain stopped just as I walked by, causing me to jump. I was definitely a little anxious, and the sudden lack of noise was just as startling to me as an air horn going off.

As soon as I turned the corner by the edge of the Rose Garden, closer to the west edge of the One Acre Lawn, I stopped. This is just where Mrs. Suarez took her last breath. I took a few steps toward the flagstone path and leaned over the railing to look down the waterfall.

Suddenly, I had a vision of Mrs. Suarez lying in the waterfall. It was almost surreal—like I was actually in the twilight zone of the night of the ball forty years ago. I could see her beautiful hair fanned out over her shoulders and her red dress drenched in water.

Looking through all the old pictures, reading the medical examiner's diaries, talking with Chief Cerrazo, and the jewelry delivery really got to me. The thought of something so evil and violent happening in this beautiful setting seemed sacrilegious to me.

Then I heard the Carillon Tower clock chime—it was 8:15, and Jonathan would be arriving any minute. I needed to get my notepad and get back to the safety of my apartment.

I looked over my right shoulder and saw the white notepad on the stage. I jogged over, scooped it up, and then ran back home.

As I hopped over the knee-high wall between Peaceland Park and Mr. Z's house, Jonathan drove into the driveway, and the chief was sitting on my steps.

"How nice to see you both," I said between gasps of catching my breath. All this going to the gym really wasn't helping build my capacity for air since I rarely got on the treadmill. I was more of a stretching and light-weights girl.

"What are you doing?" the chief asked.

He looked pissed off. "I tried calling both your home and cell phone and there was no answer, so I had your peeping Tom across the street come over to check on you, and he had to get Mr. Zilenski to let him in to determine if you were hit over the head and lying unconscious."

"Sam, what is going on? Why is the chief of police hanging out on your steps?" asked Jonathan. He looked a little jealous. Or maybe just totally freaked out—I couldn't really tell the difference.

"Why don't you both go out to the backyard, and we can have some lemonade," I said very calmly as I leaned over to give Jonathan a kiss on the cheek.

"It's nice to see you," I said. And I gave him a pat on the butt—I thought that may help make light of the fact the chief of police was there.

I walked into the kitchen, tossed my notepad on the floor near my bag. Then, I took a few clean glasses out of the dishwasher and lemonade out of the refrigerator and returned to the table and chairs where Mr. Z liked to read his morning paper.

The chief had lit the citronella candle on the table, and the backyard was also dimly lit from the surrounding house lights.

I started by explaining to Jonathan that the chief had an officer watching me for a few days since I received the necklace.

"You received a mystery piece of jewelry, and you have to be under police surveillance? That must have been some necklace!" Jonathan said.

"It wasn't just any piece of jewelry. It was a replica of what Mrs. Suarez wore the night she was murdered," the chief said. "Sam, I think you are in real danger. No more walks in the park—or going anywhere—without an officer tagging along."

He continued by telling us how he reviewed the medical examiner's diaries and the notes from Mr. Suarez's interview and compared that to the files from 1969.

"Sam, I hope Jonathan is planning to stay with you tonight because if he isn't, I'm going to have the officer move from across the street to your couch," he said. "Mrs. Suarez was murdered. It was no accident. So many people thought it was a murder, but no one was able to provide the proof or evidence in such a short amount of time, and the case was closed."

"Jonathan, I'm sorry to tell you this, but your grandfather did a crummy job of solving this incident. It was long before the ability to test DNA and other forensic science advances, but once you look at the files, the crime scene photos, and read through Dr. Roberts's diaries, there's no doubt in my mind that Mrs. Suarez was murdered."

"How do you think it happened?" Jonathan asked.

"I think Mrs. Suarez was strangled and then pushed over the railing. And then I think after her body got to the other side of the railing, the murderer placed her in a position to make it look like she drowned," the chief said. "Here are some pictures of the crime scene. "

He had pulled out a file folder of black and white shots that included very close-up gruesome photos of Mrs. Suarez lying in the top of the waterfall. He took out a pocket flashlight so we could see it better in the summer twilight.

"Where did you get these from? I asked the chief. "They aren't the ones from Dr. Roberts's files."

"These are from Jonathan's grandfather's private files. After I joined the force, I had asked him about this case. I never felt right about it even years later when I finally graduated from the police academy, and he said I could have his files when he retired."

"But that never happened. He died two and a half months before he could file for retirement," Jonathan said. His grandfather was not the nicest man, and although alcohol was his best friend, it didn't bring out the best in him. "So how did you get the files?"

"I went to your grandmother and offered to help her go through his files. She didn't want to go through all this stuff. He had cabinets and cabinets of files. So many that she didn't know where to start. She was going to shred everything, and I suggested I take care of it for her."

"We soon realized that he had all those cabinets because he kept original photos and evidence of many crimes over the years," the chief said.

"Why would he keep all that information at his house?" Jonathan said.

"It wasn't for disaster recovery purposes," the chief said, trying to make light of the moment. "It was so he could have his own stash of information on people. Ya know," and he paused while nodding his head a bit, "to put the squeeze on."

Jonathan suddenly turned white as a ghost. "Are you telling me that my grandfather blackmailed people?"

"Jonathan, I am sorry that you had to find out this way, but didn't you think it was a bit odd that your grandfather was a lifelong civil servant, your grandmother never worked, and yet they always had a new Cadillac, a minimansion up the street here overlooking the Westfield River, and also the lake house in Otis? How do you think he had all that money on a policeman's salary? He had a lot of dirt on many people in town, and we found a few disturbing things about this case, in particular. I really can't get into details just yet, but we need to find out who killed Mrs. Suarez, and we need to find out soon."

"I never would have thought he was an extortionist. I thought he was just very good at saving and buying things when the markets were down," Jonathan said. He was about to start sobbing when I noticed something in the pictures.

"Chief, there's no way Mrs. Suarez could have fallen through this railing toward the waterfall. Look at the way the wood is splintered in this picture," I said.

We all looked very carefully at the black and white photos. Even though the photos were very old, we could tell that the railing was stained a dark color—probably the similar brown color that's still there today. The contrast between the outside and the inside of the wood was so distinct that you could tell the railing was pushed from the waterfall side and then splintered away from Mrs. Suarez's body.

"You are right, Sam, there's no way that Mrs. Suarez could have fallen against the railing and then into the waterfall," Jonathan said. He was getting color back in his face as we switched gears back to the case rather than his corrupt grandfather.

"We have all the evidence that this was not an accident, but we don't have much evidence as to who was the murderer," the chief said. He went on to explain that there wasn't anything that he could find in the police files or the medical examiner's files that pointed to any specific suspects.

"Sam, you said that you found out Mrs. Suarez wasn't well liked by some. Who told you that?" Jonathan asked.

I told them how Violet mentioned that when she worked in the kitchen she would sometimes hear visiting salespeople say nasty things about Mrs. Suarez. "But she also said they were just catty women and were quite proper even with their spiteful spurts."

"But what about the note from Violet's husband? Who was supposed to drive her home the night of the Black Squirrel Ball? First it seemed like it was Violet's husband, Bob, but then you said that it was Pat O'Connor. Do you think it was him?" I asked the chief.

"There's absolutely no way it was Pat. He was about 120 pounds soakin' wet when he was that age, and he was as meek as a mouse," the chief said. "But he must know who drove Mrs. Suarez home—or who was supposed to drive her home. I have to get to that nursing home tomorrow and talk to him and find out what happened."

"Chief, do you think we're looking at this from the wrong angle?" I asked.

"What do you mean, Sam," he replied.

"Do you think someone may have killed Mrs. Suarez to hurt Mr. Suarez? Someone who had a vengeance against him? He is still sick over the death of his wife forty years later. Do you think that's because he thinks he is responsible?" I asked.

"Do you think he killed her?" Jonathan asked.

The chief and I both responded with a resounding no. And then we looked at each other with a little surprise that we were in sync.

"I don't think he killed her, but maybe someone killed her to get at him or get back at him. He was a successful man in town, and maybe he wasn't as well liked as we think he was," I said.

The chief said that he didn't remember too much about Mr. Suarez, except that he was a bit mysterious. Mr. Suarez was a chemist who created some of the top-selling cleaning products for Formula 333. His educational training in Mexico focused on using herbs and flowers for cleaning components and fragrances

"He was quite secretive on his research. Very few people worked with him and knew exactly what he did. He kept a very loyal but small crew around him in the labs. Yet, his wife was very outgoing about her sales work." The chief described their different personalities as polar opposites.

"I still remember watching them dance the night of the Black Squirrel Ball. The band played a tango and they lit up the dance floor. It was like they were performing for everyone. They were quite the couple." He was telling the story as he stared into space—like he was seeing an old movie being shown against the back of the house.

"Sam, since you are so involved in this, I'm going to need your help," he said as he came back to the present. He asked me to set up a visit with Mr. Suarez tomorrow, but not to let on to any details. "Just ask to sit with him to talk. Try to get him to visit you without Dax and Esther. I want him to just talk to you, but you'll have officers near you. I think he'll share more information with you since he has taken such a shine to you. I have a feeling he still thinks of me as the same department that botched the investigation forty years ago."

"I'm not comfortable with this at all," Jonathan said. He once again seemed to have a bit of jealousy showing. For a fairly boring accountant, he had suddenly shown signs of passion.

"Sam, I think you are in a dangerous situation. I think you should stay with me at my apartment tonight."

"That's a good idea, but we'll still have surveillance on you," the chief said. "And we know who has access to information to date, and we have surveillance on all of them."

"Even Doree and her husband?" I asked.

"Yes, even them. But they don't know they're being watched so don't mention it." The chief went on to say that they aren't suspects, but the police are following them for their own safety.

"Jonathan, I appreciate your concern for Sam, but she'll never be out of sight—or sound—of my team. We'll have her wired and will be within jumping distance at all times."

The chief gave me my instructions on where to meet Mr. Suarez the next day and how to get him there.

It was about 10:00 p.m. by the time the chief left, and I was exhausted, plus I needed my rest for the next day. I packed up a bunch of clothes in case I was going to be at Jonathan's for a few days. I followed him in my car, and I was sure we were both followed by the chief.

When we got to his apartment, we barely talked before we fell asleep; we were both mentally worn out by what just transpired. And I thought that Jonathan and I could wait one more day to have our big talk.

If he was going to stay in town, there would be no reason to have the discussion tonight. And if he was moving to Miami, I wouldn't have to feel rejected by the man I loved while being scared that a murderer was still in town. I'd rather just be scared out of my wits than scared and heartbroken. Plus, I think Jonathan was a bit overwhelmed that his boring corporate-working girlfriend of a few weeks ago was now a fund-raising murder-solving sleuth and his grandfather was a money-hungry crook.

There's only so much one person can take in one day.

CHAPTER 25

WHEN I CALLED MR. SUAREZ first thing in the morning, I was able to convince him to meet me at Peaceland Park. I wasn't sure he was going to accept my invitation since he hadn't been back for forty years.

The chief suggested that I first go to my mother's house, and he would have officers from his team meet me there to wire me up. That way, if someone was following me, the person wouldn't see who was already there and figure out I was getting bugged.

"Why are police officers coming to my house with all sorts of radio equipment and spy stuff?" she asked when I called her to set up the details. My mom was a bit overdramatic about stuff like that. But then again, it isn't every day that the local police are using your daughter as a decoy to find a murderer, so I knew I really shouldn't be too hard on her and her over-protectiveness.

Jonathan wanted to come with me to the park, but the chief thought that was only going to make Mr. Suarez uneasy. I agreed with the chief. I wouldn't want to meet up with someone's close relative who did me wrong—especially to this extent.

Getting ready was a bit of a challenge. When I woke up that morning, I had a feeling like it was the first day of school. A little anxiety, a little excitement, and I had to really think about what I was going to wear. Jonathan was the one who suggested loose clothing so the wires wouldn't show.

"Stop fussing about your hair. It's not like Mr. Suarez or the person who killed Mrs. Suarez will care if your hair is out of place," he said.

"I'm a little nervous, if you couldn't tell, and I want to look my best."

He was insisting on driving me to my mom's and staying there while I was at the park.

I said, "Let's think about this. If you go with me to my mom's and if I'm being followed, don't you think the bad guy will become suspicious if you stay there and I go to the park alone? Since when have you had social engagements with my mom?"

He just rolled his eyes, turned towards me, held my face in both of his hands and said, "I love you very much, and I hope everything goes well." He kissed me like he hadn't kissed me in months—maybe ever. Wowza!

"Is there more of that left over for tonight?" I asked. My head wasn't really in the detective mood anymore. I had thoughts of ripping our clothes off right there after that kiss. It had been so long since we'd had a night of passion. If I only knew trying to solve a forty-year-old mystery would get his juices flowing.

"I'll meet you at your apartment tonight, and I'll make you dinner. Whatever else happens is up to you," he said. He gave me a kiss on the cheek and wished me luck, and I drove away.

The ride to my mother's house seemed much longer than any other day. I'm not sure if I was preoccupied in thought about meeting Mr. Suarez and the murderer possibly following me or daydreaming about getting back to Jonathan, but I wasn't paying attention to how slow I was driving.

Getting wired at my mom's was uneventful. There was a female officer available to assemble the tape and gadgets. My mother didn't even want to be in the same room because she was so fidgety. She kept asking the officers if they'd like a glass of water or a freshly baked chocolate chip cookie.

It was about eleven-thirty by the time I was done, and I had asked Mr. Suarez to meet me at the lily pond at noon. The pond was on the river side of the park, at the south side of the duck pond with a wide pathway in between. The chief thought it was a good spot because there was a parking area nearby, making it easy for Mr. Suarez to reach at his frail age. Plus, he said there were plenty of spots along the duck pond on and above the elevated walkways for officers staged as passersby to watch out and be ready to react if something went wrong.

I pulled into the entrance near my apartment off of Kensington Avenue, bore left onto the entrance road, and got a spot right near the walkway near the Rotary Eternal Light for Peace. There's a simple white lamp post with a red light bulb. It was dedicated by the U.S. ambassador to Italy. As I walked by, I took a minute to read the bronze plaque at the bottom.

I needed a little peace myself. I took a deep breath, filling my lungs with the warm summer air, and I heard, "Hello there, Sam." It was Frank O'Connor. He actually looked a little chipper, with a spring in his step.

"Hi, Frank. How are you today?" I asked. And I almost really cared, compared to when he was in a committee meeting snipping at all my hard work.

"I'm fine, thank you. I was just strolling through the park, feeding the squirrels," he answered, showing me a plastic bread bag filled with cracked corn, nuts, and some things that looked like squished berries. "Ever since I was a kid and the black squirrels were first in the cages at the barn, I've come to feed them. They're the craziest little critters."

"What are you doing here?" he asked.

I suddenly was much more nervous than I had been all morning. I couldn't say that I was meeting Mr. Suarez because he might want to come along—especially since Frank thought I couldn't close the donation request of Mr. Suarez. But then I couldn't say I wasn't meeting with him because he might not be leaving Peaceland Park, and what if he saw me with him?

"Mr. Suarez wanted to meet with me to talk about the ball." There, I said something. Hopefully he won't follow me, I thought. Hopefully he won't ask to join me.

"It's about time you closed this deal. Well, good luck, then, and get top dollar from that old fool," he said in the crabby tone I was more used to than his fleeting moment of sweetness.

"Thanks, Frank. I'll do my best," I said and took off along the path between the wildflower garden and the rose garden. The two gardens contrast one another like grumpy old Frank O'Connor and the very kind Mr. Suarez. One is dark and shallow, and the other is vivid and colorful.

I walked down the Midwestern Trail, a walking trail that follows the slope of the steep hill behind the Pavilion and the One Acre Lawn. It's one of my favorite parts of the park, since it borders the back yard of the house my grandparents lived in when my grandfather worked there.

I was one of the youngest grandchildren, and I wasn't allowed to venture too far off by myself so this was the section of Peaceland Park I was most familiar with. As I walked along, I remembered that one of Grandpa's workers designed a beautiful garden that Grandma cherished. It was in the shape of a heart and was designed at her request—it must have been Mugsy since he did the same for Mrs. Suarez. It's now mostly marshy and cattails, a sign that the water that used to flood around the lily pond was being diverted.

Even from about one hundred yards away, I could see someone with thinning hair on top of his head, reflecting the shine from the sun, sitting on a bench near the lily pond. How ironic that a man who walked with a cane was sitting near the crooked cane tree, a tree that does not have bending or straight branches, but twisted branches that look like very stiff grapevines.

I picked up my step a little and gave a wave when I got about half way to Mr. Suarez. He didn't respond until I was a bit closer, and then he started to brace himself on the bench's arm with his left hand and his cane with his right hand to get up to greet me.

"Sam, what a beautiful day, and you look just as lovely," he said with his

Hispanic accent. I enjoyed the way he spoke to me. If he was about thirty years younger, I could fall in love with him just because of his linguistics.

"Hello, Mr. Suarez. It's nice to see you, too," I said as he held out his hand to take mine and give me a soft kiss on the cheek. He continued to hold my hand as I sat next to him on the bench, sitting at an angle so I could face him.

"I love this spot. I can still remember the Easter my cousin Maggie fell into the Lily Pond, pretty new dress, white patent leather shoes, and all when she was about seven years old. My grandfather must have been looking at something close to the edge, and she wanted to look, too. However, he was wearing his work boots and she was wearing new shoes and slid right in." We both chuckled as I made a swooping hand gesture.

"I asked you to join me here not to tell you about my cousin, but because I really wanted to talk to you about your wife. Police Chief Cerrazo has determined that her death was definitely a murder. However, the suspect list is very, very short."

I then took his hand in my two and held it. "Mr. Suarez, I know this may be very painful, but do you know anyone who would have wanted her dead?"

There, I just said it. The police team who wired me suggested that I ease into asking Mr. Suarez the questions the chief wanted me to review with him, but that wasn't my style. Even though Mr. Suarez didn't know me very well, in order for me to be genuine, I had to be direct.

I noticed that his eyes were getting wet and glassy, and he looked up toward the endless blue sky.

"There wasn't anyone who would want to hurt Pauli. She was a beautiful and caring woman. Sure, there were some who were a bit jealous of her success as a salesperson, but no one would actually hurt her. Those green-eyed catty women were threatened by her self-confidence and drive compared to their trivial need to make money to buy the next fancy new car or fur coat. But no one would actually cause her physical harm."

He continued to look troubled as he spoke, laboring over many words.

"I know this is hard to imagine, but did anyone have a romantic interest in Mrs. Suarez?" I was thinking that maybe Mugsy—who was a bit "off," as Esther told me, and created a heart-shaped garden for her while he worked at the house in Connecticut.

"There were many men who had an eye for Pauli, but I don't think anyone would have wanted to hurt her, or actually take action on their affection for her," he said with a bit stronger accent than usual. I thought the emotion of it all might have impacted his clarity of speech.

"However, there were some people who wanted to hurt me," he said, looking right into my eyes, with his squinting a bit for effect.

"I was a successful chemist, and my products were the big sellers of the day. In the days of working for Formula 333, I was pushing for natural products, using plant extracts and oils to enhance the cleaning product's effectiveness, but most importantly not to contaminate our water and soils."

"Many in Formula 333 didn't like using these ingredients, because it was more expensive. Mr. Smith was supportive of using the ingredients, but he would not raise prices to customers."

"Therefore, the sales staff was very angry as these new or improved products were introduced, because the only way to keep prices the way they were, and the overall profit margins the same, was to cut the commissions."

He continued to tell me how he would get threatening notes and messages from sales people all around the company that he was costing them their beach house, their next new car, or their kids' boarding school tuition.

"Did Mr. Smith know?" I asked.

"Sure he did. He even had someone investigating the situation, and he told me that nothing would happen to me and that I should just keep up the good work."

Mr. Suarez said that during the summer of the first Black Squirrel Ball, Mr. Smith announced that all the products would be converted to environmentally friendly ingredients—which was very forward thinking for such a traditional company like Mr. Smith's, particularly at that time.

"He felt it was going to be a competitive advantage and that the salespeople would be able to sell more units, and, therefore, their commissions would stay the same or even grow," he said.

Mr. Suarez said that he received some intimidating notes prior to that summer, but the notes and messages increased as Mr. Smith continued to announce the changes at the summer sales conferences.

"It wasn't until the day before the ball that I received a note stating that my Pauli would be harmed," he said and began to weep. "I showed the note to Mr. Smith, and he said he would have a company driver escort her at all times so she wouldn't have to worry about anything."

"How was a company driver going to help? Why not get the police involved?" I asked.

"Everyone in town knew the police chief back then was a no good *burro*. The company drivers were young men who would take care of her and make sure she got to her appointments and visits safely."

"Why weren't you with your wife the night of the ball? If you were worried for her safety, wouldn't you want to be with her as much as possible?"

I asked. After I asked the last question, I realized that I probably had asked him the question that he had been struggling with for the last forty years.

"You're right, Sam. I should have been with her, and for not being there for her, I'll hold myself just as much responsible for her death as the bastard who pushed her into the waterfall."

He told me that Mr. Smith wanted him to meet with the private investigator and the senior sales management team, who were all in town that one night for the ball. Mr. Smith wanted to ensure that all resources were being used for Mr. and Mrs. Suarez's safety.

"I never thought that while we were planning how to keep Mrs. Suarez and me safe that she was being killed," he said and began to cry. He had his head in his hands, and his aging back was even more curved as he shook uncontrollably.

"I never should have left her alone. I never should have left her in the hands of those young, innocent kids. It wasn't their fault, but they weren't security personnel. They just knew how to drive cars, open doors, and be on time to pick up the executives and their wives. They weren't trained to deal with killers."

"Mr. Suarez, were there any leads as to specific individuals who could be responsible for the threats?"

"No. After Pauli died, I didn't get any more notes, and I left Formula 333 a few months after. I just couldn't live here knowing that my research and my work were responsible for her death."

"What did you do after you left here? What did you do for work?"

"I never worked again," he said bluntly, with a shrug of his shoulders.

I wondered how he afforded such a beautiful home near the ocean if he hadn't worked for forty years. Whether he was successful or not for the first part of his career—or actually for a few years of his total career, how could he live that long without any income?

"When I started at Formula 333, Mr. Smith and Mr. O'Connor made a deal with me that the patents I filed were shared with me—they were not just Formula 333's. We developed licensing agreements with many other companies five years after each product was introduced by Formula 333. When I began, Mr. Smith wanted me to always be inventing new products and stay with the company for the long term. He thought if I shared in the future profits that I would be motivated to continue to invent new products that could be sold to others after our five-year product development cycle. I had always intended to stay with Formula 333 and pursue the concept of cleansers without harmful chemicals."

"After I left, he stood by his word, and when he sold formulas to other companies, I got half of the fees—even though that wasn't his ... or my intention with our agreement. And that's how I could afford not to work. A few months after Pauli's death, Mr. Smith came to my office and told me that I shouldn't have to be burdened with losing my wife and staying in the area where there were painful memories for me."

"How many people knew about this deal?"

"Just Mr. Smith, me, and the chief financial officer, George O'Connor."

"Frank O'Connor's father?" I asked.

"Yes. He is such a nice man—what a gentleman. I just exchanged letters with him last month."

"The intention of the deal was a golden handcuff, not a parachute—right?" I asked, trying to keep him on track of solving his wife's murder rather than catch up on old times.

"Right. No one in their right mind would have allowed their researcher to take half of licensing fees from their pocketbook if the researcher left," he said. He was still wiping away a few tears and blowing his nose after the wailing episode a few minutes ago.

"Frank was a driver, wasn't he?"

"Yes. Again—why?"

"Did he ever drive Mrs. Suarez?"

"Yes, and I ask for the third time—why?" Again, his accent got in the way of his question. He said yes with a hard "j" sound, and when he said "third" is sounded like "turd." It was a bit distracting, and I almost got off track in my thoughts.

"It just seems very odd that Frank's father knew of this arrangement and knew that you were responsible for the revenue opportunities with the company, and Frank also was one of the drivers responsible for Pauli's safety. Did you ever find out if the threatening notes were from the field sales force or from a home office author?"

"I never really thought of it, but now that you say it," he looked up at the sky, but with a more energized gaze then before, "they must have been local messages, because all external mail was screened by the mailroom and someone would have found them before they came to me."

"So, it might not have been from a sales associate; it could have been from someone within administration."

"But even the internal mail was opened and sorted, so unless it was from someone in the mailroom." He stopped and his eyes widened, his mouth opened, and he sucked in two full lungs of air and said, *"Ah mi Dios!* It was Frank."

He just shook his head, and his eyes welled up with tears again.

Mr. Suarez continued, "It makes all the sense in the world. Frank must have learned about the agreement from his father somehow, and then he took matters into his own hands. If I left Formula 333, Frank must have thought that I would not receive any of the licensing fees, and profits from future sales would have been greater."

"Wait until I get my hands on that weasel. He is going to suffer and suffer a long, long time," he said as he grasped his hands and started to stand up, forgetting to grab his cane for his unsteadiness.

"Mr. Suarez, this is all based on conjecture and hunches. We need to let the police do their job and ensure that justice is served," I said as I guided him back down on the bench.

Just then, Chief Cerrazo came running toward us from the elevated walkway and steps along the duck pond, waving his arms. When he got to us, he was a bit out of breath.

As he was huffing, he said, "I just met with Pat O'Connor, and he said Frank was assigned to drive Mrs. Suarez home that night. Frank may have been the last person to see Mrs. Suarez alive."

"I told you, Samantha, Frank killed her," Mr. Suarez said.

"Well, I didn't say that, but he is my next person of interest that I need to question," the chief said in a breathy rhythm.

"After you read the transcript from our conversation, you'll put all the pieces together," I said to the chief.

"Transcript, are we being taped?" Mr. Suarez asked. His eyes weren't as glassy when he glared at me for a split second.

"Yes, I'm sorry we were deceptive, Mr. Suarez, but I wasn't sure you were telling me the whole truth the other day," the chief said.

"You thought I killed my lovely Pauli?" he said standing with both hands on his hips, yelling at the chief. He was still not using his cane.

"Never," the chief said with great force in his voice and also moving his arms like he was calling a baseball play safe. "We never thought you killed your wife. It's just that we weren't sure if you were holding back information, and I thought you might be more forthright to a lovely young lady whom you seemed to connect with rather than an officer of the same police force who you felt wronged your wife's murder investigation."

"Although that Chief O'Malley was a snake, I wouldn't hold his poor behavior and excuse of service against a fine man like you," Mr. Suarez said to Chief Cerazzo as he held out his hands to shake the chief's right hand.

"Thank you, Mr. Suarez, thank you for that vote of confidence. And I don't think we have this case solved just yet, but I think we're very close. We need to confirm a few other details," he said, "but we are very close indeed."

CHAPTER 26

As the police team de-wired me at my mom's house, she was full of questions, but I just told her I was exhausted from the meeting.

"Did you at least solve the case?" she asked. I'm not sure if she was annoyed at me for not giving her the details or anxious to have this saga over with.

"We're pretty sure we figured it out. The chief has a little more work to do, but I think he's close," I said. "I'm going home, I'm going to crank up the air conditioner, and Jonathan is coming over later to make me dinner."

"I'm glad Jonathan is in town and will look after you tonight," my mom said. I wasn't sure she would want to know what details we had planned.

"Thanks, Mom. We're all set now. The police didn't think anyone was following me, so there's no need for surveillance anymore."

"Are you sure? What if they were wrong?"

"I'm confident that who they're looking for is not after me." That's the best I could do to calm her fears, but since they thought they knew who killed Mrs. Suarez, it wasn't me who was going to be followed—it was Frank O'Connor.

On my way home, I stopped at the vegetable stand and picked up some fresh watermelon. I thought that would be a nice bedroom snack to have on hand to help if we needed a sugar rush or hydration.

When I got into my apartment, I immediately turned the window air conditioners on high in the living room and bedroom. I wanted the place to be like an icebox when Jonathan got there, I could immediately jump to the evening's activities.

It was only about 4:00 p.m., which would give me enough time to clean up the apartment, take a shower, and get into ready for tonight. I wasn't much for fancy Victoria's Secret type lingerie, but I was pulling out all the stops for tonight and had a simple navy blue short slip that was nice and fitted on top and flowing from the bustline down. It was just the right balance of sexy and sophisticated.

I thought, "I might have been overthinking all of this, but I was so ready for a passionate evening. It was a hell of a day or two, and I needed some way to relax. I only hoped Jonathan was looking forward to the night as much as I was."

As I stepped out of the shower, I heard the phone ring. Maybe Jonathan wanted to come over early, I thought.

I ran to the phone on my nightstand, stubbing my toe on the edge of my bed, and it wasn't Jonathan. It was Mr. Suarez.

"Sam, I can't thank you enough for solving the case," he said.

"Well, Mr. Suarez, it hasn't totally been solved just yet. The chief still needs to put together some details so he can make an arrest. We just need to hold tight for a day or two so that can happen."

"I'm confident Jake will put together the details, and Frank will get his just due," he said with a strong voice and emphasis on *his*.

"I want to thank you for your persistence and willingness to ask questions others were too reluctant to ask so many years ago. I want to support the Black Squirrel Ball."

What a day! I helped solve a forty-year-old murder, I was planning for a night with Jonathan, and then I was closing the deal on the gift from Mr. Suarez.

"Life cannot get better than this," I thought.

"I'd like to meet you again at the park and talk about how we can memorialize Pauli at this year's ball," he said.

"Great. How about ten tomorrow morning?" I suggested quickly. I wanted to wear my hair up for when Jonathan arrived, but then have it look just as nice when I took it out of the hairpins, and in order to do that, I had to blow it dry a certain way and time was ticking away.

"No, I'd really like to meet you there tonight. How about five o'clock?"

It was like the world stopped. Sort of like when the skunk sprayed my blanket. I just sighed. Loudly.

"Is there something wrong, Sam?"

I thought, "This man just learned who killed his wife, and he wanted to donate money to Peaceland Park in order to share her memory, and all I wanted to do was jump my boyfriend in less than two hours. How insensitive am I?"

"No, I just walked by the air conditioner, and the blower is on high so it's pretty loud," I said as a lame cover-up.

"I'll be glad to meet you at five, but is there any way to meet a little earlier—maybe in about ten minutes?"

"Oh, OK. I'll see you in the rose garden, near the Carillon Tower?" he said.

I quickly put my hair up in a hair clip—I'd have to settle for the messy look a little later, but for now, I could look well put together with a summer slip dress, sandals, and a pair of earrings. I grabbed my shoulder bag, jumped in the car, and was at the bench near the Carillon Tower in seven and a half minutes.

I didn't call Jonathan or leave him a note. I planned on taking care of business with Mr. Suarez and getting back in plenty of time.

Mr. Suarez was walking along the flagstone pathway about a minute after I got there. He seemed to gain an inch or two in height since I had seen him earlier. The weight of not knowing who killed his wife was finally lifted off his shoulders.

"Well, aren't you prompt!" he said to me.

"I have a date tonight, but I wanted to make sure we were able to spend some time talking about what to do in Mrs. Suarez's memory here in Peaceland Park," I said. I thought that was a nice way of saying, 'I appreciate your potential gift, but let's get going because I have hot and steamy plans.'

"Oh, if you have a date, we could have done this another time."

I thought, 'Now he says it. Oh well, too late.' But I was worried it would be now or never.

"No problem. I have been hoping that you would support the Black Squirrel Ball, so I've been thinking of a few ideas. What did you have in mind?"

"Pauli always loved the One Acre Lawn. She had some of her most successful sales endeavors recognized on the stage there. I'd like to make a donation to renovate the stage into a small band shell and name it the Pauli Suarez Band Shell," he said. "Is that doable?"

"I don't see why not. The park's strategic plan for this next year includes fixing up the stage, but I'm not sure they had all that in mind."

"Whatever it takes. That's what I'll pay. How much do you think they will need?" he asked.

All I had to do was say a number. Any number. These are the fund-raising moments that can be matched in excitement only to the fervor of an intense orgasm.

"I think $50,000 would do it, for sure. I don't have quotes or bids, but if you want to redo the stage, add the band shell, and also include the sound system, $50,000 would be a great start."

I wasn't sure how much any of that would cost, but we were hoping for $25,000 from him; Peaceland Park planned on updating the stage with the operating funds next year, and hopefully another $25,000 would get it to where he wanted it. If I started out proposing $50,000, he may land on $25,000—just like a real estate negotiation.

He responded, "Sounds great! Let's start at $50,000 and see what that can do. Then, if the park needs more, I'll make up the difference to add the best sound system and acoustic band shell."

With the other smaller individual gifts we received the past week or so, that would put us right over the $100,000 goal. I was doing a happy dance in my head but still trying to look cool and sophisticated in the summer heat.

By far, that was one of the best days of my life. Who cares about graduating from college or pitching a new business venture to a Fortune 500 CEO?

It was truly a great day.

"Sam, this was a very special place for Pauli and me, and we so enjoyed listening to music at the concerts in the Pavilion and the One Acre Lawn. I want others to have beautiful memories like ours in this majestic place," he said. "Let's go over to the stage and take a look. I have a few ideas."

It was almost 5:00 p.m. by the time we got over to the One Acre Lawn and crossed to the far side toward the stage. Mr. Suarez had more of a spring in his step than earlier that afternoon, but the spring didn't bounce him along any faster.

He stepped up to the front middle of the stage and looked out on the lawn and closed his eyes.

"I can remember the song that the band played that night. It was "Por Una Cabeza," by Gardel and Le Pera. It was a song that we danced to at our wedding in Mexico City."

He put his cane over his wrist and pretended to dance while he hummed the music he was referring to. He had his eyes closed and seemed to be in a different place. Or maybe he was in the same place, but forty years ago.

It was lovely to watch him so happy remembering a good memory between him and his wife. I was smiling, watching him glide across the stage like he was floating on air.

He looked like that only until he tripped on a crack in the concrete stage and went over the side of the stage—right over the embankment. Head over teakettle and down the steep hill.

"Oh, my God. Are you OK?" I leaned over the side of the stage to see if he was moving and still alive. He was quiet for about ten seconds, and then he started to laugh hysterically.

"I'm fine," he said as he got to his knees and pulled himself up on his feet. He even giggled a bit. "I was so caught up in the moment that I forgot it was so close to the edge of the stage."

"Wait right there, I'll come get you." I scurried down the side of the bank, got my hands under his arms, and helped him to his feet. We got hold of a small tree, pulled ourselves up, braced our feet against some rocks and edged our way up to the top of the bank, where we were greeted by Frank.

"You don't have to go any farther," he said, holding a small gun toward the two of us. "You, my dear, should have stuck with your corporate job rather than take on this new adventure of playing Jessica Fletcher from *Murder, She Wrote*. Your ambition to "solve the case" was more important than your goal of raising money for Peaceland Park, and look where you are now."

He usually spoke with an evil tone, but this time Frank was beyond evil. His eyes looked red. Not the white parts with bloodshot streaks, but the irises looked red—like he was in a photo without red-eye reduction. His voice was very deep and rough, like every word was rubbed against sandpaper as it came out of his mouth.

"Mr. Suarez, you got much more than you ever deserved from Formula 333, and, yes, that's why I killed your precious Pauli."

I was holding onto Mr. Suarez's arm and could feel us shaking in unison.

"Frank, I didn't get anything more than I earned," Mr. Suarez insisted as he moved another step up the hill. "You should have just stuck to your own business. Your father, George, was the one responsible for my compensation."

"George? George O'Connor was a schlep. He was so generous to everyone else and didn't look out for his family, and we lost our opportunities. You were the one making all the money from Formula 333, and your precious Paulita was getting all the attention," Frank said.

He told us how he would "investigate office files" in the executives' offices when he was supposed to be emptying wastebaskets and dusting at night. In one of the files that he was "privy to," as he said, he found the employment agreement Mr. Suarez made with Formula 333.

"If you left town, the company would be more profitable, and that would have made George O'Connor, and the whole O'Connor clan, richer and more important," Frank said like a petulant child.

"So you did this to make yourself a better businessman? Frank, your father was the one who drew up the agreement. He was in full support of that deal. It was to keep me creating new products and keep me at Formula 333 instead of going to a competitor," Mr. Suarez said as he inched forward to keep from losing his balance again.

"Don't you move any farther, you aren't going anywhere except inside this stage you love so much," Frank said.

"Inside? What do you mean inside?" I asked him like he was crazy. I almost forgot he had a gun in front of us and that he probably was crazy.

"To the left of you, there's a door to the storage area," Frank said.

There was a metal door about four feet high on the hill side of the stage. I was intrigued by the fact there was a storage area under the stage, and I wondered what was in there, but I certainly didn't want to go into it.

"Get in there. I'm going to take care of you now for good. I've waited for this day for forty years," Frank said as he looked straight through Mr. Suarez. He pointed the gun toward the door and then back toward us.

"We'd better do what he says, or he might kill us," I said.

"He's going to kill us anyway, so I don't see why we should go in and die in the dark instead of out here in daylight," Mr. Suarez said. His accent was more prominent now than ever. He must revert when he's nervous.

"I'm not going to kill you out here. Someone will hear the gunshot and find you quickly," Frank said. "I want you to suffer, just like I've suffered working so hard and not getting my just due from Formula 333."

"Just due? What are you talking about? You've done well for yourself, working your way up from driver and mail clerk. You had it easy. Your parents gave you everything a child could want, growing up in a lovely four-bedroom house, a barn full of horses, and you and your siblings had good educations in boarding schools and private colleges," Mr. Suarez told Frank. "Your parents were good people and wanted you to learn the value of a dollar by working during the summers and so you could learn the business. You were nothing but a selfish brat then, and you still are today."

"You don't know anything about me or my parents. Now stop stalling and get into that room. Your doomsday is today ... or maybe in a few days, once the rats and squirrels get to you."

I noticed there was a bunch of cracked corn and berries around the entrance of the storage room. That's what he was doing earlier—setting a trap for our deaths. We were going to be nibbled at by those little black rodents.

"This is what you were doing today, when I saw you with your bag of squirrel feed?" I asked.

"Yes. I was preparing your tomb," Frank said.

I was still shaking, but I was also very confused. Frank had been planning this all along.

"How did you know that we would end up here?"

"I didn't know you would end up here on your own until I heard Mr. Suarez call you a little while ago. I have been listening to your every word." He pulled the earbud part of the listening device out of his ear. "How do you think that skunk really got into your apartment?"

"Mr. Z said it was from the dryer vent. Was it you?" I asked.

Frank said, "I thought that I would leave you a present while I was getting one for myself—the stinky one was for you and the other present was so I could hear your every word. I placed bugs in your kitchen, living room, and bedroom. Then, I let another skunk into your car to smell it up just for fun."

It was probably a good thing Jonathan and I went to his apartment instead of staying at my apartment, just in case we did have the energy for a romp. Although, I thought, "considering I might die soon, I really shouldn't care if someone heard me having sex compared to never having sex again."

"And I thought the necklace would have really scared you off, but all it did was put a tail on you from the Westfield Police. I noticed that ended this afternoon after you two met on your little rendezvous. What was that about anyway?" Frank asked.

At that point, I realized that he didn't know that the police knew he killed Mrs. Suarez. He may have heard everything said inside my apartment since the skunk was escorted into my home, but he didn't hear the review of the medical examiner's files from prior to the skunk encounter, my conversation with Mr. Suarez in the park earlier that day, or the review of Chief O'Malley's found evidence from my backyard conversation with the chief and Jonathan the previous night.

He continued, "I heard every word from your apartment since the skunk intruders were left. I heard about the details on the flowers, the catering, the music, and how Chief Cerrazo re-opened the case. But without any evidence, there isn't much of a case, is there? Everything was destroyed forty years ago. Otherwise, this would have been an open and shut investigation back then." His eyes sunk deeper in his brow as he segued from talking about ball details to the evidence he thought was no longer available.

"Now let's stop this jabbering, and you two get in there." He motioned to us as we climbed toward the steep incline right outside of the door.

I peered inside and was hit with the disgusting smell of stinky feet and rotten onions inside the hidden room. "It smells terrible in there," I said.

"Not as bad as it will in a few days when your bodies have decomposed, and the earthworms start nibbling at your toes and fingers."

I cringed, thinking of the creepy crawlies invading my body. My Uncle Tony once said to me, "You spend your whole life flicking bugs off of you, why would you want to let them in when you're dead?" I thought that was a great testimonial for cremation.

It must have been close to 6:00 p.m. when we were forced into the dark, damp room. It had a dirt floor, and there were about twenty old, rusty, metal folding chairs.

"Give me your pocketbook," Frank said to me as he beamed a flashlight in my eyes, and I tossed it to him. There went my lifeline of a cell phone, along with my survival tools of a small jackknife and my ladylike defense spray of hairspray.

"And you," he said toward Mr. Suarez. "Empty your pockets. Give me your wallet and your cell phone."

"Here, here's my wallet. Why don't you steal my money—go ahead and take more of something that doesn't belong to you—just like you stole my lovely wife from me," Mr. Suarez said, raising his voice.

"You keep your voice down, old man. If you don't, I'll give you a shock to help keep you quiet," Frank said as he held out a Tazer gun and blasted it to make sure we knew he meant business.

"Where's your cell phone?" Frank demanded to Mr. Suarez.

"I don't have one of those stupid things. I like to call people from the comfort of my home or send personal letters," he responded quite calmly.

"Fine. Then it's now time to die." He turned toward me. "It's too bad you couldn't have just stuck to the plan and raised money rather than getting into researching Mrs. Suarez's death. You brought this on yourself, and you deserve to die for it," Frank said.

He turned away, closed the door behind him, and we could hear him click a padlock shut.

We sat there for a few minutes, listening to the squirrels in the corners, eating the cracked corn and nuts. Once they were done eating that, they wouldn't be hungry for a while. But at some point, they might be interested in another snack.

By now, Jonathan would be at my apartment and might be pretty pissed off that I wasn't waiting for him with baited breath and in my blue silk slip. Or without my blue silk slip. Either way, I wasn't there waiting for him. Instead, I was locked in a small dungeon awaiting death.

"What should we do?" I whispered.

"Well, we can't yell since he is right outside here," Mr. Suarez said.

"Do you really not have a cell phone, or was that just a way to keep it?" I asked. I so hoped he was lying to Frank.

"I don't lie to people—even if they're crazy murderers," he said in such a sweet voice. His accent was not as strong as it was when he was talking with Frank. He must be a little calmer now.

I was glad one of us had calmed down because I sure hadn't.

"Sam, I don't have a cell phone because I don't need one." He reached around his neck and pulled out a necklace with a small plastic box attached to it. It was an emergency call transponder.

"I pressed it when I fell down the hill, and someone should be on their way any minute. It can track me to within fifty feet, and I can keep hitting it until they find us."

"I thought those were only good for a certain distance within and right around your home," I said.

"I helped a high school kid who mows my lawn come up with this idea for a science fair. It is a cell phone chip with a direct dial number to an emergency line that will be routed to the nearest 911 dispatch with my location," he said. "I felt bad—the kid didn't win because he was so nervous making the verbal presentation that he vomited all over the judges' table."

"Can you talk to someone via that thing? What if they can't find us under here?" I asked. For a minute, I was really intrigued by the technology. I almost forgot that we were going to die a slow death.

"I can't talk through it, but I have hope that they'll find me. I once fell on the beach, and the paramedics found me in about ten minutes."

"Do you think he is still out there?" I asked. I noticed a slim ray of light through a small crack near the top of one corner, but I couldn't see anything.

"I bet he got out of here pretty quickly, and he'll probably get up to George's house on the lake before anyone can figure out we're gone."

"Well, someone is aware I'm missing by now because I was supposed to meet my boyfriend at 6:00 p.m. and I told him I wouldn't be late. Jonathan will call the police, and they'll start looking for me soon, if they haven't already. Plus, I would think the 911 dispatcher may put one and one together and figure out we're together."

"You make it sound so simple," he said.

"I have hope, too, and we have your lucky charm around your neck," I said, secretly convincing myself that I would not be a rodent's best meal within the next forty-eight hours.

Through the very dim light, I could see that he was sulking back into his chair.

"I really miss my Pauli. It seems like just yesterday that we were dancing under the grand tent, enjoying the music, our friends, and this beautiful place. Although it was the place of my wife's death, and maybe my death as well, this park is something very special to everyone who visits."

"It has colorful and well maintained gardens, winding pathways to encourage visitors to enjoy holding hands while conversing and walking, all the while it is preserving history," he said.

"Mr. Smith had a vision for Peaceland Park, and he was able to inspire so many other people to contribute funds. Many people think he was solely responsible for starting the park, but it was with the support of his sales team, executives, and the hard work of the blue-collar park staff that made this such a beautiful place. Mr. Smith definitely led the charge, but he had a way to encourage others to take action and be a part of the park's future."

Mr. Suarez went on to tell me stories about the sales conferences that were held at the park, and how my grandfather was such an integral part of making sure everyone felt welcome and was comfortable. After all, many of the participants had never before been too far from their homes and some visited from as far as California, Puerto Rico, Texas, Mexico, and parts of South America.

"I can still remember coming up for lunch—the menu was the same every week—and on Tuesdays they would have mashed potatoes. You know, your grandfather was in charge of so many things here, but it was the ladies in the kitchen, including your grandmother, who kept the visitors really happy and well fed. I've traveled to many places and had the good fortune of eating in many four-star restaurants. I've never had mashed potatoes as good as your grandmother's."

He reached out and held my right hand.

I started to cry. Now I felt like giving up.

"We're going to be just fine, Samantha." And he patted my hand with a reassuring touch as an attempt to be strong for me. And then I cried harder.

Unfortunately, I am a crier. I cry when I laugh, and I cry when I'm upset or mad, and I definitely cry when I feel helpless. I couldn't stop sobbing.

Because it was the middle of summer, there was light still coming through the cracks of the stage's foundation, even though it was probably almost 7:00 p.m. Dusk would come about 9:00 p.m., and then it would get dark. My eyes adjusted just enough so I could see that the squirrels seemed just as scared of us, in the opposite corner, as we were of them. I've never been scared of squirrels, but Frank did plant the idea that they were carnivores and would be happy to pick away at us during our dying moments. I don't think that is true, but I guess I'll never know because I'll be unconscious by then.

I thought of how disgusting it would be when we were found; parts of our extremities would be nibbled off by the offspring of those little critters that my father helped escape from their cage so many years ago. If he didn't let them out, there wouldn't be any squirrels to eat us, and there also wouldn't have been a Black Squirrel Ball to begin with and Mrs. Saurez wouldn't have been killed and maybe I would have been destined to continue to work in my corporate hellhole—I would have still been miserable, but I would have been alive.

I could trace it all back to those silly squirrels.

And then I started thinking that it was a good thing I wanted to be cremated because there would be no way to have an open casket at my wake. I would just hope that there was more of a focus on memorializing my spirit than spending lots of money on flowers. I don't like smelly things, and I hoped my mother would remember that.

My mind kept wandering, thinking about what music the choir at church would sing and who might say my eulogy. Maybe my brother and sister would tag team. Or maybe my Aunt Reggie and Aunt Ruth would join forces. Either partnership would do a nice job.

I thought I would cry through the night and then pass out and die of starvation and dehydration.

Mr. Suarez was quiet. He didn't move or weep or even try to talk. He sat in perfect stillness and kept hitting that stupid alert button around his neck.

It seemed like hours went by, and we didn't hear anyone. I would have thought that the chief or Jonathan or Mr. Z would have realized both Mr. Suarez and I were missing and started tracking the most likely locations.

But I doubt this dank creepy place is on anyone's top ten locations of where they would look for us. My only hope was that someone had found Frank by now, captured him, and he told the police where we were, and they were on their way.

As I kept crying, and even though I was terrified, I was so emotionally tired I fell asleep dreaming of who would find and save Mr. Suarez and me.

CHAPTER 27

FINALLY. I WAS RID OF that perky little redhead with all her optimism, organization, and project planning nagging, along with the old man. It was about time I finished what I started forty years ago when I killed Paulita Suarez.

I had just left the One Acre Lawn and was quickly going to the car. I had my trail planned out. I didn't want anyone to recognize me, so I left the lawn via the Midwestern Trail, being careful not to slide down the steep embankment.

I took Patrick's Crown Vic out of his garage that morning and left mine in his barn. It's not like the do-gooder needs it since he had the stroke. He's going to live out his last days eating applesauce and strained peas in the nursing home and getting sponge baths from the crazy nurses' aide with the multicolored hair.

That Samantha is such a pain in the ass. It's a good thing that she got screwed up with Mr. Saurez and solving Paulita's death because it gave me a reason to kill her. I couldn't stand how she always had an agenda at every meeting that included "to-do" lists for all the committee members. My job was to make sure they didn't overspend. I wasn't actually going to do anything.

I had two more years until retirement, and then I would be done with Formula 333 and those stupid fund-raisers. There shouldn't be any need for any fund-raisers. People should pay to go into the park rather than have everything free. For decades, I have worked so that a portion of my salary supported that ridiculous place, and what do I have to show for it?

Nothing.

And nothing in life should be free. If people want to smell the roses, they should pay for the fertilizer.

I got into the car and realized the gas tank was empty.

With all this planning, I couldn't believe I forgot to check the gas tank. I had to get to the O'Connor cottage in Otis in a jiffy and lay low for a few days while the police searched for Samantha and Mr. Suarez. Once they weren't found, the evidence against me would be unfounded, and I wouldn't be arrested for the murder of Pauli Suarez. Without those two, they wouldn't have a case against me for Pauli's murder.

I didn't think I would even make it to the little gas station in Russell, so I had to go down Granville Road, turn right onto Mill Street, and go down the hill to the gas station on South Maple Street.

I pulled in and realized that I couldn't use my credit card—if anyone was looking for me, I would be traced. Damn. I didn't think through all these details.

I grabbed the fishing hat in the back seat of Patrick's car and pulled it down as low as it could go, and then put on his sunglasses that were folded into the visor. I took a quick look in the rearview mirror and thought, "No one will recognize me." The place was pretty deserted.

I pulled $10 from my money clip and walked in quickly but without drawing attention to myself.

As I entered the convenience store, I noticed a car pulling up at the pump next to me. I knew right away that it was a 1951 Ford—a teal blue metallic finish that Artie Goodson painted years ago. I wasn't sure who owned it now or who was driving it, but I remember my friend Artie restoring it to mint condition. Then his mean Broom-Hilda wife sold it before his body was cold in the ground five years ago. He died from lung cancer—he was always smoking while he was working in his garage, and it hit him hard. She sold the cars, the tools, and the garage and moved to Florida within a month of his funeral.

That bitch.

I walked out of the store after paying the cashier. I even talked in a really low voice and a southern redneck accent so no one would overhear me and think it was me. There was only one guy in the store over by the hot dog machine, and he looked like he was wearing hearing aids.

When I got to the gas pump, I noticed the tires and rims on the car were different than what Artie had. They were not the restored originals but some fancy new style that didn't fit with Artie's philosophy. He would be pissed to see his hard work ruined with those high stylin' new wheels.

Why can't people just leave well enough alone and appreciate good work?

I pumped my gas and wouldn't look at the guy. I didn't want him to see me, and if I did make eye contact with him, I would probably have told him to piss up a rope for changing the wheels like that.

After I pumped the gas, I slowly left the gas station and headed up to Otis. I hadn't been to the cottage in a while, but I checked in with Patrick yesterday at the nursing home to make sure none of his kids were going to be there. I also wanted to get the key to his fishing boat. I needed the low profile boat to get into the stumps—where many of the ski boats and pontoon party boats can't get to—later in the week.

I had already stocked my cooler with enough food for a few days, and we always had three days worth of dry goods. If I went fishing early each morning, I could stay up there without going to a store for about a week.

And Mr. Suarez and Samantha would be good and dead by then. If the rodents and squirrels don't get them first, they'll die from suffocation in that concrete box after a few days.

I already had all the materials I needed to transport the bodies in plastic bags from the One Acre Lawn to the car and then to Otis to the boat. Once I got the bodies in the boat, I'd go out with the foot pedal motor in the middle of the night so I'd be very quiet. Then, when I got to the middle of the lake, I could turn the trolling engine on and slowly coast down to the end of the lake called the stumps.

That's where I'd dump their dead and decaying bodies.

I bought biodegradable bags and I planned on lining them with fish food. That way, the bass and trout would finish off what the black squirrels and rats didn't eat.

No one would find their bodies for a long, long time. The stumps is a part of the reservoir where there are tree stumps on top of one another under the water. Even with sonar, it would be very hard for anyone to find their bodies, and only a few boats—like Patrick's—could get into that part of the lake.

I went over every task in my mind as I drove up past the park again. I could only depend on myself this time, not like forty years ago. I wish my father was here to help me like he did then. It was good to know someone of his stature and with his connections had your back, but that ended long ago.

As I stepped on the gas after bearing left onto Bates Road and then past Russell Pond, I thought that it was a good thing I took Pat's old Crown Victoria to the shop a couple of weeks ago to fix the muffler. Everyone on this side of town would have heard the car and noticed me.

Once I turned onto Route 23, it would normally take about fifteen more minutes, but I got stuck behind a slow-moving hay truck. About half way up, the stupid farmers' bales of hay on the top of the trailer tipped and fell off right in front of the car. I had to swerve to the right and almost hit a retaining wall as the GD bales fell off the top.

I would have called the cops on those punks and got them pulled over, but I didn't want to have to give my name. And if I was a thoughtful chap, I would have parked on the side of the road and moved the bales of hay that fell off in the middle of the road.

About a half hour later, I rolled into the gravel driveway and parked the car in the shed. I didn't want any of the neighbors to think Patrick was out of the nursing home and start calling to visit. If they thought it was me, they'd stay away.

I brought the cooler into the house and started to unpack when the phone rang. I wasn't going to answer it, until I noticed the caller ID as the infamous George O'Connor. Everyone loved him, too. They were two peas in a freakin' pod.

I picked up the phone and answered, "Yeah—Frank here."

"Frank, I've been looking all over Westfield and Otis for you all day. What are you doing?" George asked in between gasps of air. He was older than dirt and should have been contributing to it by now.

"What do you care what I'm doing? I came up to the house to go fishing," I said.

"I care because the police are coming to arrest you."

"Arrest me?" I thought to myself. Even if they did arrest me, they couldn't prove anything since there wasn't any evidence.

George said, "Chief Cerrazo called your sister and me earlier this afternoon to tell us that you killed Paulita Suarez. I always thought you had something to do with it, but I never really knew how. And I never wanted to believe you were responsible for her death."

"No one killed that crazy Mexican. She fell through the fence. If it was anyone's fault, it was that park ranger, Mr. Cummings. He should have kept up on the fences and walkways," I said.

"The chief has pictures from the medical examiner's files that show the railing was broken from the inside, not the outside. Pauli's death was no accident."

I thought, "What did he mean about pictures? All the evidence was destroyed forty years ago."

"And Pat told the chief that you were the last one to see Mrs. Suarez," George said between labored breaths. "Frankie, it's over."

I hated when anyone called me Frankie. Only one person could call me that, and he wasn't here to solve this problem like he did forty years ago.

"Frankie? Frankie? Are you listening to me? I'm begging you to go peacefully. If you cooperate, they may go easy on you." He was pleading with me like a little girl asking her mommy for a puppy dog. It was pathetic.

"If the cops come for me, I'll do what I have to do," I said and slammed the phone down on the receiver.

I grabbed the cooler, pulled a blanket off the couch, and checked that I had Pat's boat keys in my pocket. I would take off for a cove and hide out there until it was clear that the old man was BS-ing me.

I turned around to grab a shotgun from the gun cabinet and red lights hit the wall in front of me.

They weren't coming for me.

They were already there.

"Frank, put your hands in the air and don't take another step," Chief Cerrazo said.

CHAPTER 28

IT SEEMED LIKE HOURS PASSED before they found us, but when they did, I couldn't have been happier.

The squirrels and rats didn't get me, but the mosquitoes had a colony in the concrete foundation, and I was their Thanksgiving dinner.

Jonathan and Mr. Z found us around midnight. I was dreaming that I was in a wooden soapbox with a tap dancer on top, but it was Jonathan and Mr. Z on the stage.

Mr. Suarez woke me up to start screaming, and they heard us through the cracks in the concrete.

"Samantha, is that you?" I heard Mr. Z say. "We're here—Jonathan and me—we'll get you out in a jiffy."

They kicked and banged against the metal door, but it didn't budge. "We'll call the security guys to bring some bolt cutters," Jonathan said.

Unlike the wait in the stinky dark room that seemed to last forever, the security guys must have been on the edge of the lawn because they had the door open in seconds.

Jonathan helped Mr. Suarez out of the room, cupping the top of his head so he didn't hit it as he stooped out of the little door, and then led him by the arm to the lawn until they were both on solid footing.

A security guard who I did not recognize helped me out of the door and toward the group.

"How did you find us?" I asked.

"A phone number from Connecticut kept coming up through the 911 emergency line and after five times, the dispatcher put a trace on it and found out it was from Mr. Suarez's cell phone," Mr. Z said.

Mr. Suarez's necklace aid really did work.

"This is my cell phone," Mr. Suarez said proudly as he showed everyone his pendant.

"We have about fifty volunteers helping search for you both throughout the park," Jonathan said.

"I'll call Chief Cerrazo and tell him you are both safe and sound. He'll be happy to have an end to this night," the security guard said as he sauntered over to his electric-powered golf cart and drove across the lawn while talking into his radio.

"But what about Frank? Is he still around here? I want to get out of here as fast as we can," I said as Jonathan put his arm around me.

Mr. Z said, "Don't you worry, young lady, Frank is where Frank is supposed to be. He's in jail."

CHAPTER 29

NO MATTER HOW MUCH PLANNING time is spent on a project, it always seems like you miss a detail or two.

Frank certainly missed a few important details in his plan to scare Mr. Suarez out of town forty years ago, and then he didn't do such a great job killing Mr. Suarez and me a few weeks ago. I'm glad he was a poor planner, or else I may have died.

After Chief Cerrazo arrested Frank in Otis, Frank admitted to assaulting Mrs. Suarez but said he didn't mean to kill her. He said that when he left Peaceland Park that night, he went straight to Police Chief O'Malley's house.

According to the recap from Chief Cerrazo, the young Frank told Chief O'Malley that if the police chief didn't cover up Mrs. Suarez's murder, Frank was going to tell everyone that the chief was his real father.

When Chief Cerrazo called George O'Connor to tell him that Frank was captured, George explained that he and his wife adopted Frank from a wayward woman who was their housecleaner. After the woman gave her son up, she left town, and was never heard from again.

George told Chief Cerrazo that his wife handled all the details of the adoption and he didn't know who Frank's biological father was. But Frank somehow found out, and based on Chief O'Malley's actions forty years ago, the chief did not want anyone to know that he was the father of an illegitimate child—and a murderer at that.

How and when Frank found out remains a mystery since Frank didn't share any more details with anyone.

And Gareth was quite a hero in the capture of Frank. He was the one who figured out where Frank was going after he left Mr. Suarez and me to die when he was out for a drive in his hot rod and noticed my red shoulder bag in the back seat of the car next to his at the gas station.

He called the police, and they had a tail on Frank in seconds.

Frank may have caused Mrs. Suarez's death accidentally, but she died at his hands, nonetheless. He was charged and pled guilty to second-degree murder and was sentenced to life in prison with a possibility for parole in fifteen years.

He didn't plan well at all.

But everything for the Black Squirrel Ball was planned perfectly.

Even though I was distracted by Mrs. Suarez's murder investigation and was almost killed during our planning process, the fortieth anniversary Black Squirrel Ball was better than anything I could have imagined.

The weather was gorgeous. It was about eighty degrees, but there was a slight breeze every so often—just enough to keep the bugs from taking flight.

I didn't wear a red dress with the ruby and diamond necklace that was left in my house, but I did have a lovely turquoise blue dress that I accessorized with my dichroic glass earring and necklace set.

All my friends and family members were there. Aunt Reggie and Uncle Paul, my mom and dad and sister and brother were at my table with Jonathan. My Uncle Joe and his wife, and Aunt Ruth and her husband Uncle Tony sat with Mr. Suarez, Esther and Dax, and Violet and Chief Cerrazo. I thought the widow and widower might have a good time together. Gareth, his business partner Bill, and their raffle prize-winning clients were whooping it up at tables near us with their family members, too.

And Tom was enjoying showing those "east of the river" people how nice the "west of the river" was at his table.

Even Lucinda was having a great time with her new grandson from Italy.

As I was walking through the crowd, greeting people at the cocktail hour, I heard, "Come; meet my new grandson, Salvatore. Isn't he handsome?" the crotchety old lady said. It was nice to see her so happy, considering she's usually pretty nasty, and it was nice to finally meet the mystery man.

I said, "It's nice to see you all enjoying yourselves, and it's a pleasure to meet you, Salvatore." Later in the evening, I saw Sal and Isabella twirling on the dance floor—she looked like a red-headed version of Cinderella, with Prince Charming all dressed up and gliding across the dance floor.

Mike, my friend from my old job, and his family loved the event. I saw them at the cocktail hour, enjoying the appetizers.

"I can't believe you were trapped in cube world just a few months ago, and now you are the talk of the town!" Mike said. "My kids and friends are having a great time, and we plan on this being an annual event." He looked very handsome in an off-white casual suit with a Tommy Bahama floral shirt, brown woven loafers and no socks. I'm guessing that his wife Kerry helped him get dressed tonight because there is no way he could have put that together based on the uniform of white button-down shirts and dark grey pants he always wore to work.

Everyone was having a grand time, and there was no reason why they wouldn't. And then, I caught sight of Jerry and his boyfriend. At first I thought it might have been a very tall Phyllis Diller impersonator and a guy who looked like Herve Villechaize—Tattoo from *Fantasy Island*.

"Hello," Jerry sang to me as he came skipping—literally—over to me. As usual, he swept me up into a big hug, twirled me around twice, and gently placed me back on Planet Earth.

"Sammy, this is my dear sweetheart, Bubba," Jerry said. Jerry wasn't wearing a dress, but was wearing very flouncing white sheer pants and a pink silk wrap blouse with a rhinestone necklace. "And this is my murder-mystery solving friend, Samantha Cummings."

"You can call me Sam," I said as Bubba gently took my hand to his little mouth and kissed it.

"Hello, Sam. I've heard so much about you," Bubba said in a deep voice that would fit Jerry's body better than his four foot two inch tall body. He was dressed in a white suit—which made him look even more like Tattoo. I almost choked from laughter, and then I realized that this guy was for real.

"We are having a fabulicious time tonight. I especially love this new signature drink—The Black Squirrel. You really outdid yourself," Jerry said.

Since I'm not one to enjoy alcohol, I couldn't take credit for the addition to the ball. My mom and Aunt Reggie came up with a new drink. I didn't remember all the ingredients, but it had some berry and nut liqueurs with a splash of soda, along with a blackberry garnish along the top. I'm not sure if it really was a new drink or just something new to them, and they called it The Black Squirrel. In any case, people were drinking them all over the tent.

"I love the fruity and nutty tastes together. It was like it was made just for us," Jerry said as he patted Bubba on the head and gave him a wink.

"I can't wait until the band starts so we dance," Bubba said as he gave Jerry a once-over with his eyes like he was a jelly donut. I started to think of that visual, and I was thankfully startled by a hand on my shoulder.

"Excuse me, Samantha? Samantha Cummings? I thought that was you," a tall, tan-skinned man with black hair and eyes as brown as Hershey kisses said to me.

"I'm so glad my mother asked me to escort her to the ball," he said. It took about twenty seconds for me to place him. It was Chris Morozick—the kid who took me for a walk through Peaceland Park the night before our high school prom.

"Chris, I almost didn't recognize you. I'm so glad you could make it," I said. I was glad. Very glad. He was drop-dead gorgeous. He did look awfully familiar to me, but not from high school.

"Would you please save a dance for me later?" he asked.

"Sure. That will be great," I stammered, and he walked away with two glasses of champagne. He must have been getting his mother a drink.

"Wow—how did you get Chris Morozick to come to the ball?" Jonathan asked me as he handed me a fancy glass filled with Coke with a lemon. It looked more like a cocktail with a piece of fruit in it.

"His mother was on the invitation list," I said very matter-of-factly, not wanting to let on that I was entranced by Chris's request for a dance.

It all started coming back to me a bit more once I saw him. Chris moved away to live with his father for our senior year of high school, and I lost touch with him. Therefore, I didn't realize until I saw him that he was the one and only Chris Morozick, the PGA newcomer of 2008.

Seeing him was a pleasant diversion, but I needed to get back to the details of the night.

The food was outstanding. Hors d'oeuvres of fresh shrimp wrapped in sugar snap peas, Ipswich clams casino, Nebraska lamb chops, free-range chicken satay skewers, miniature bison wellingtons, bruschetta, and water chestnuts wrapped in bacon. We had beef tenderloin and sea scallops for entrees—a little surf and turf on every plate—with native green beans in butter sauce. And for dessert, we had individual warm blueberry pudding cakes served with locally made vanilla ice cream and blueberries. Yours truly, Aunt Reggie, Esther, my sister who came into town for the ball a little early, and my mom spent the whole day at the blueberry patch earlier in that week.

The music was fantastic. The eight-piece band, with a singer, trumpeter, trombonist, saxophonist, bass player, keyboard player, lead guitar, and drummer, kept the party rocking all night long. They played oldies, big band music, and a few newer favorites. The dance floor was crowded the entire night. I even had the pleasure of dancing a polka with Mr. Z.

And the decorations were spectacular. Toward the end of the planning, Doree had to "step back a bit" because she was getting overtired. I think she was pregnant, but she didn't announce it yet.

I hope she's pregnant, and I was glad she had to "step back," as she put it, because she was starting to drive Violet crazy with all her new ideas. Once Doree was out of the picture, Violet could focus on getting everything done rather than entertaining Doree's "idea of the day."

Violet had hundreds of white Chinese lanterns lining the pathways from the parking lot, through the rose garden, and then along the path to the One Acre Lawn where the incredibly large tent encompassed the entire acre. It looked like one huge tent, but it was actually a group of tents that descended in height from the center to each edge. The tent had more lanterns hanging throughout, and the little white lights inside the clear Lucite flower arrangement vases were a big hit.

With the donation from Mr. Suarez, we were able to have the stage completely renovated with a band shell in time for the ball.

"I can't believe how much better the band sounds with that acoustic shell," Dax said to me before we went on stage to start the historical video of Peaceland Park. "I feel like I'm in an opera house instead of the middle of a park."

Dax and I had put in countless hours in the weeks prior to the ball creating the video, collecting snippets of voice-overs and old photos and researching historical documents from the registry of deeds, and the Smith's family documents. He reluctantly agreed to introduce the video, which added even more drama to the surprise we had for him.

At the end of the video, chronologically detailing the beginning of Peaceland Park, the development of the gardens and the pond, the construction of the Carillon Tower, the improvements to the pavilion and the grounds, along with event pictures from the 1940s through to 2008, the video included a montage of tributes to Dax.

He joined Esther at their first-row table after he introduced the video, and I could see him from the side of the stage getting teary-eyed and laughing. A few people shared some good jokes at his expense, and a few of his cronies told stories about him working at the park when he was just a kid. It was everything Esther, the committee, and I had hoped for.

"You really got me, Samantha. I was doing all that work on the video, and then you went and made fun of me!" he said to me as he gave me a big squeeze.

"We weren't making fun of you, just having fun with you," I said with a chuckle and a kiss on the cheek. "You've done so much for Peaceland Park, everyone wanted you to know how appreciated you are."

"Did someone say something about appreciation?" Mr. Suarez said as he snuck up on us. "Sam, may I have this dance? I'd like to show you my appreciation with a tango."

"Of course. I'm more of a polka kind of girl, but I'll give it a whirl," I said reluctantly, because I didn't know how to dance the tango.

We danced to an upbeat tango, and although I've only seen him walk slowly and with a cane, the music made his frailness disappear. He took my right hand in his left, put his right hand around my waist and led me through a beautiful dance which I will never forget. He led me with such grace and confidence that I felt I could enter a ballroom dance contest with him.

At the end of the dance, Mr. Suarez took me over to the side of the lawn, near the Angel of Independence statue, and said, "Sam, I went to visit George O'Connor this morning, and we had a lovely talk."

"I know it may seem odd that I visited him considering the circumstances, but he called me yesterday and asked to see me," he said. "It was the most healing experience for my soul."

Mr. Suarez continued to tell me that Mr. O'Connor was horribly sorry for his adopted son's actions and said that if he had ever known or suspected that Frank had killed Pauli, he would have gotten to the bottom of it long ago.

"He also wanted to show his appreciation for justice being served. He was a good friend to both Pauli and me, and he wants that friendship to be memorialized," he continued. "He couldn't make it tonight, but he asked that I give this to the heroine of the Black Squirrel Ball."

Mr. Suarez handed me a sealed envelope.

I took a deep breath and opened the envelope. Inside was a hand-written note:

Dear Ms. Cummings,

You've done a wonderful job with the 40th Anniversary Black Squirrel Ball and bringing a good friend's death to justice.

Please accept this gift in Pauli's memory toward the ball's fund-raising goal.

Your grandfather would be very proud of you and your dedication to your friends, family, and Peaceland Park.

Sincerely,

George O'Connor

I started to tear up at the thought that my grandfather would be proud of me. That thought was more valuable to me than any amount of fund-raising in the world. And especially coming from Mr. O'Connor, who knew my grandfather many years ago. I remembered seeing pictures of them in their bowling league shirts from the 1960s and 1970s.

Inside the envelope was a check for $25,000.

Mr. Suarez smiled at me and said, "George is a good and generous man, and he wants the O'Connor name to be remembered in Peaceland Park for the good in the family, not the bad. I think it's wonderful that he is supporting the park in Pauli's memory."

Unexpectedly, Jonathan came up behind me and slipped his hand around my waist.

"May I have the next dance?" he whispered in my ear.

Mr. Suarez said, "Go—enjoy your big night. You deserve it," and he gave me a kiss on the cheek.

"Sure, let's go," I said to Jonathan as he led me to the dance floor filled with all my family and friends.

It was a spectacular evening—even better than I had planned!

CHAPTER 30

JUST THE NIGHT BEFORE, I was on top of the world, dancing with my boyfriend to Frank Sinatra's "The Way You Look Tonight" and with my friends and family around me. Mrs. Suarez's death was solved as a murder, and the Black Squirrel Ball had raised more than our goal of $100,000.

We raised $135,000! That was awesome.

But this morning was a big letdown.

Jonathan stayed over and the magic continued through the night, but he had to leave early to go back to New York City for his latest assignment. The past few weeks had been wonderful between us, but I'd bet things will go back to the way they were once he gets an opportunity to go to Miami, Dallas, or Chicago.

I was thinking that it might be time for the Samantha/Jonathan show to end, and for me to move on to something—or, better said, someone else. I couldn't get Chris Morozick out of my mind that morning.

And then it hit me that I didn't have a job anymore. I would get the final payment from the ball committee later that week, but other than a few thank you notes to write, I didn't have anything to do. I was going to be bored.

I went to church and met up with my mom and dad for breakfast. Both in church and at the breakfast restaurant, people kept coming up to me, congratulating me on solving Mrs. Saurez's murder and coordinating such a spectacular event.

It was nice to be a local celebrity, and I enjoyed my fifteen minutes of fame.

As I was leaving the restaurant to go to my car, Gareth caught my eye and waved me over to his table. He was having breakfast with his parents and a few of his other relatives who I recognized from around town and the night before, although I didn't remember all their names.

He's such a nice guy. Hardworking, good looking, and very personable.

"I want you to meet my uncle," he said. "This is Albert Tubbins."

"Mr. Tubbins, it's nice to meet you again." I did recall meeting Albert a few years ago at a Chamber of Commerce breakfast and had seen him from time to time at community events.

"Samantha, it's nice to see you again, too," he said as he got up from his seat and shook my hand. He was a man of large stature, about six feet, four inches, with glasses, a pleasant smile, and a strong handshake. His white hair was a bit thin, but combed in a way that was not hiding his very shiny head. For such a large man, he had lovely, welcoming blue eyes that made me feel quite at ease, even when he almost crushed my hand in his.

"Your ball last night was absolutely wonderful, and I'd like you to do your magic with the Hospital Masquerade this October. Here's my card. Please call me tomorrow so we can work out the details of your employment."

And just like that, I had another adventure before me.

ABOUT THE AUTHOR

Amy Liptak Caruso lives in Southwick, Massachusetts with her husband and near her close-knit family. She works in financial services and volunteers with nonprofit organizations, including Stanley Park.

Amy's grandfather, Louie Liptak, Sr., was an establishing employee of Stanley Park and was associated with the park until he died in 1979.

Printed in the United States
by Baker & Taylor Publisher Services